Little GREEN Men

LITTLE GREEN MEN VOLUME 1: GO BIG OR GO HOME!

Published by Ape Entertainment, San Diego, CA (www.ApeComics.com). Proudly printed in the USA.

Little GREEN Men

created by
BRENT ERWIN & DAVID HEDGECOCK

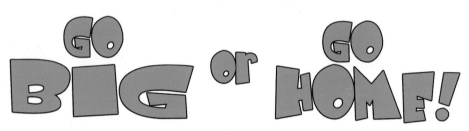

GO BIG or GO HOME!

story, pencil, inks, colors, letters by
JAY FOSGITT

APE ENTERTAINMENT

David Hedgecock
Co-Publisher
DHedgecock@Ape-Entertainment.com

Brent E. Erwin
Co-Publisher
BErwin@Ape-Entertainment.com

Jason M. Burns
Editor-in-Chief
KFreeman@Ape-Entertainment.com

Kevin Freeman
Managing Editor
KFreeman@Ape-Entertainment.com

Troy Dye
Submissions Editor
TDye@Ape-Entertainment.com

Jay Carvajal
On-Line Marketing Manager
JCarvajal@Ape-Entertainment.com

Company Information:
Ape Entertainment
P.O. Box 7100
San Diego, CA 92167
www.ApeComics.com

For Licensing / Media rights contact:
William Morris Agency
Scott L. Agostoni
email: sla@wma.com

APE DIGITAL COMIC SITE:
Apecmx.com

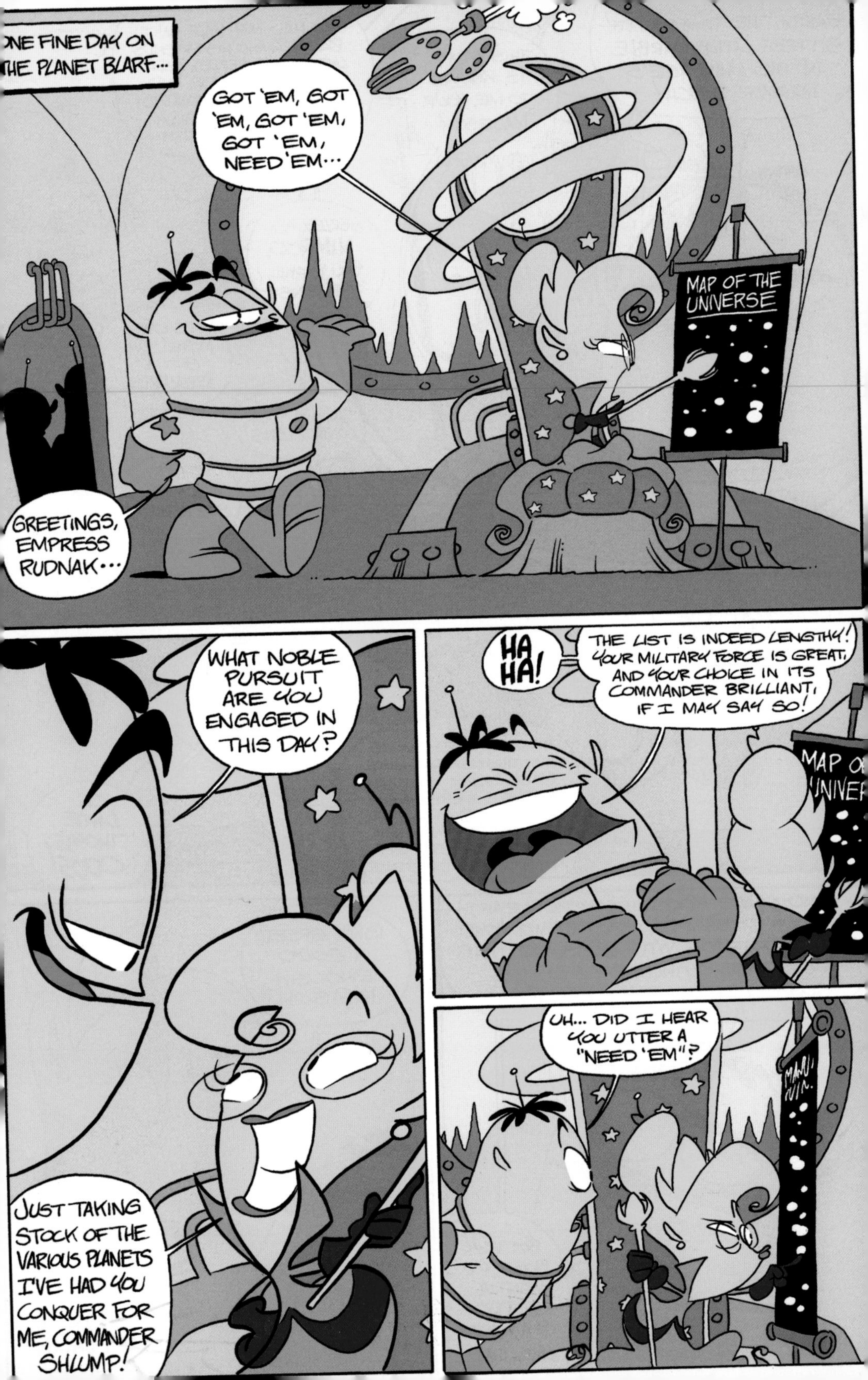
ONE FINE DAY ON THE PLANET BLARF...
GOT 'EM, GOT 'EM, GOT 'EM, GOT 'EM, NEED 'EM...
MAP OF THE UNIVERSE
GREETINGS, EMPRESS RUDNAK...
WHAT NOBLE PURSUIT ARE YOU ENGAGED IN THIS DAY?
JUST TAKING STOCK OF THE VARIOUS PLANETS I'VE HAD YOU CONQUER FOR ME, COMMANDER SHLUMP!
HA HA!
THE LIST IS INDEED LENGTHY! YOUR MILITARY FORCE IS GREAT, AND YOUR CHOICE IN ITS COMMANDER BRILLIANT, IF I MAY SAY SO!
UH... DID I HEAR YOU UTTER A "NEED 'EM"?

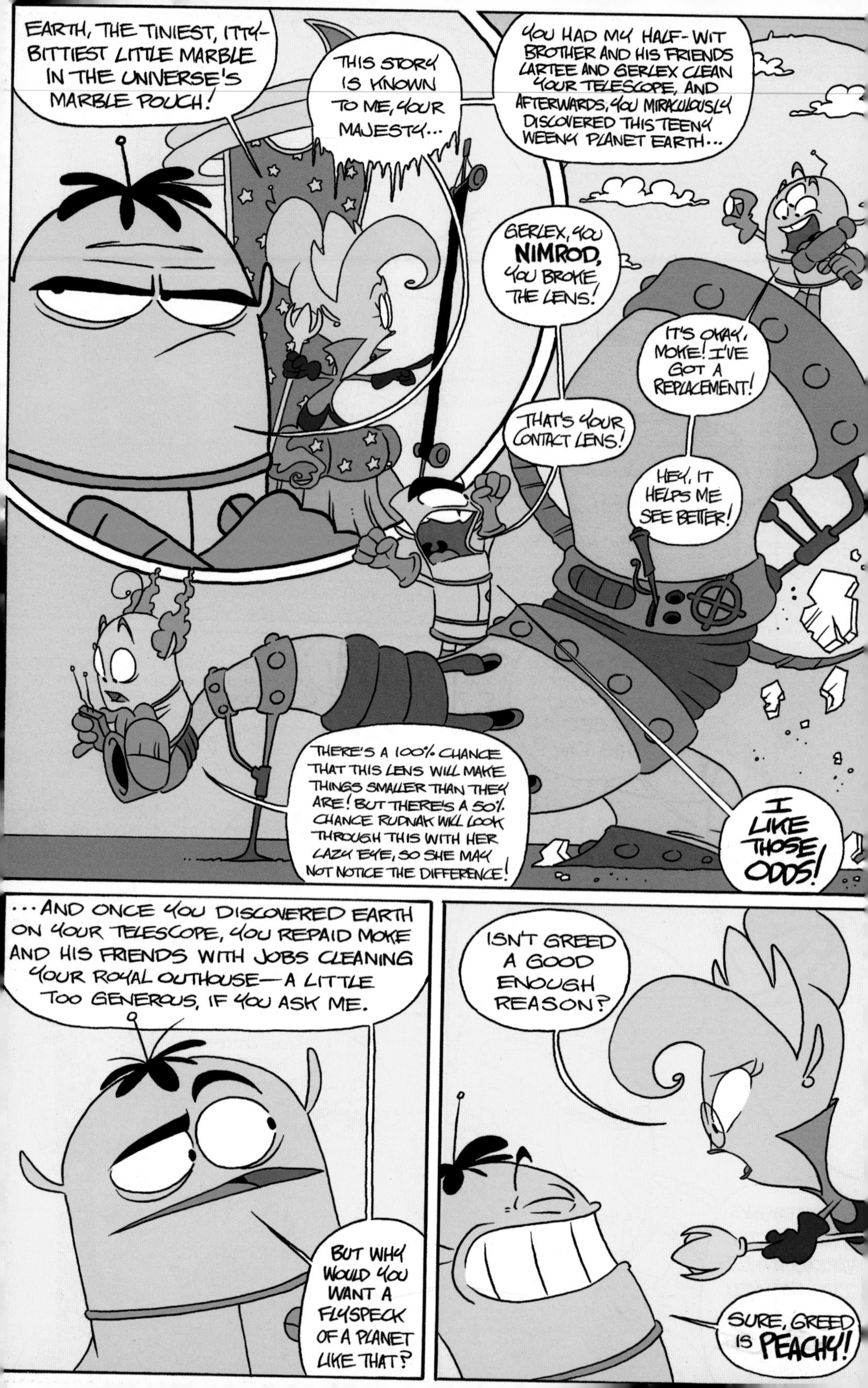
EARTH, THE TINIEST, ITTY-BITTIEST LITTLE MARBLE IN THE UNIVERSE'S MARBLE POUCH!
THIS STORY IS KNOWN TO ME, YOUR MAJESTY...
YOU HAD MY HALF-WIT BROTHER AND HIS FRIENDS LARTEE AND GERLEX CLEAN YOUR TELESCOPE, AND AFTERWARDS, YOU MIRACULOUSLY DISCOVERED THIS TEENY WEENY PLANET EARTH...
GERLEX, YOU **NIMROD**, YOU BROKE THE LENS!
IT'S OKAY, MOKE! I'VE GOT A REPLACEMENT!
THAT'S YOUR CONTACT LENS!
HEY, IT HELPS ME SEE BETTER!
THERE'S A 100% CHANCE THAT THIS LENS WILL MAKE THINGS SMALLER THAN THEY ARE! BUT THERE'S A 50% CHANCE RUDNAK WILL LOOK THROUGH THIS WITH HER LAZY EYE, SO SHE MAY NOT NOTICE THE DIFFERENCE!
I LIKE THOSE ODDS!
...AND ONCE YOU DISCOVERED EARTH ON YOUR TELESCOPE, YOU REPAID MOKE AND HIS FRIENDS WITH JOBS CLEANING YOUR ROYAL OUTHOUSE—A LITTLE TOO GENEROUS, IF YOU ASK ME.
BUT WHY WOULD YOU WANT A FLYSPECK OF A PLANET LIKE THAT?
ISN'T GREED A GOOD ENOUGH REASON?
SURE, GREED IS **PEACHY**!

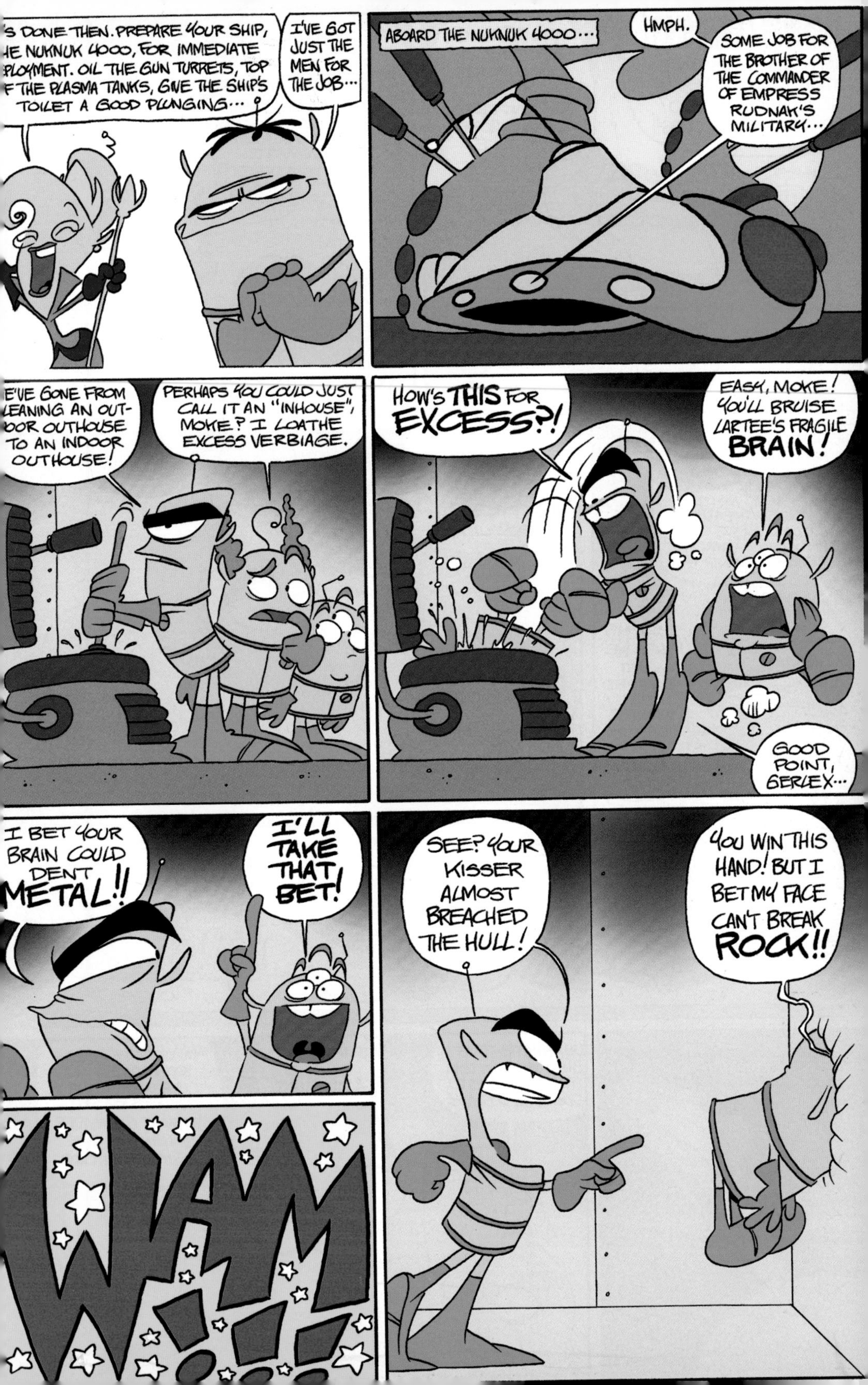
'S DONE THEN. PREPARE YOUR SHIP, HE NUKNUK 4000, FOR IMMEDIATE EPLOYMENT. OIL THE GUN TURRETS, TOP F THE PLASMA TANKS, GIVE THE SHIP'S TOILET A GOOD PLUNGING...
I'VE GOT JUST THE MEN FOR THE JOB...
ABOARD THE NUKNUK 4000...
HMPH.
SOME JOB FOR THE BROTHER OF THE COMMANDER OF EMPRESS RUDNAK'S MILITARY...
E'VE GONE FROM LEANING AN OUT-OOR OUTHOUSE TO AN INDOOR OUTHOUSE!
PERHAPS YOU COULD JUST CALL IT AN "INHOUSE", MOKE? I LOATHE EXCESS VERBIAGE.
HOW'S THIS FOR EXCESS?!
EASY, MOKE! YOU'LL BRUISE LARTEE'S FRAGILE BRAIN!
GOOD POINT, GERLEX...
I BET YOUR BRAIN COULD DENT METAL!!
I'LL TAKE THAT BET!
WAM!!
SEE? YOUR KISSER ALMOST BREACHED THE HULL!
YOU WIN THIS HAND! BUT I BET MY FACE CAN'T BREAK ROCK!!

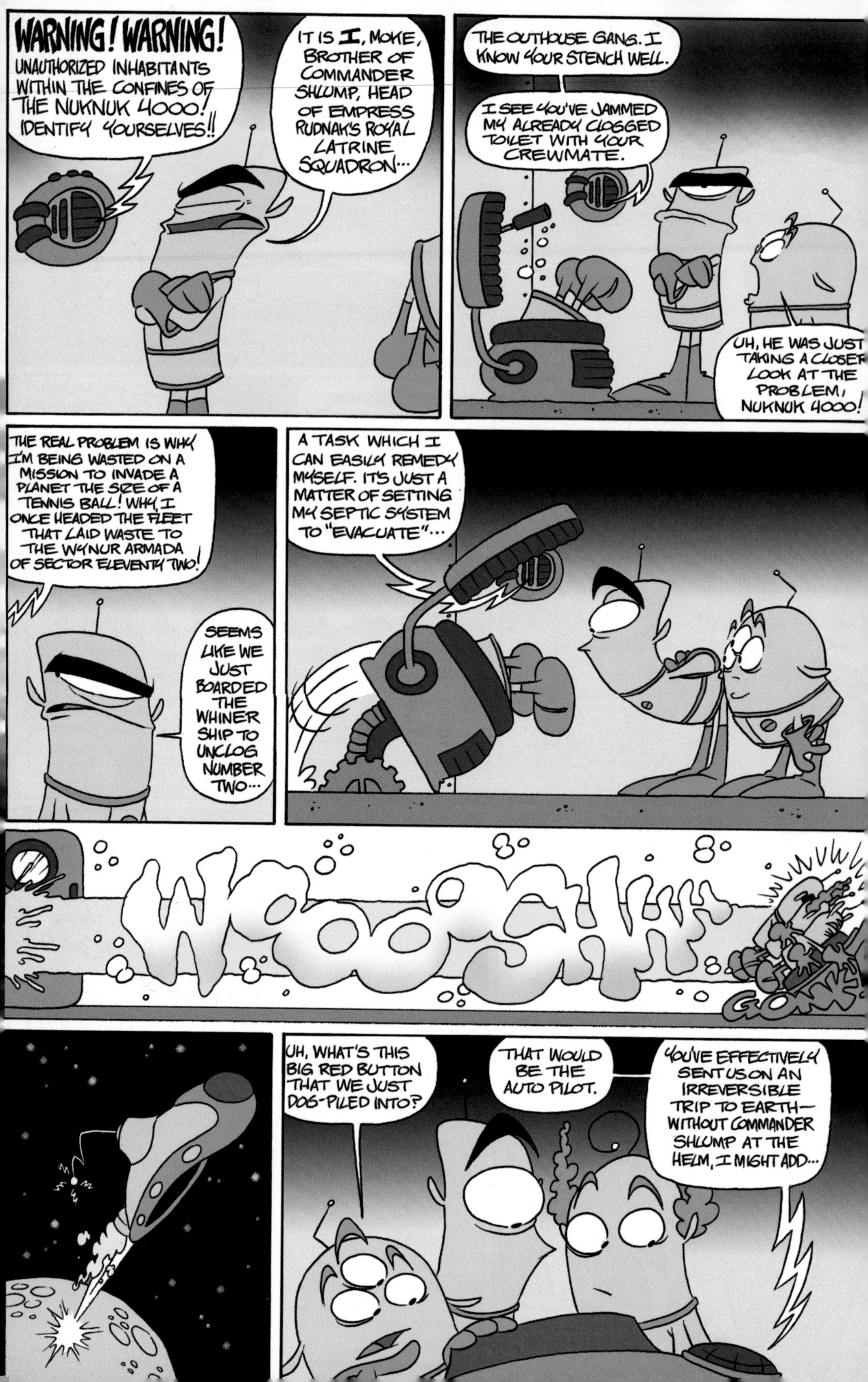
WARNING! WARNING!
UNAUTHORIZED INHABITANTS WITHIN THE CONFINES OF THE NUKNUK 4000! IDENTIFY YOURSELVES!!
IT IS I, MOKE, BROTHER OF COMMANDER SHLUMP, HEAD OF EMPRESS RUDNAK'S ROYAL LATRINE SQUADRON...
THE OUTHOUSE GANG. I KNOW YOUR STENCH WELL.
I SEE YOU'VE JAMMED MY ALREADY CLOGGED TOILET WITH YOUR CREWMATE.
UH, HE WAS JUST TAKING A CLOSER LOOK AT THE PROBLEM, NUKNUK 4000!
THE REAL PROBLEM IS WHY I'M BEING WASTED ON A MISSION TO INVADE A PLANET THE SIZE OF A TENNIS BALL! WHY, I ONCE HEADED THE FLEET THAT LAID WASTE TO THE WYNUR ARMADA OF SECTOR ELEVENTY TWO!
SEEMS LIKE WE JUST BOARDED THE WHINER SHIP TO UNCLOG NUMBER TWO...
A TASK WHICH I CAN EASILY REMEDY MYSELF. IT'S JUST A MATTER OF SETTING MY SEPTIC SYSTEM TO "EVACUATE"...
WOOOSHHH
GONK
UH, WHAT'S THIS BIG RED BUTTON THAT WE JUST DOG-PILED INTO?
THAT WOULD BE THE AUTO PILOT.
YOU'VE EFFECTIVELY SENT US ON AN IRREVERSIBLE TRIP TO EARTH— WITHOUT COMMANDER SHLUMP AT THE HELM, I MIGHT ADD...

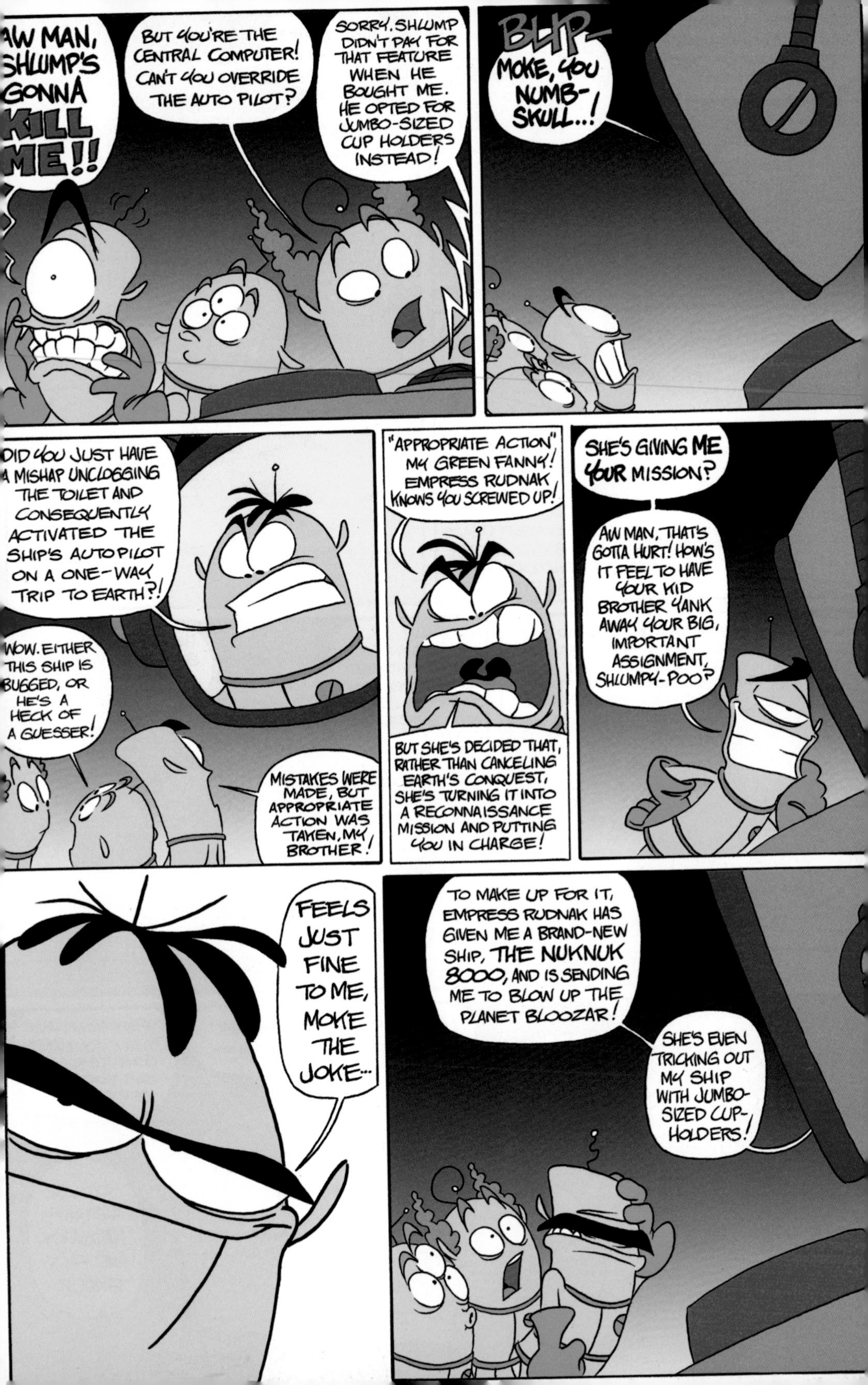
AW MAN, SHLUMP'S GONNA KILL ME!!
BUT YOU'RE THE CENTRAL COMPUTER! CAN'T YOU OVERRIDE THE AUTO PILOT?
SORRY. SHLUMP DIDN'T PAY FOR THAT FEATURE WHEN HE BOUGHT ME. HE OPTED FOR JUMBO-SIZED CUP HOLDERS INSTEAD!
BLIP—
MOKE, YOU NUMB-SKULL...!
DID YOU JUST HAVE A MISHAP UNCLOGGING THE TOILET AND CONSEQUENTLY ACTIVATED THE SHIP'S AUTOPILOT ON A ONE-WAY TRIP TO EARTH?!
WOW. EITHER THIS SHIP IS BUGGED, OR HE'S A HECK OF A GUESSER!
MISTAKES WERE MADE, BUT APPROPRIATE ACTION WAS TAKEN, MY BROTHER!
"APPROPRIATE ACTION" MY GREEN FANNY! EMPRESS RUDNAK KNOWS YOU SCREWED UP!
BUT SHE'S DECIDED THAT, RATHER THAN CANCELING EARTH'S CONQUEST, SHE'S TURNING IT INTO A RECONNAISSANCE MISSION AND PUTTING YOU IN CHARGE!
SHE'S GIVING ME YOUR MISSION?
AW MAN, THAT'S GOTTA HURT! HOW'S IT FEEL TO HAVE YOUR KID BROTHER YANK AWAY YOUR BIG, IMPORTANT ASSIGNMENT, SHLUMPY-POO?
FEELS JUST FINE TO ME, MOKE THE JOKE...
TO MAKE UP FOR IT, EMPRESS RUDNAK HAS GIVEN ME A BRAND-NEW SHIP, THE NUKNUK 8000, AND IS SENDING ME TO BLOW UP THE PLANET BLOOZAR!
SHE'S EVEN TRICKING OUT MY SHIP WITH JUMBO-SIZED CUP-HOLDERS!

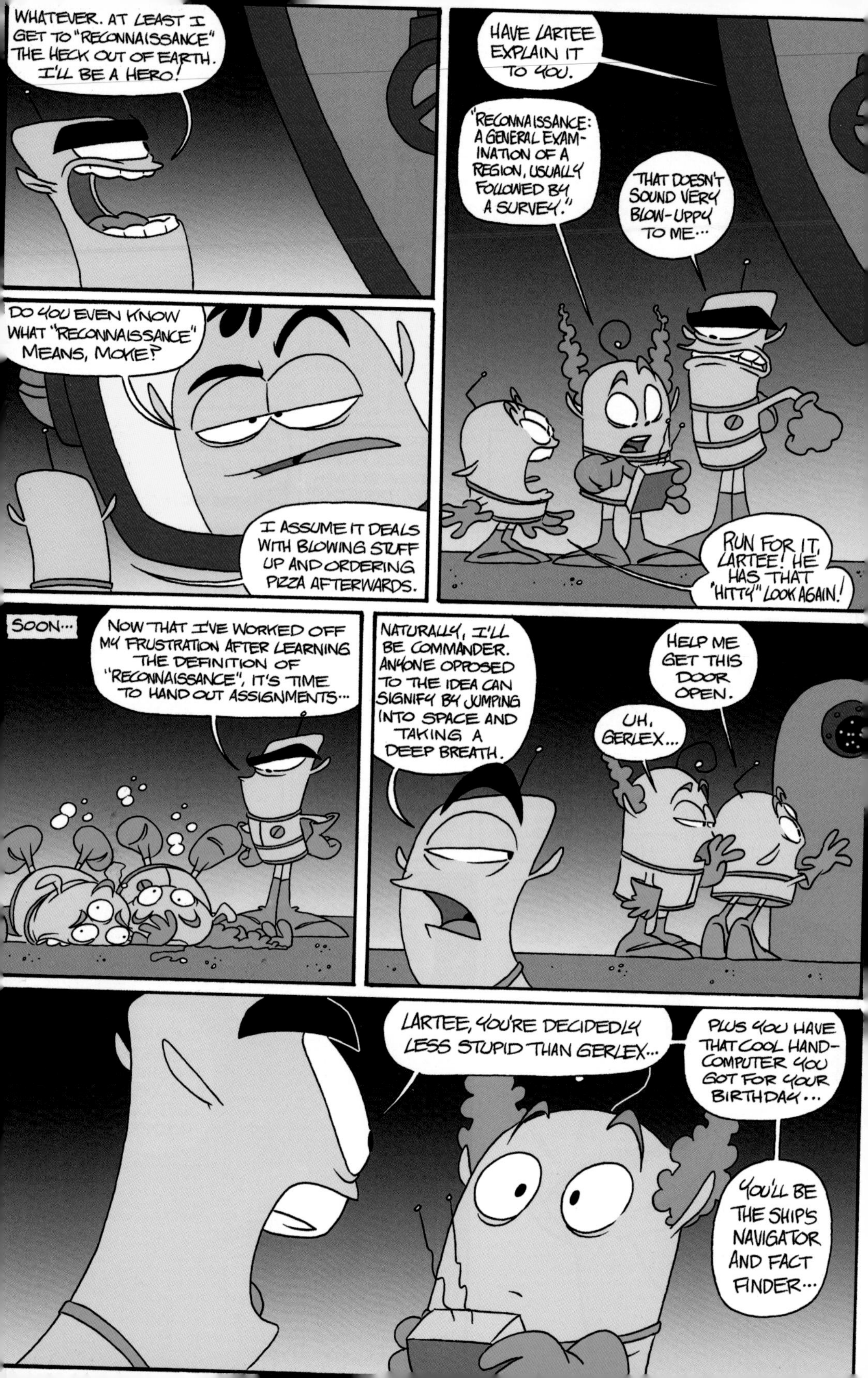
WHATEVER. AT LEAST I GET TO "RECONNAISSANCE" THE HECK OUT OF EARTH. I'LL BE A HERO!
DO YOU EVEN KNOW WHAT "RECONNAISSANCE" MEANS, MOKE?
I ASSUME IT DEALS WITH BLOWING STUFF UP AND ORDERING PIZZA AFTERWARDS.
HAVE LARTEE EXPLAIN IT TO YOU.
"RECONNAISSANCE: A GENERAL EXAMINATION OF A REGION, USUALLY FOLLOWED BY A SURVEY."
THAT DOESN'T SOUND VERY BLOW-UPPY TO ME...
RUN FOR IT, LARTEE! HE HAS THAT "HITTY" LOOK AGAIN!
SOON...
NOW THAT I'VE WORKED OFF MY FRUSTRATION AFTER LEARNING THE DEFINITION OF "RECONNAISSANCE", IT'S TIME TO HAND OUT ASSIGNMENTS...
NATURALLY, I'LL BE COMMANDER. ANYONE OPPOSED TO THE IDEA CAN SIGNIFY BY JUMPING INTO SPACE AND TAKING A DEEP BREATH.
HELP ME GET THIS DOOR OPEN.
UH, GERLEX...
LARTEE, YOU'RE DECIDEDLY LESS STUPID THAN GERLEX...
PLUS YOU HAVE THAT COOL HAND-COMPUTER YOU GOT FOR YOUR BIRTHDAY...
YOU'LL BE THE SHIP'S NAVIGATOR AND FACT FINDER...

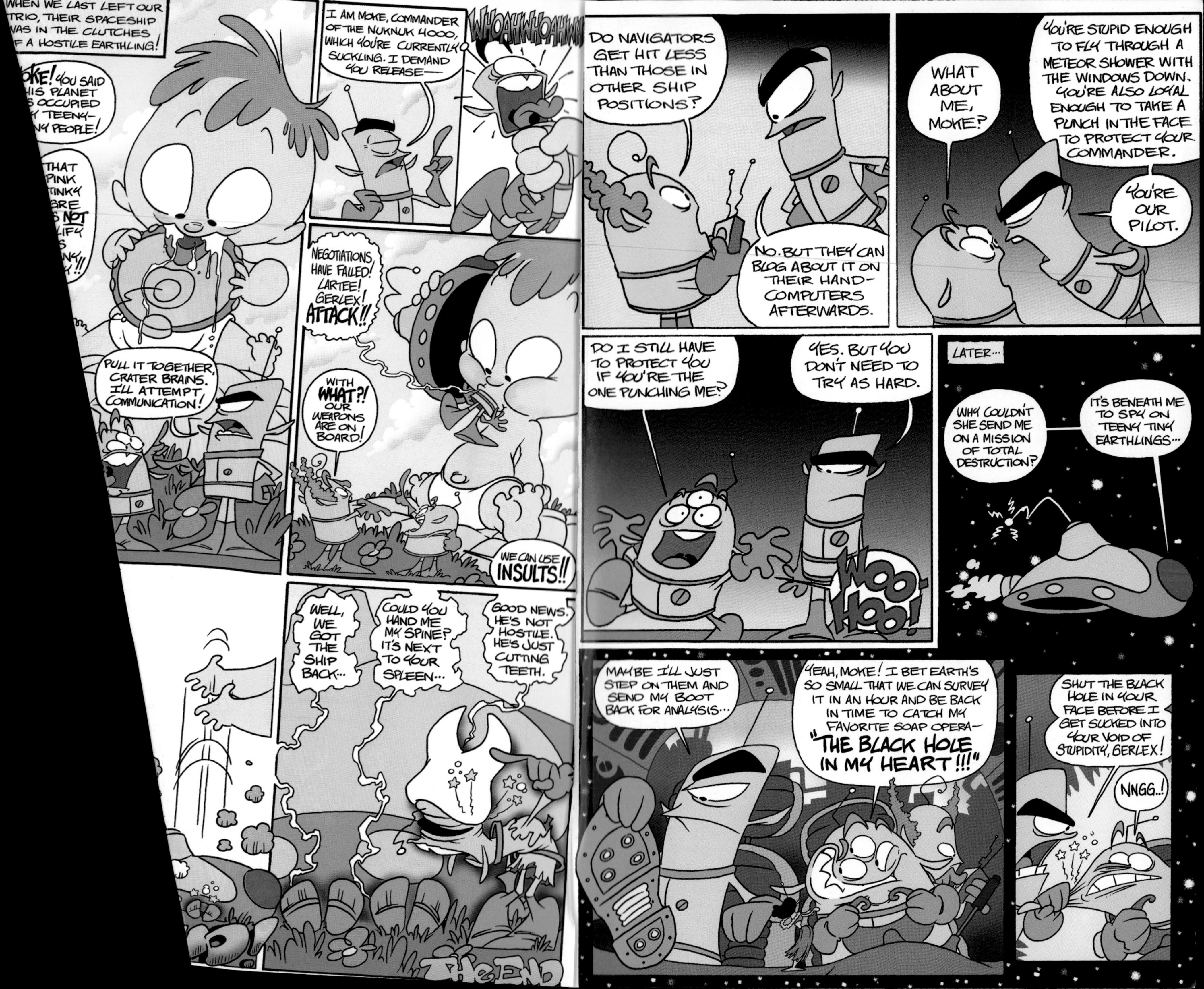
WHEN WE LAST LEFT OUR TRIO, THEIR SPACESHIP WAS IN THE CLUTCHES F A HOSTILE EARTHLING!
OKE! YOU SAID HIS PLANET S OCCUPIED Y TEENY- NY PEOPLE!
THAT PINK TINKY GRE S NOT LIFY S
PULL IT TOGETHER, CRATER BRAINS. I'LL ATTEMPT COMMUNICATION!
I AM MOKE, COMMANDER OF THE NUKNUK 4000, WHICH YOU'RE CURRENTLY SUCKLING. I DEMAND YOU RELEASE—
WHOAHWHOAHWH
NEGOTIATIONS HAVE FAILED! LARTEE! GERLEX! ATTACK!!
WITH WHAT?! OUR WEAPONS ARE ON BOARD!
WE CAN USE INSULTS!!
WELL, WE GOT THE SHIP BACK...
COULD YOU HAND ME MY SPINE? IT'S NEXT TO YOUR SPLEEN...
GOOD NEWS. HE'S NOT HOSTILE. HE'S JUST CUTTING TEETH.
THE END
DO NAVIGATORS GET HIT LESS THAN THOSE IN OTHER SHIP POSITIONS?
NO. BUT THEY CAN BLOG ABOUT IT ON THEIR HAND-COMPUTERS AFTERWARDS.
WHAT ABOUT ME, MOKE?
YOU'RE STUPID ENOUGH TO FLY THROUGH A METEOR SHOWER WITH THE WINDOWS DOWN. YOU'RE ALSO LOYAL ENOUGH TO TAKE A PUNCH IN THE FACE TO PROTECT YOUR COMMANDER.
YOU'RE OUR PILOT.
DO I STILL HAVE TO PROTECT YOU IF YOU'RE THE ONE PUNCHING ME?
YES. BUT YOU DON'T NEED TO TRY AS HARD.
WOO-HOO!
LATER...
WHY COULDN'T SHE SEND ME ON A MISSION OF TOTAL DESTRUCTION?
IT'S BENEATH ME TO SPY ON TEENY TINY EARTHLINGS...
MAYBE I'LL JUST STEP ON THEM AND SEND MY BOOT BACK FOR ANALYSIS...
YEAH, MOKE! I BET EARTH'S SO SMALL THAT WE CAN SURVEY IT IN AN HOUR AND BE BACK IN TIME TO CATCH MY FAVORITE SOAP OPERA— "THE BLACK HOLE IN MY HEART!!!"
SHUT THE BLACK HOLE IN YOUR FACE BEFORE I GET SUCKED INTO YOUR VOID OF STUPIDITY, GERLEX!
NNGG..!

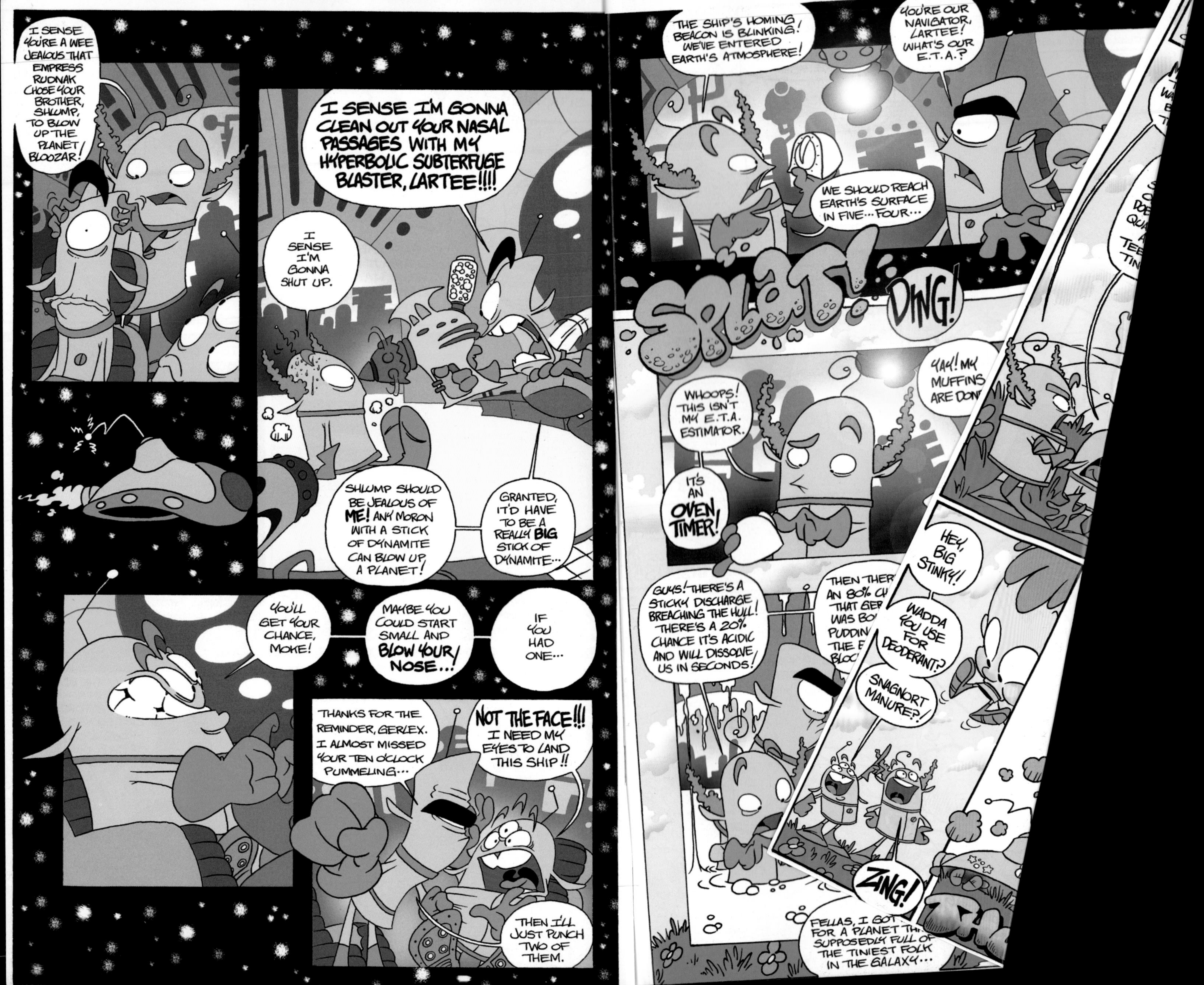
I SENSE YOU'RE A WEE JEALOUS THAT EMPRESS RUDNAK CHOSE YOUR BROTHER, SHLUMP, TO BLOW UP THE PLANET BLOOZAR!
I SENSE I'M GONNA CLEAN OUT YOUR NASAL PASSAGES WITH MY HYPERBOLIC SUBTERFUGE BLASTER, LARTEE!!!!
I SENSE I'M GONNA SHUT UP.
SHLUMP SHOULD BE JEALOUS OF ME! ANY MORON WITH A STICK OF DYNAMITE CAN BLOW UP A PLANET!
GRANTED, IT'D HAVE TO BE A REALLY BIG STICK OF DYNAMITE...
YOU'LL GET YOUR CHANCE, MOKE!
MAYBE YOU COULD START SMALL AND BLOW YOUR NOSE...!
IF YOU HAD ONE...
THANKS FOR THE REMINDER, GERLEX. I ALMOST MISSED YOUR TEN O'CLOCK PUMMELING...
NOT THE FACE!!! I NEED MY EYES TO LAND THIS SHIP!!
THEN I'LL JUST PUNCH TWO OF THEM.
THE SHIP'S HOMING BEACON IS BLINKING! WE'VE ENTERED EARTH'S ATMOSPHERE!
YOU'RE OUR NAVIGATOR, LARTEE! WHAT'S OUR E.T.A.?
WE SHOULD REACH EARTH'S SURFACE IN FIVE... FOUR...
SPLAT! DING!
WHOOPS! THIS ISN'T MY E.T.A. ESTIMATOR.
IT'S AN OVEN TIMER!
GUYS! THERE'S A STICKY DISCHARGE BREACHING THE HULL! THERE'S A 20% CHANCE IT'S ACIDIC AND WILL DISSOLVE US IN SECONDS!
HEY, BIG STINKY!
WADDA YOU USE FOR DEODERANT?
SNAGNORT MANURE?!
ZING!

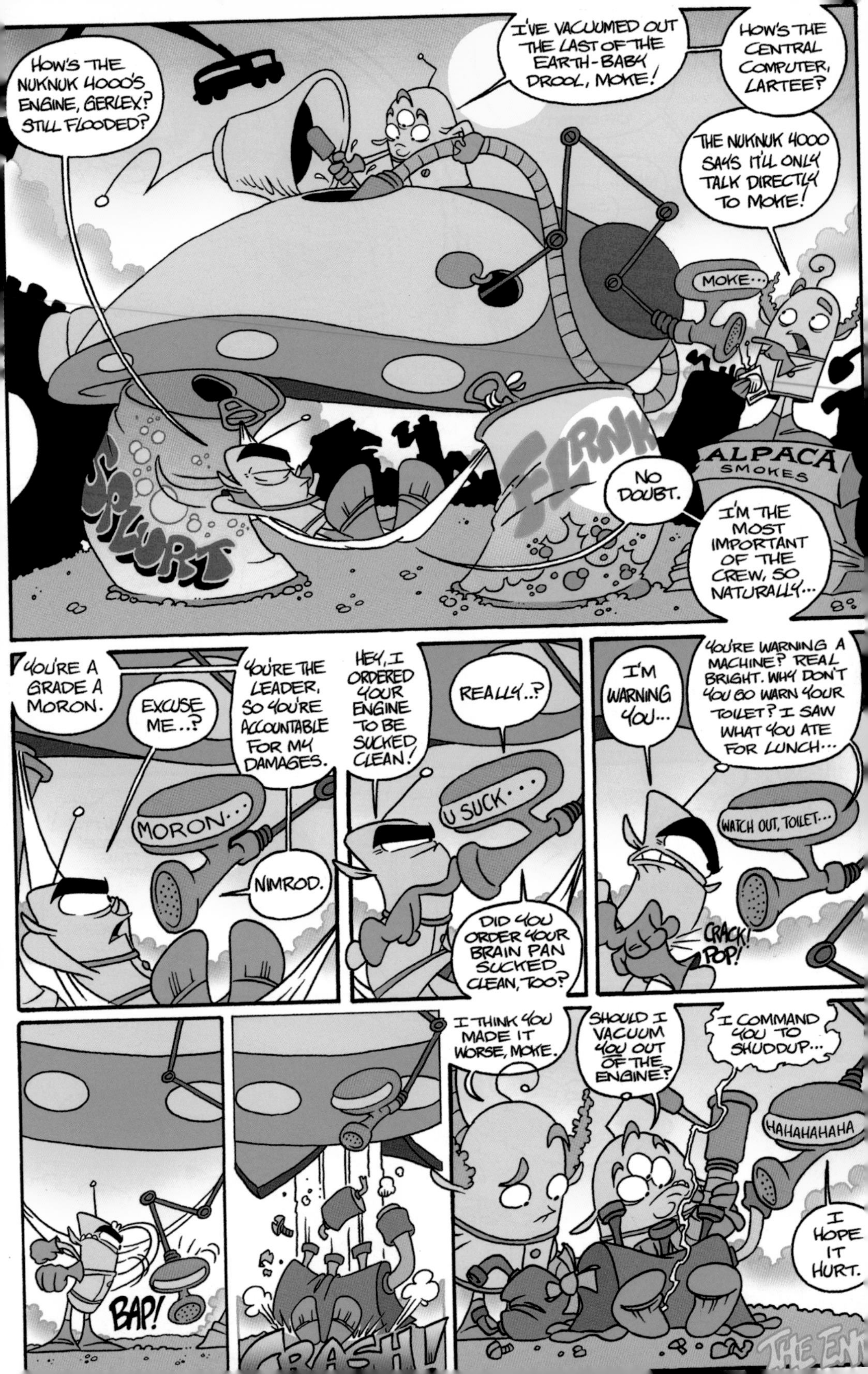
HOW'S THE NUKNUK 4000'S ENGINE, GERLEX? STILL FLOODED?
I'VE VACUUMED OUT THE LAST OF THE EARTH-BABY DROOL, MOKE!
HOW'S THE CENTRAL COMPUTER, LARTEE?
THE NUKNUK 4000 SAYS IT'LL ONLY TALK DIRECTLY TO MOKE!
MOKE...
SPLURT
FLRNK
ALPACA SMOKES
NO DOUBT.
I'M THE MOST IMPORTANT OF THE CREW, SO NATURALLY...
YOU'RE A GRADE A MORON.
EXCUSE ME...?
MORON...
YOU'RE THE LEADER, SO YOU'RE ACCOUNTABLE FOR MY DAMAGES.
NIMROD.
HEY, I ORDERED YOUR ENGINE TO BE SUCKED CLEAN!
REALLY...?
U SUCK...
DID YOU ORDER YOUR BRAIN PAN SUCKED CLEAN, TOO?
I'M WARNING YOU...
YOU'RE WARNING A MACHINE? REAL BRIGHT. WHY DON'T YOU GO WARN YOUR TOILET? I SAW WHAT YOU ATE FOR LUNCH...
WATCH OUT, TOILET...
CRACK! POP!
BAP!
CRASH!
I THINK YOU MADE IT WORSE, MOKE.
SHOULD I VACUUM YOU OUT OF THE ENGINE?
I COMMAND YOU TO SHUDDUP...
HAHAHAHAHA
I HOPE IT HURT.
THE END

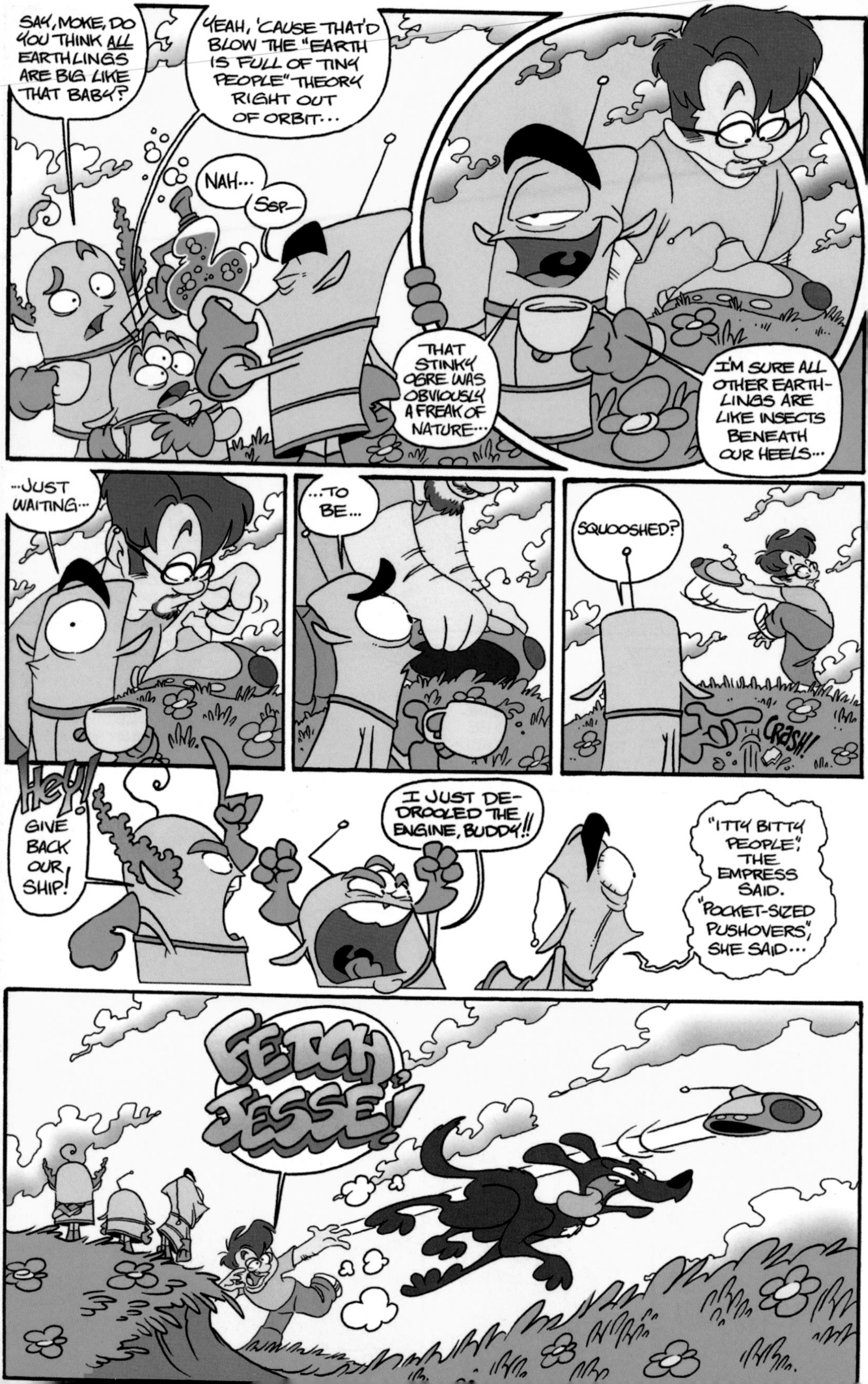
SAY, MOKE, DO YOU THINK ALL EARTHLINGS ARE BIG LIKE THAT BABY?
YEAH, 'CAUSE THAT'D BLOW THE "EARTH IS FULL OF TINY PEOPLE" THEORY RIGHT OUT OF ORBIT...
NAH...
SSP—
THAT STINKY OGRE WAS OBVIOUSLY A FREAK OF NATURE...
I'M SURE ALL OTHER EARTH-LINGS ARE LIKE INSECTS BENEATH OUR HEELS...
...JUST WAITING...
...TO BE...
SQUOOSHED?
CRASH!!
HEY!
GIVE BACK OUR SHIP!
I JUST DE-DROOLED THE ENGINE, BUDDY!!
"ITTY BITTY PEOPLE," THE EMPRESS SAID. "POCKET-SIZED PUSHOVERS," SHE SAID...
FETCH, JESSE!

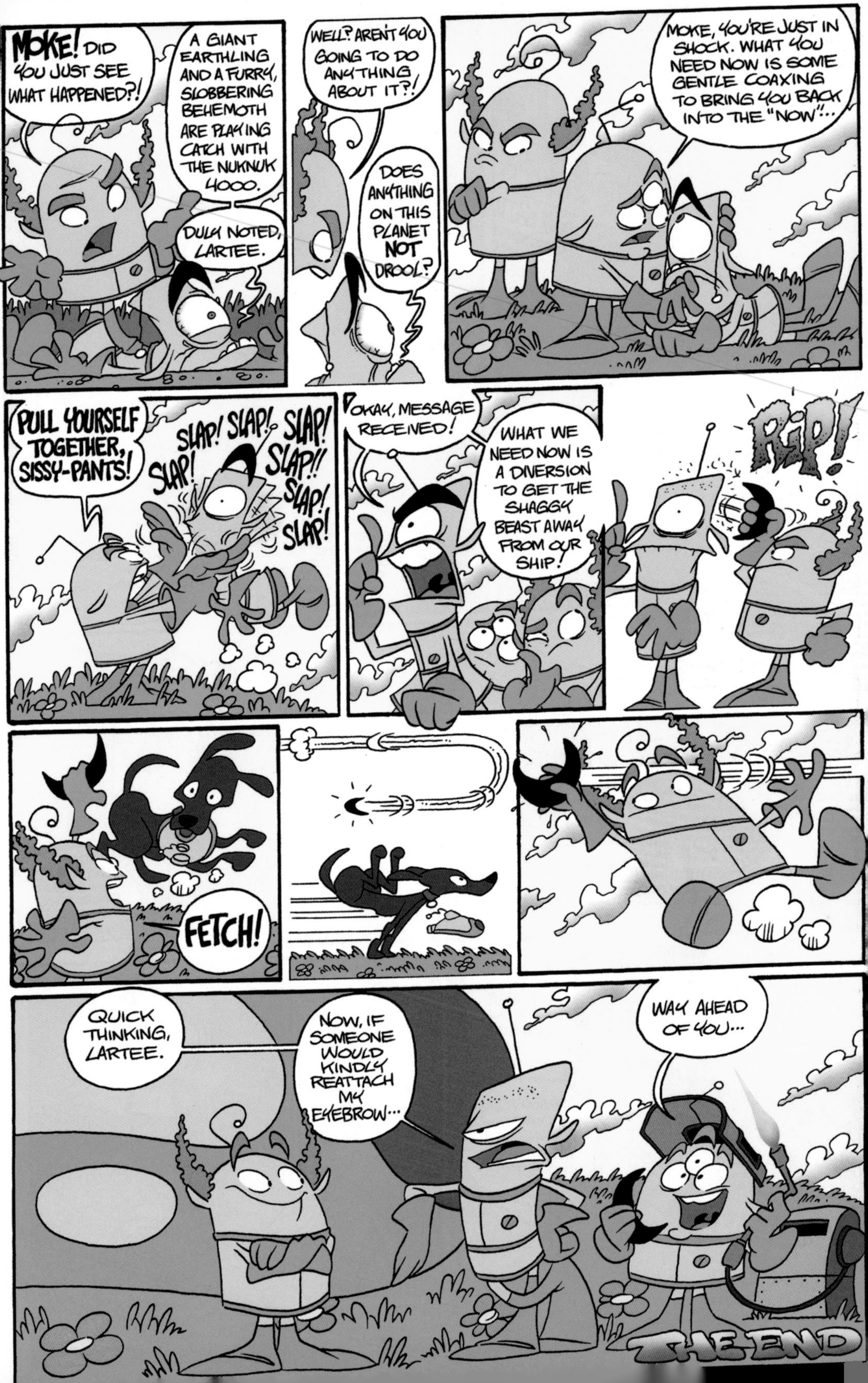
MOKE! DID YOU JUST SEE WHAT HAPPENED?!
A GIANT EARTHLING AND A FURRY, SLOBBERING BEHEMOTH ARE PLAYING CATCH WITH THE NUKNUK 4000.
DULY NOTED, LARTEE.
WELL? AREN'T YOU GOING TO DO ANYTHING ABOUT IT?!
DOES ANYTHING ON THIS PLANET NOT DROOL?
MOKE, YOU'RE JUST IN SHOCK. WHAT YOU NEED NOW IS SOME GENTLE COAXING TO BRING YOU BACK INTO THE "NOW"...
PULL YOURSELF TOGETHER, SISSY-PANTS!
SLAP! SLAP! SLAP! SLAP! SLAP!! SLAP! SLAP!
OKAY, MESSAGE RECEIVED!
WHAT WE NEED NOW IS A DIVERSION TO GET THE SHAGGY BEAST AWAY FROM OUR SHIP!
RIP!
FETCH!
QUICK THINKING, LARTEE.
NOW, IF SOMEONE WOULD KINDLY REATTACH MY EYEBROW...
WAY AHEAD OF YOU...
THE END

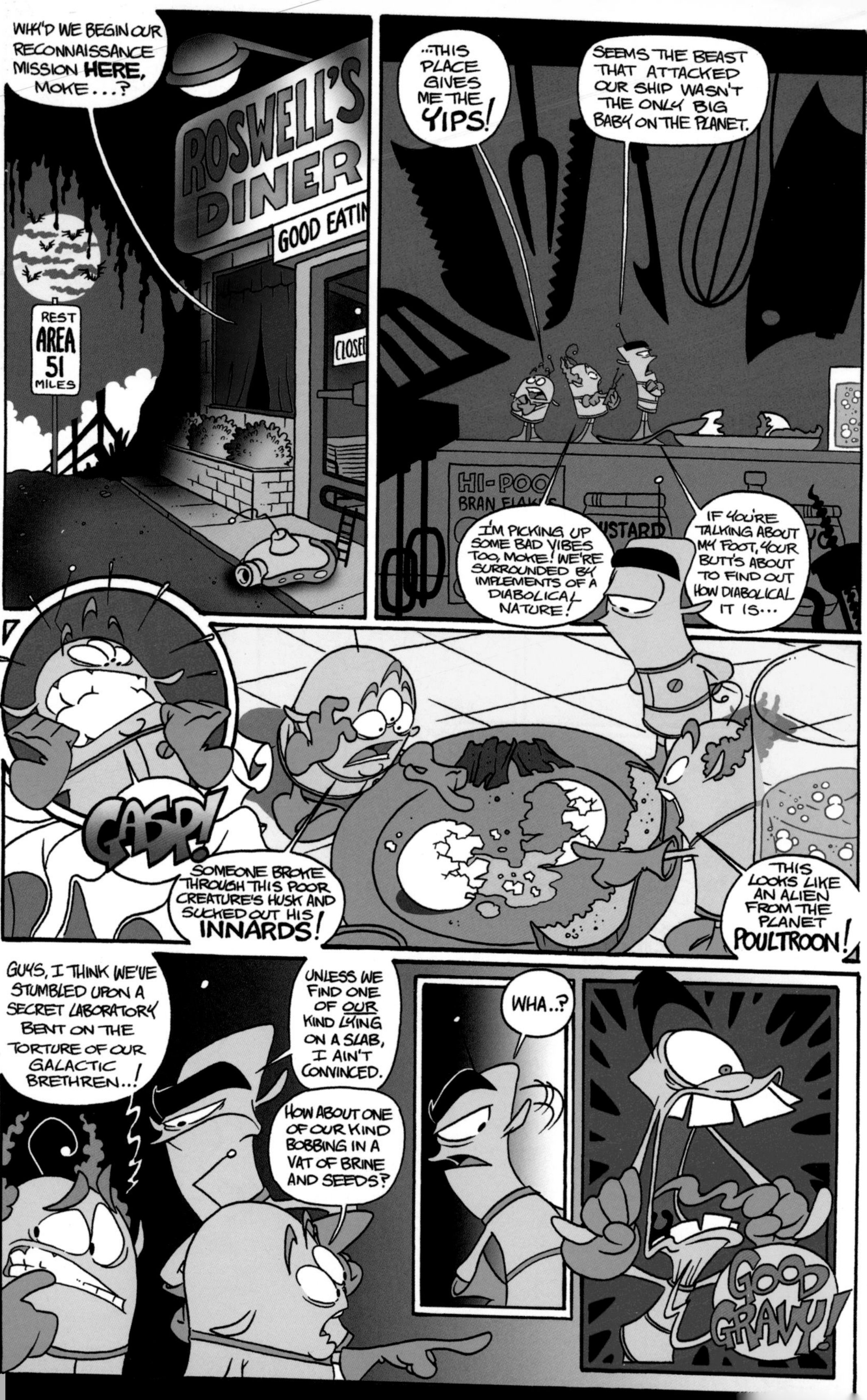
WHY'D WE BEGIN OUR RECONNAISSANCE MISSION HERE, MOKE...?
ROSWELL'S DINER
GOOD EATIN
REST AREA 51 MILES
CLOSED
...THIS PLACE GIVES ME THE YIPS!
SEEMS THE BEAST THAT ATTACKED OUR SHIP WASN'T THE ONLY BIG BABY ON THE PLANET.
HI-POO BRAN FLAKES
MUSTARD
I'M PICKING UP SOME BAD VIBES TOO, MOKE! WE'RE SURROUNDED BY IMPLEMENTS OF A DIABOLICAL NATURE!
IF YOU'RE TALKING ABOUT MY FOOT, YOUR BUTT'S ABOUT TO FIND OUT HOW DIABOLICAL IT IS...
GASP!
SOMEONE BROKE THROUGH THIS POOR CREATURE'S HUSK AND SUCKED OUT HIS INNARDS!
THIS LOOKS LIKE AN ALIEN FROM THE PLANET POULTROON!
GUYS, I THINK WE'VE STUMBLED UPON A SECRET LABORATORY BENT ON THE TORTURE OF OUR GALACTIC BRETHREN...!
UNLESS WE FIND ONE OF OUR KIND LYING ON A SLAB, I AIN'T CONVINCED.
HOW ABOUT ONE OF OUR KIND BOBBING IN A VAT OF BRINE AND SEEDS?
WHA..?
GOOD GRAVY!

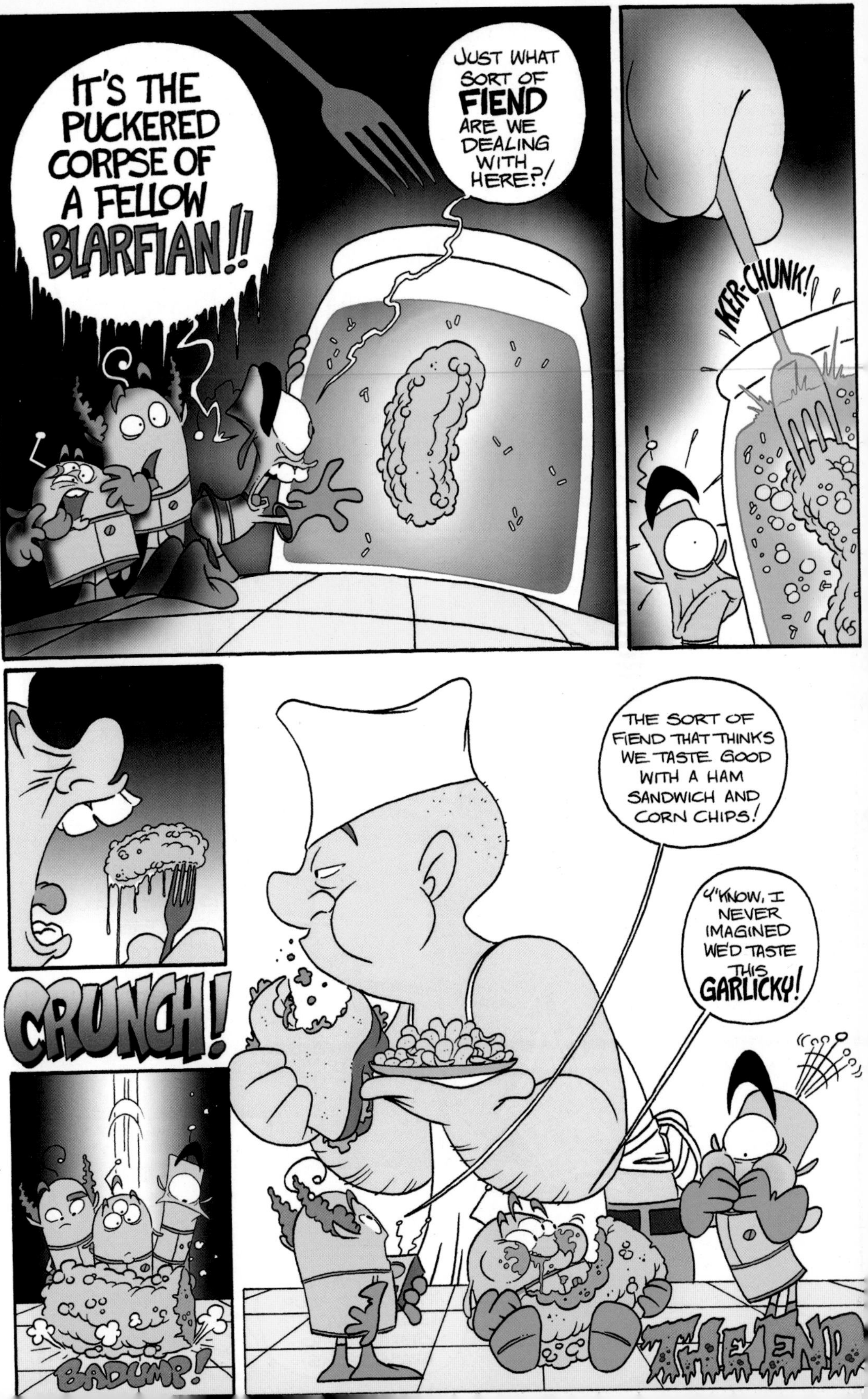
IT'S THE PUCKERED CORPSE OF A FELLOW BLARFIAN!!
JUST WHAT SORT OF FIEND ARE WE DEALING WITH HERE?!
KER-CHUNK!
CRUNCH!
BADUMP!
THE SORT OF FIEND THAT THINKS WE TASTE GOOD WITH A HAM SANDWICH AND CORN CHIPS!
Y'KNOW, I NEVER IMAGINED WE'D TASTE THIS GARLICKY!
THE END

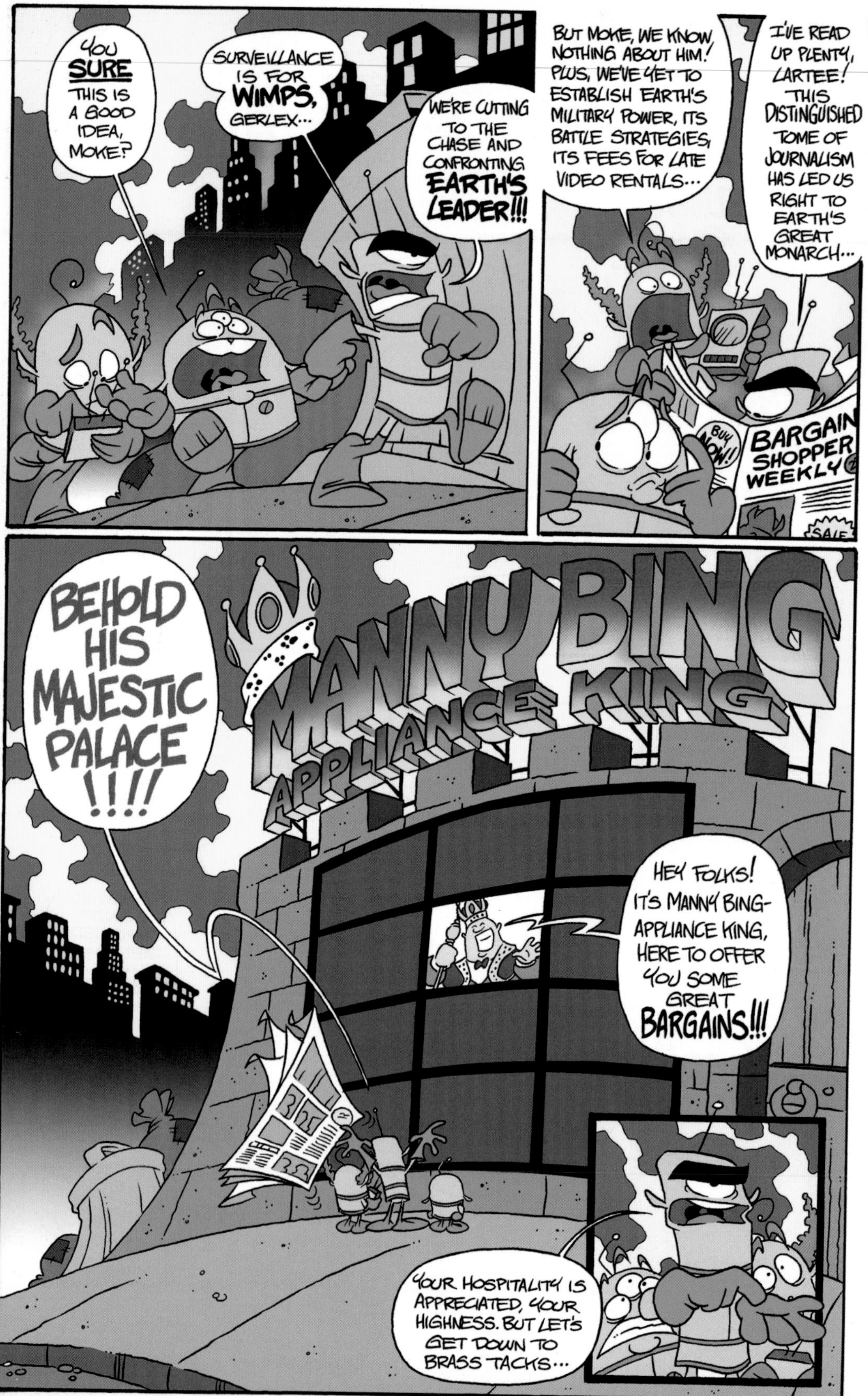

YOU SURE THIS IS A GOOD IDEA, MOKE?
SURVEILLANCE IS FOR WIMPS, GERLEX...
WE'RE CUTTING TO THE CHASE AND CONFRONTING EARTH'S LEADER!!!
BUT MOKE, WE KNOW NOTHING ABOUT HIM! PLUS, WE'VE YET TO ESTABLISH EARTH'S MILITARY POWER, ITS BATTLE STRATEGIES, ITS FEES FOR LATE VIDEO RENTALS...
I'VE READ UP PLENTY, LARTEE! THIS DISTINGUISHED TOME OF JOURNALISM HAS LED US RIGHT TO EARTH'S GREAT MONARCH...
BUY NOW!!
BARGAIN SHOPPER WEEKLY
SALE
BEHOLD HIS MAJESTIC PALACE!!!!
MANNY BING
APPLIANCE KING
HEY FOLKS! IT'S MANNY BING- APPLIANCE KING, HERE TO OFFER YOU SOME GREAT BARGAINS!!!
YOUR HOSPITALITY IS APPRECIATED, YOUR HIGHNESS. BUT LET'S GET DOWN TO BRASS TACKS...

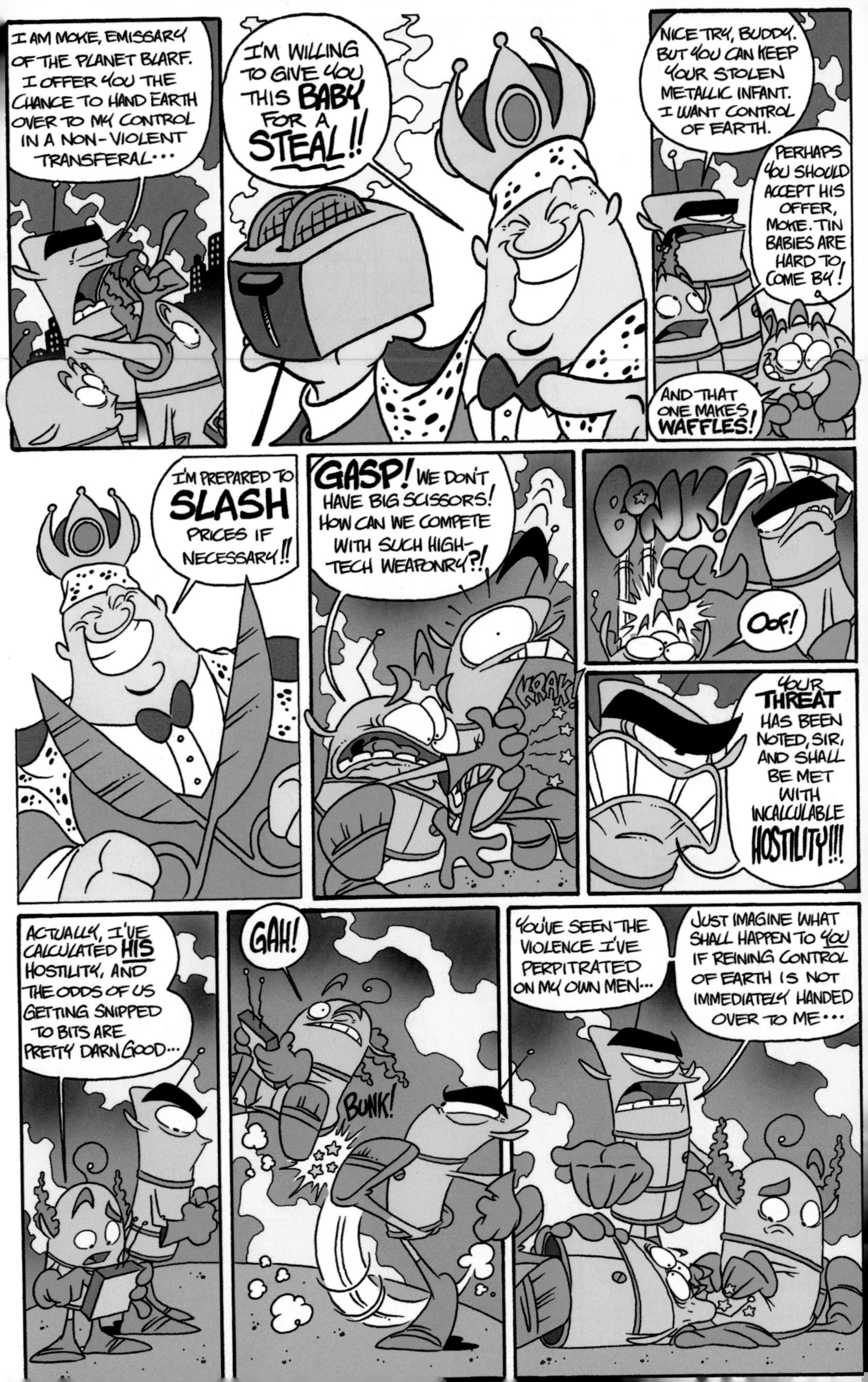

I AM MOKE, EMISSARY OF THE PLANET BLARF. I OFFER YOU THE CHANCE TO HAND EARTH OVER TO MY CONTROL IN A NON-VIOLENT TRANSFERAL...
I'M WILLING TO GIVE YOU THIS BABY FOR A STEAL!!
NICE TRY, BUDDY. BUT YOU CAN KEEP YOUR STOLEN METALLIC INFANT. I WANT CONTROL OF EARTH.
PERHAPS YOU SHOULD ACCEPT HIS OFFER, MOKE. TIN BABIES ARE HARD TO COME BY!
AND THAT ONE MAKES WAFFLES!
I'M PREPARED TO SLASH PRICES IF NECESSARY!!
GASP! WE DON'T HAVE BIG SCISSORS! HOW CAN WE COMPETE WITH SUCH HIGH-TECH WEAPONRY?!
KRAK!
BONK!
BAM
OOF!
YOUR THREAT HAS BEEN NOTED, SIR, AND SHALL BE MET WITH INCALCULABLE HOSTILITY!!!
ACTUALLY, I'VE CALCULATED HIS HOSTILITY, AND THE ODDS OF US GETTING SNIPPED TO BITS ARE PRETTY DARN GOOD...
GAH!
BUNK!
YOU'VE SEEN THE VIOLENCE I'VE PERPITRATED ON MY OWN MEN...
JUST IMAGINE WHAT SHALL HAPPEN TO YOU IF REINING CONTROL OF EARTH IS NOT IMMEDIATELY HANDED OVER TO ME...

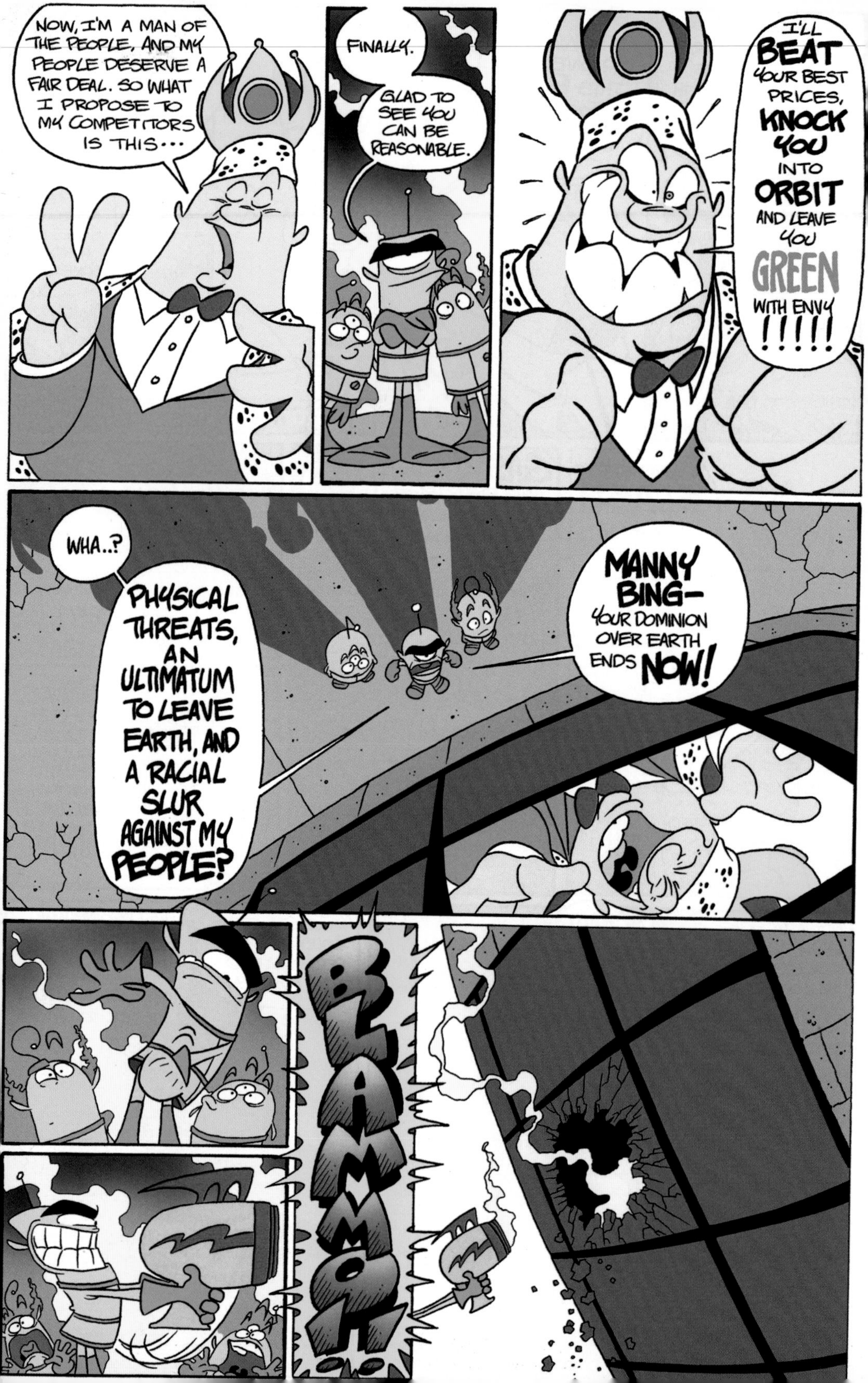
NOW, I'M A MAN OF THE PEOPLE, AND MY PEOPLE DESERVE A FAIR DEAL. SO WHAT I PROPOSE TO MY COMPETITORS IS THIS...
FINALLY.
GLAD TO SEE YOU CAN BE REASONABLE.
I'LL BEAT YOUR BEST PRICES, KNOCK YOU INTO ORBIT AND LEAVE YOU GREEN WITH ENVY!!!!!
WHA..?
MANNY BING- YOUR DOMINION OVER EARTH ENDS NOW!
PHYSICAL THREATS, AN ULTIMATUM TO LEAVE EARTH, AND A RACIAL SLUR AGAINST MY PEOPLE?
BLAMMO!

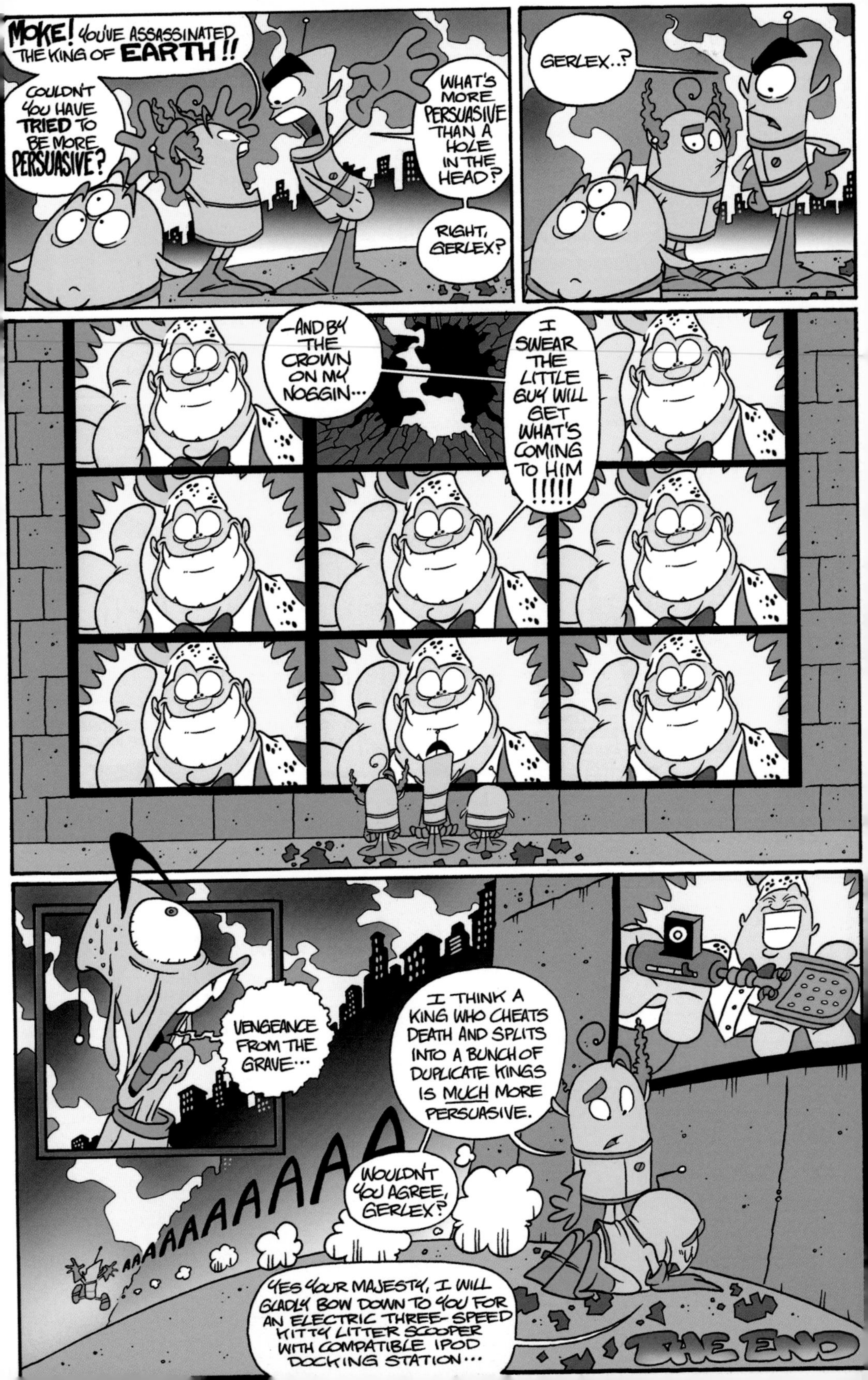

MOKE! YOU'VE ASSASSINATED THE KING OF EARTH!!
COULDN'T YOU HAVE TRIED TO BE MORE PERSUASIVE?
WHAT'S MORE PERSUASIVE THAN A HOLE IN THE HEAD?
RIGHT, GERLEX?
GERLEX..?
—AND BY THE CROWN ON MY NOGGIN...
I SWEAR THE LITTLE GUY WILL GET WHAT'S COMING TO HIM!!!!!
VENGEANCE FROM THE GRAVE...
I THINK A KING WHO CHEATS DEATH AND SPLITS INTO A BUNCH OF DUPLICATE KINGS IS MUCH MORE PERSUASIVE.
WOULDN'T YOU AGREE, GERLEX?
AAAAAAAAAAAAA
YES YOUR MAJESTY, I WILL GLADLY BOW DOWN TO YOU FOR AN ELECTRIC THREE-SPEED KITTY LITTER SCOOPER WITH COMPATIBLE IPOD DOCKING STATION...
THE END

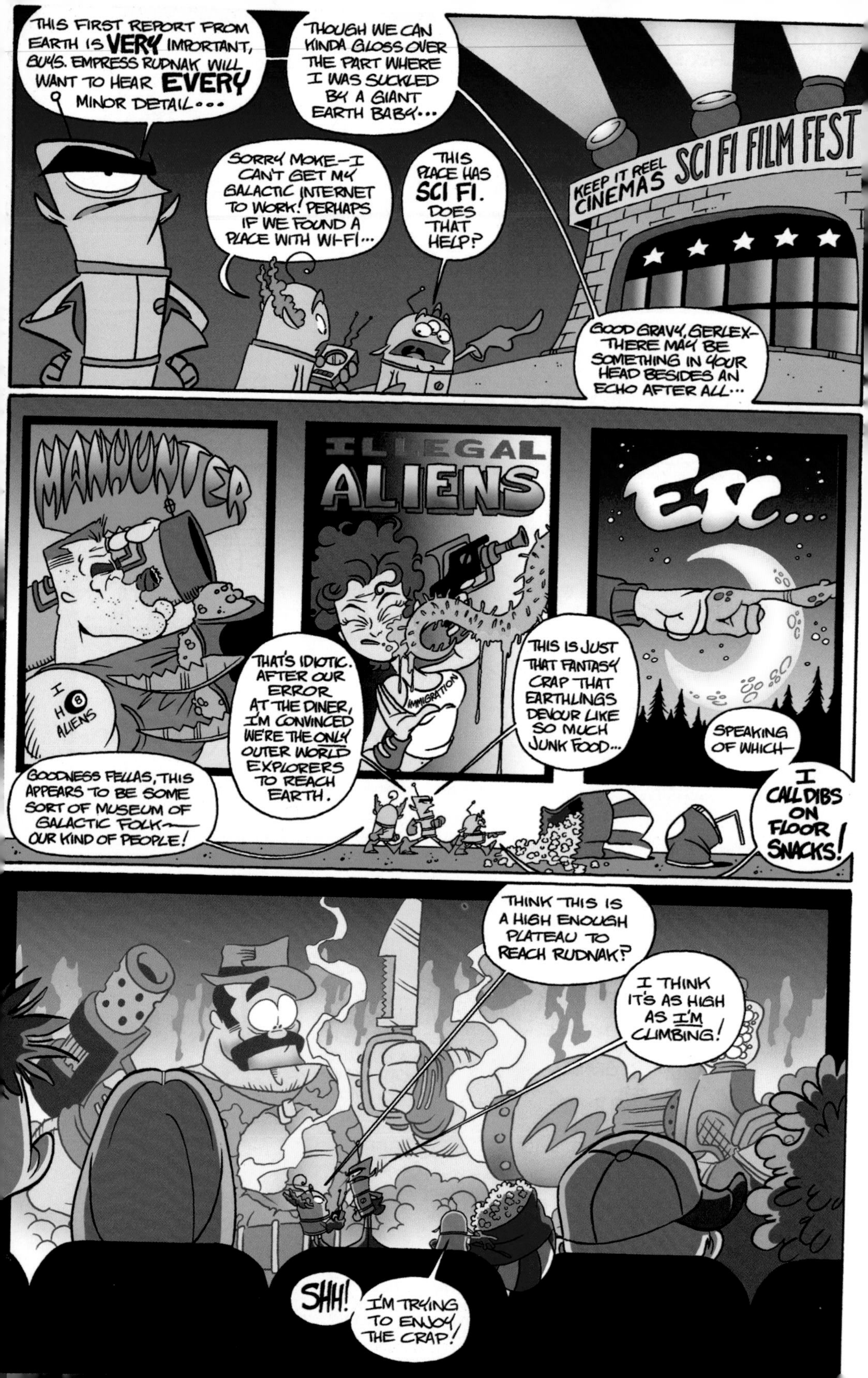
THIS FIRST REPORT FROM EARTH IS VERY IMPORTANT, GUYS. EMPRESS RUDNAK WILL WANT TO HEAR EVERY MINOR DETAIL...
THOUGH WE CAN KINDA GLOSS OVER THE PART WHERE I WAS SUCKLED BY A GIANT EARTH BABY...
SORRY MOKE—I CAN'T GET MY GALACTIC INTERNET TO WORK! PERHAPS IF WE FOUND A PLACE WITH WI-FI...
THIS PLACE HAS SCI FI. DOES THAT HELP?
KEEP IT REEL CINEMAS SCI FI FILM FEST
GOOD GRAVY, GERLEX—THERE MAY BE SOMETHING IN YOUR HEAD BESIDES AN ECHO AFTER ALL...
MANHUNTER
I H8 ALIENS
ILLEGAL ALIENS
IMMIGRATION
ETC...
GOODNESS FELLAS, THIS APPEARS TO BE SOME SORT OF MUSEUM OF GALACTIC FOLK—OUR KIND OF PEOPLE!
THAT'S IDIOTIC. AFTER OUR ERROR AT THE DINER, I'M CONVINCED WE'RE THE ONLY OUTER WORLD EXPLORERS TO REACH EARTH.
THIS IS JUST THAT FANTASY CRAP THAT EARTHLINGS DEVOUR LIKE SO MUCH JUNK FOOD...
SPEAKING OF WHICH—
I CALL DIBS ON FLOOR SNACKS!
THINK THIS IS A HIGH ENOUGH PLATEAU TO REACH RUDNAK?
I THINK IT'S AS HIGH AS I'M CLIMBING!
SHH!
I'M TRYING TO ENJOY THE CRAP!

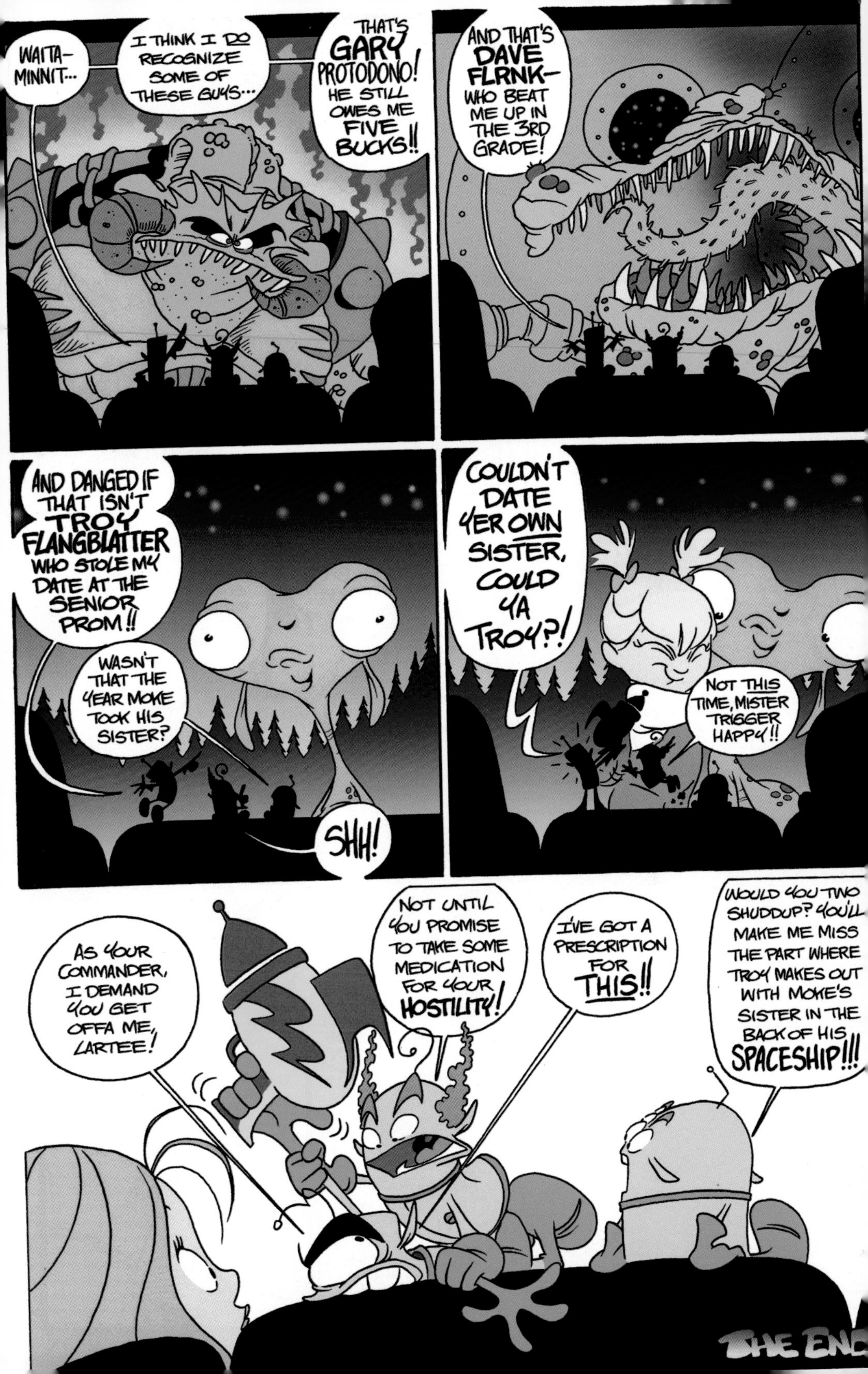
WAITA-MINNIT...
I THINK I DO RECOGNIZE SOME OF THESE GUYS...
THAT'S GARY PROTODONO! HE STILL OWES ME FIVE BUCKS!!
AND THAT'S DAVE FLRNK-WHO BEAT ME UP IN THE 3RD GRADE!
AND DANGED IF THAT ISN'T TROY FLANGBLATTER WHO STOLE MY DATE AT THE SENIOR PROM!!
WASN'T THAT THE YEAR MOKE TOOK HIS SISTER?
SHH!
COULDN'T DATE YER OWN SISTER, COULD YA TROY?!
NOT THIS TIME, MISTER TRIGGER HAPPY!!
AS YOUR COMMANDER, I DEMAND YOU GET OFFA ME, LARTEE!
NOT UNTIL YOU PROMISE TO TAKE SOME MEDICATION FOR YOUR HOSTILITY!
I'VE GOT A PRESCRIPTION FOR THIS!!
WOULD YOU TWO SHUDDUP? YOU'LL MAKE ME MISS THE PART WHERE TROY MAKES OUT WITH MOKE'S SISTER IN THE BACK OF HIS SPACESHIP!!!

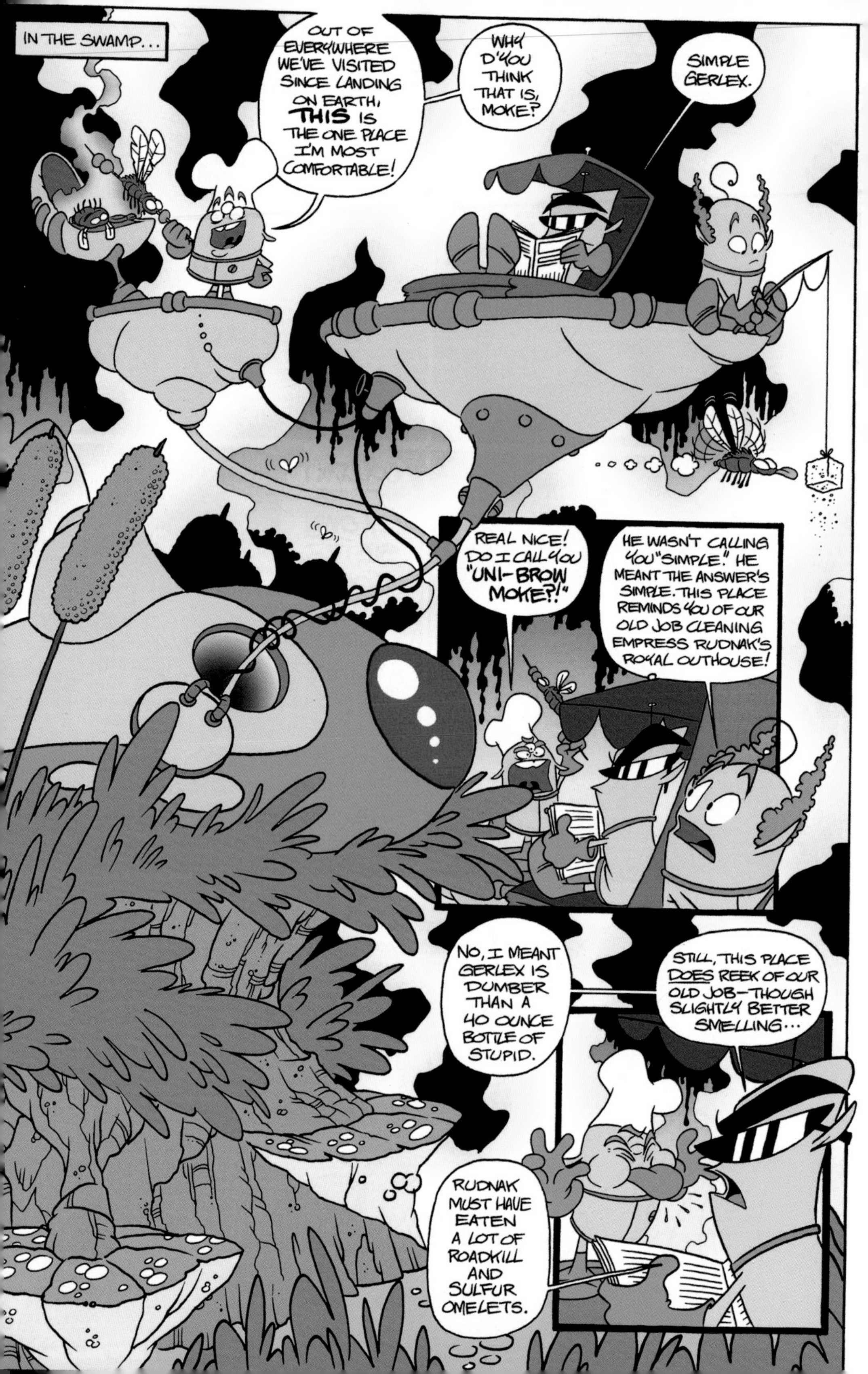
IN THE SWAMP...
OUT OF EVERYWHERE WE'VE VISITED SINCE LANDING ON EARTH, THIS IS THE ONE PLACE I'M MOST COMFORTABLE!
WHY D'YOU THINK THAT IS, MOKE?
SIMPLE GERLEX.
REAL NICE! DO I CALL YOU "UNI-BROW MOKE?!"
HE WASN'T CALLING YOU "SIMPLE." HE MEANT THE ANSWER'S SIMPLE. THIS PLACE REMINDS YOU OF OUR OLD JOB CLEANING EMPRESS RUDNAK'S ROYAL OUTHOUSE!
NO, I MEANT GERLEX IS DUMBER THAN A 40 OUNCE BOTTLE OF STUPID.
STILL, THIS PLACE DOES REEK OF OUR OLD JOB—THOUGH SLIGHTLY BETTER SMELLING...
RUDNAK MUST HAVE EATEN A LOT OF ROADKILL AND SULFUR OMELETS.

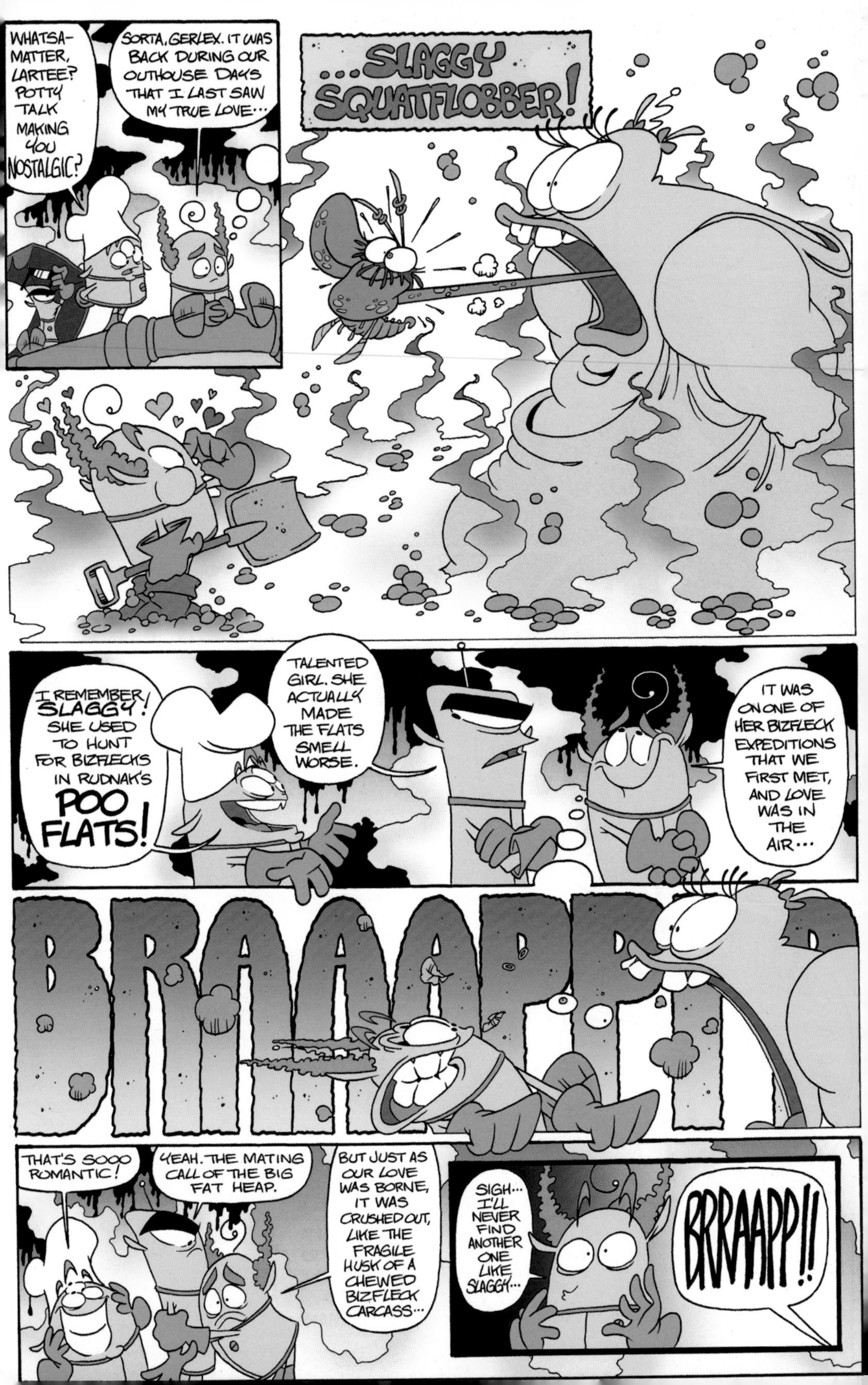
WHATSA-MATTER, LARTEE? POTTY TALK MAKING YOU NOSTALGIC?
SORTA, GERLEX. IT WAS BACK DURING OUR OUTHOUSE DAYS THAT I LAST SAW MY TRUE LOVE...
...SLAGGY SQUATFLOBBER!
I REMEMBER SLAGGY! SHE USED TO HUNT FOR BIZFLECKS IN RUDNAK'S POO FLATS!
TALENTED GIRL. SHE ACTUALLY MADE THE FLATS SMELL WORSE.
IT WAS ON ONE OF HER BIZFLECK EXPEDITIONS THAT WE FIRST MET, AND LOVE WAS IN THE AIR...
BRAAPP!
THAT'S SOOO ROMANTIC!
YEAH. THE MATING CALL OF THE BIG FAT HEAP.
BUT JUST AS OUR LOVE WAS BORNE, IT WAS CRUSHED OUT, LIKE THE FRAGILE HUSK OF A CHEWED BIZFLECK CARCASS...
SIGH... I'LL NEVER FIND ANOTHER ONE LIKE SLAGGY...
BRRAAPP!!

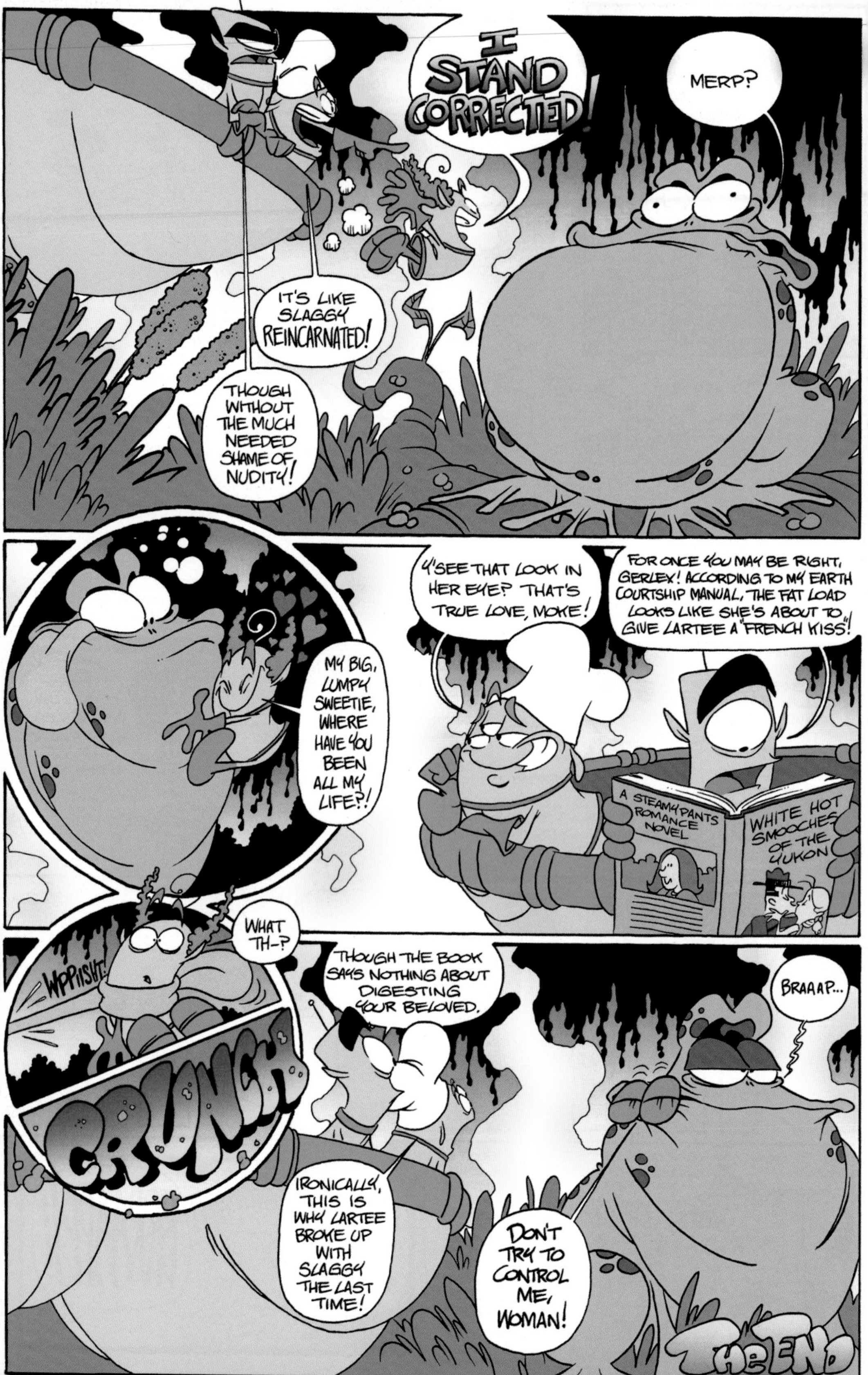
I STAND CORRECTED!
MERP?
IT'S LIKE SLAGGY REINCARNATED!
THOUGH WITHOUT THE MUCH NEEDED SHAME OF NUDITY!
Y'SEE THAT LOOK IN HER EYE? THAT'S TRUE LOVE, MOKE!
FOR ONCE YOU MAY BE RIGHT, GERLEX! ACCORDING TO MY EARTH COURTSHIP MANUAL, THE FAT LOAD LOOKS LIKE SHE'S ABOUT TO GIVE LARTEE A "FRENCH KISS"!
MY BIG, LUMPY SWEETIE, WHERE HAVE YOU BEEN ALL MY LIFE?!
A STEAMY PANTS ROMANCE NOVEL
WHITE HOT SMOOCHES OF THE YUKON
WPPISH!
WHAT TH-?
THOUGH THE BOOK SAYS NOTHING ABOUT DIGESTING YOUR BELOVED.
BRAAAP...
CRUNCH
IRONICALLY, THIS IS WHY LARTEE BROKE UP WITH SLAGGY THE LAST TIME!
DON'T TRY TO CONTROL ME, WOMAN!
THE END

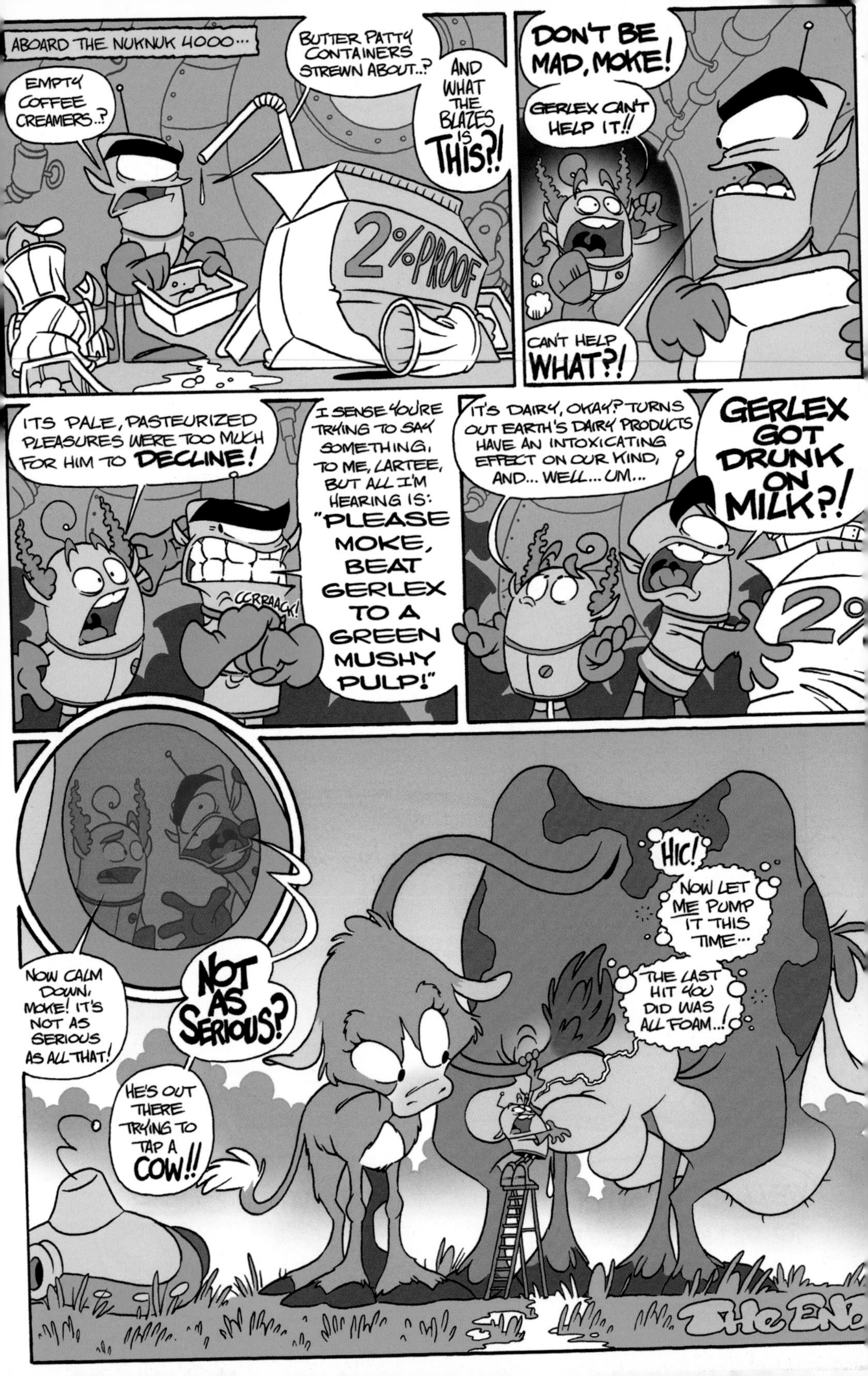
ABOARD THE NUKNUK 4000...
EMPTY COFFEE CREAMERS..?
BUTTER PATTY CONTAINERS STREWN ABOUT..?
AND WHAT THE BLAZES IS THIS?!
2% PROOF
DON'T BE MAD, MOKE!
GERLEX CAN'T HELP IT!!
CAN'T HELP WHAT?!
ITS PALE, PASTEURIZED PLEASURES WERE TOO MUCH FOR HIM TO DECLINE!
CCRRAACK!
I SENSE YOU'RE TRYING TO SAY SOMETHING, TO ME, LARTEE, BUT ALL I'M HEARING IS: "PLEASE MOKE, BEAT GERLEX TO A GREEN MUSHY PULP!"
IT'S DAIRY, OKAY? TURNS OUT EARTH'S DAIRY PRODUCTS HAVE AN INTOXICATING EFFECT ON OUR KIND, AND... WELL... UM...
GERLEX GOT DRUNK ON MILK?!
2%
NOW CALM DOWN, MOKE! IT'S NOT AS SERIOUS AS ALL THAT!
NOT AS SERIOUS?
HE'S OUT THERE TRYING TO TAP A COW!!
HIC!
NOW LET ME PUMP IT THIS TIME...
THE LAST HIT YOU DID WAS ALL FOAM..!
THE END

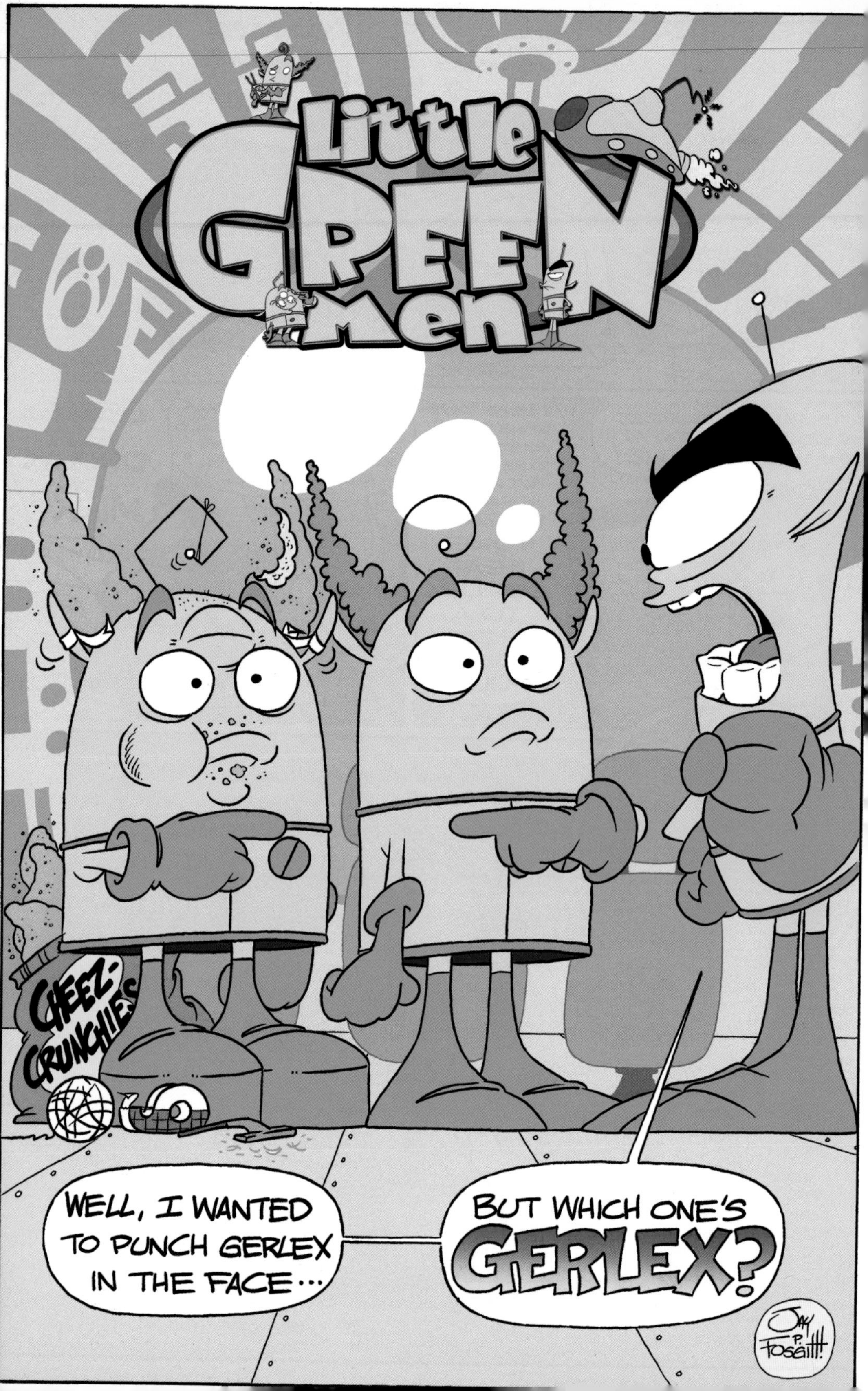
Little GREEN Men
CHEEZ-CRUNCHIES
WELL, I WANTED TO PUNCH GERLEX IN THE FACE...
BUT WHICH ONE'S GERLEX?
JAY P. FOSGITT!

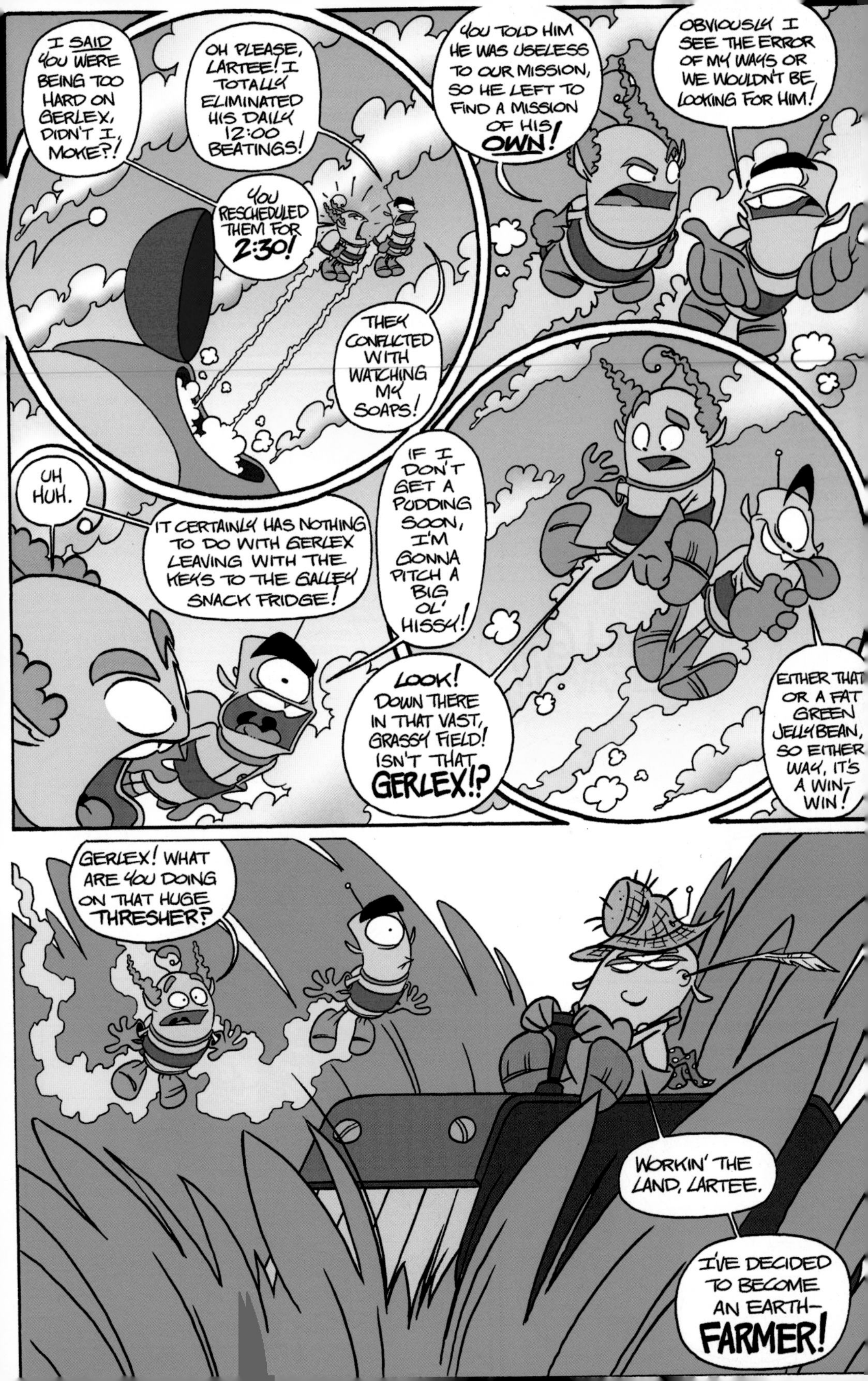
I SAID YOU WERE BEING TOO HARD ON GERLEX, DIDN'T I, MOKE?!
OH PLEASE, LARTEE! I TOTALLY ELIMINATED HIS DAILY 12:00 BEATINGS!
YOU RESCHEDULED THEM FOR 2:30!
THEY CONFLICTED WITH WATCHING MY SOAPS!
YOU TOLD HIM HE WAS USELESS TO OUR MISSION, SO HE LEFT TO FIND A MISSION OF HIS OWN!
OBVIOUSLY I SEE THE ERROR OF MY WAYS OR WE WOULDN'T BE LOOKING FOR HIM!
UH HUH.
IT CERTAINLY HAS NOTHING TO DO WITH GERLEX LEAVING WITH THE KEYS TO THE GALLEY SNACK FRIDGE!
IF I DON'T GET A PUDDING SOON, I'M GONNA PITCH A BIG OL' HISSY!
LOOK! DOWN THERE IN THAT VAST, GRASSY FIELD! ISN'T THAT GERLEX!?
EITHER THAT OR A FAT GREEN JELLYBEAN, SO EITHER WAY, IT'S A WIN-WIN!
GERLEX! WHAT ARE YOU DOING ON THAT HUGE THRESHER?
WORKIN' THE LAND, LARTEE.
I'VE DECIDED TO BECOME AN EARTH-FARMER!

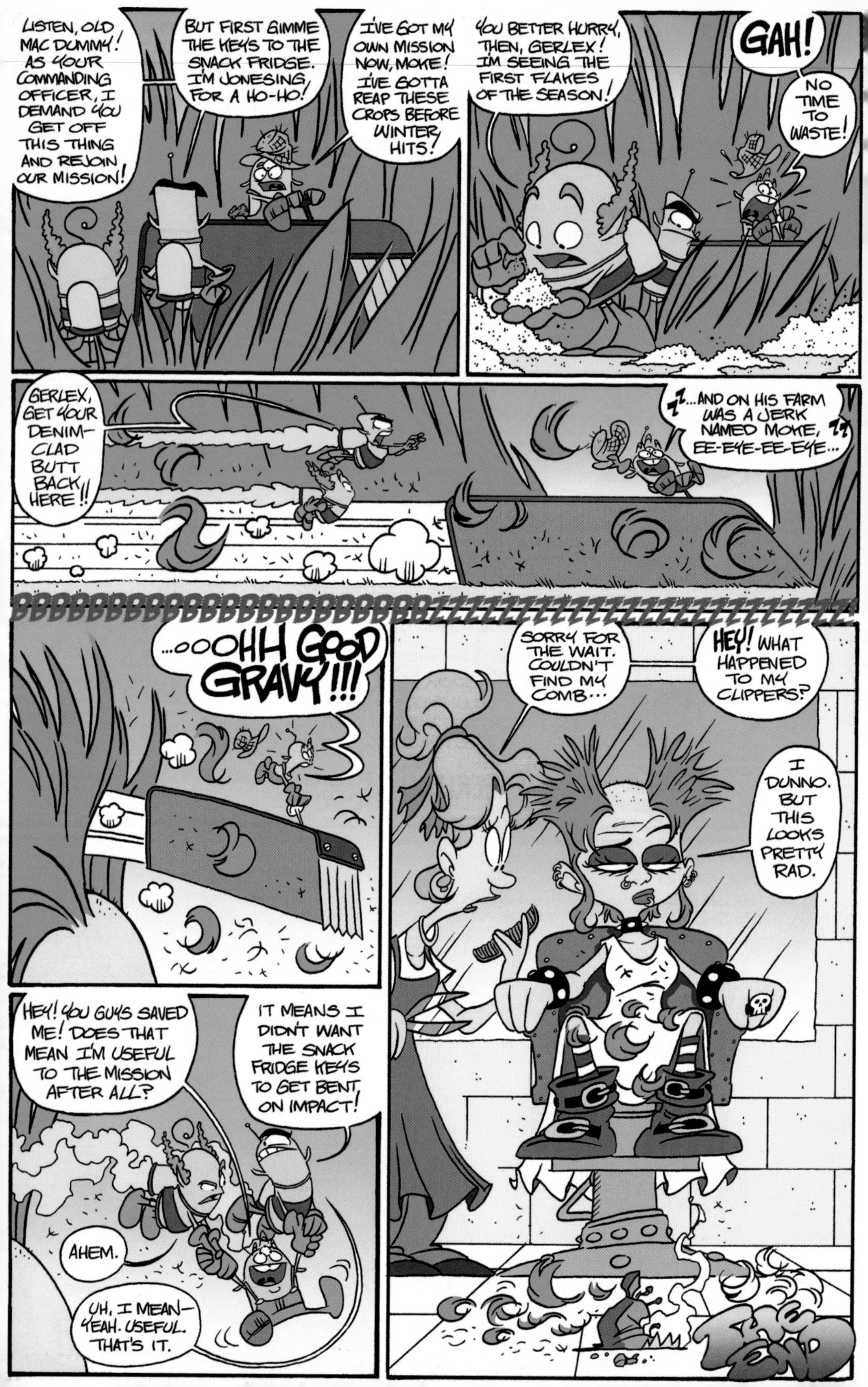
LISTEN, OLD MAC DUMMY! AS YOUR COMMANDING OFFICER, I DEMAND YOU GET OFF THIS THING AND REJOIN OUR MISSION!
BUT FIRST GIMME THE KEYS TO THE SNACK FRIDGE. I'M JONESING FOR A HO-HO!
I'VE GOT MY OWN MISSION NOW, MOKE! I'VE GOTTA REAP THESE CROPS BEFORE WINTER HITS!
YOU BETTER HURRY, THEN, GERLEX! I'M SEEING THE FIRST FLAKES OF THE SEASON!
GAH!
NO TIME TO WASTE!
GERLEX, GET YOUR DENIM-CLAD BUTT BACK HERE!!
Z...AND ON HIS FARM WAS A JERK NAMED MOKE, EE-EYE-EE-EYE...
BBBBBBBBBBBBBBBBBBBBBBBBBBBBZZZZZZZZZZZZZZZZZZZZZZZZZZZZZZZ
...OOOHH GOOD GRAVY!!!
SORRY FOR THE WAIT. COULDN'T FIND MY COMB...
HEY! WHAT HAPPENED TO MY CLIPPERS?
I DUNNO. BUT THIS LOOKS PRETTY RAD.
HEY! YOU GUYS SAVED ME! DOES THAT MEAN I'M USEFUL TO THE MISSION AFTER ALL?
IT MEANS I DIDN'T WANT THE SNACK FRIDGE KEYS TO GET BENT ON IMPACT!
AHEM.
UH, I MEAN-YEAH. USEFUL. THAT'S IT.
THE END

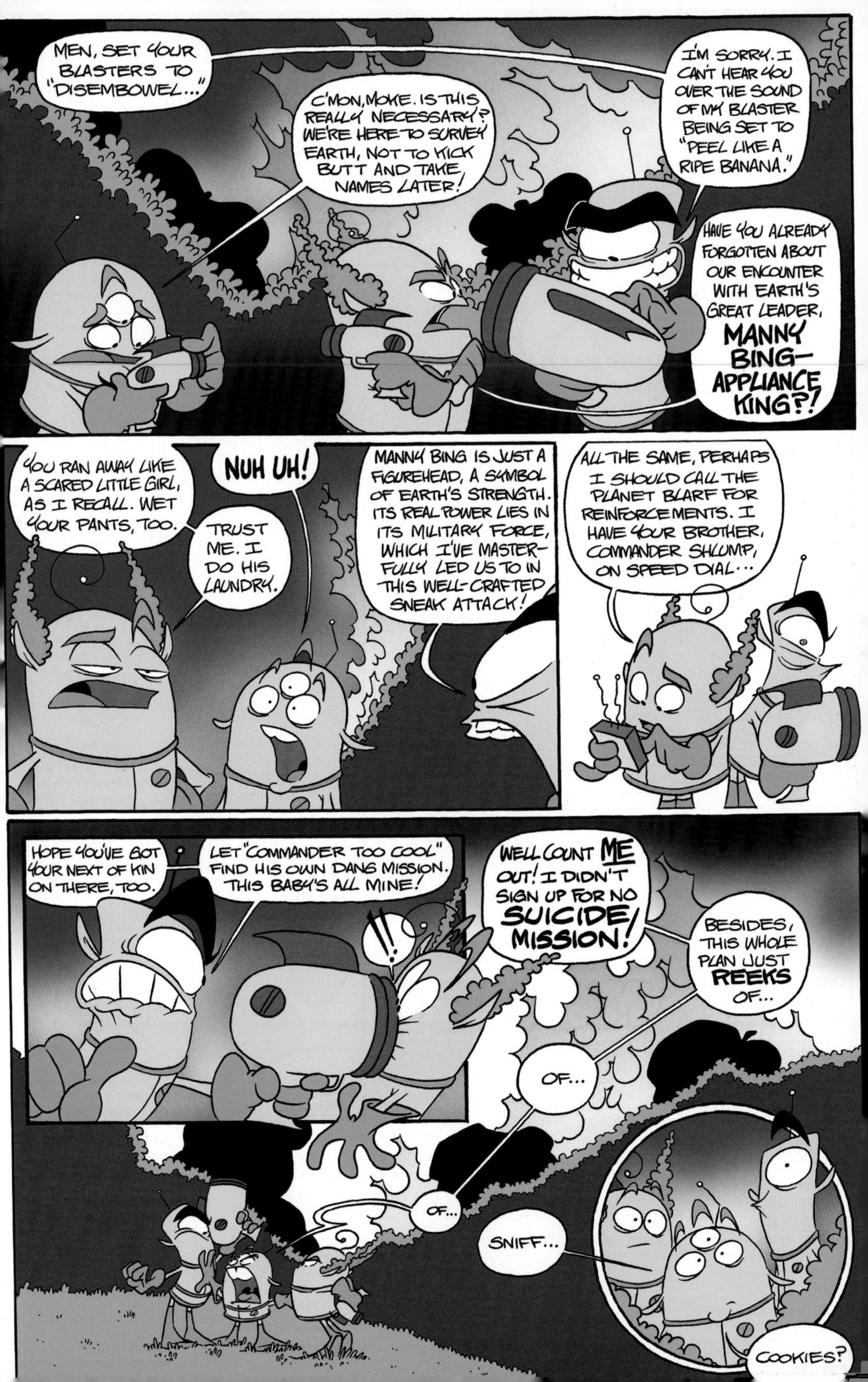
MEN, SET YOUR BLASTERS TO "DISEMBOWEL..."
C'MON, MOKE. IS THIS REALLY NECESSARY? WE'RE HERE TO SURVEY EARTH, NOT TO KICK BUTT AND TAKE NAMES LATER!
I'M SORRY. I CAN'T HEAR YOU OVER THE SOUND OF MY BLASTER BEING SET TO "PEEL LIKE A RIPE BANANA."
HAVE YOU ALREADY FORGOTTEN ABOUT OUR ENCOUNTER WITH EARTH'S GREAT LEADER, MANNY BING— APPLIANCE KING?!
YOU RAN AWAY LIKE A SCARED LITTLE GIRL, AS I RECALL. WET YOUR PANTS, TOO.
NUH UH!
TRUST ME. I DO HIS LAUNDRY.
MANNY BING IS JUST A FIGUREHEAD, A SYMBOL OF EARTH'S STRENGTH. ITS REAL POWER LIES IN ITS MILITARY FORCE, WHICH I'VE MASTERFULLY LED US TO IN THIS WELL-CRAFTED SNEAK ATTACK!
ALL THE SAME, PERHAPS I SHOULD CALL THE PLANET BLARF FOR REINFORCEMENTS. I HAVE YOUR BROTHER, COMMANDER SHLUMP, ON SPEED DIAL...
HOPE YOU'VE GOT YOUR NEXT OF KIN ON THERE, TOO.
LET "COMMANDER TOO COOL" FIND HIS OWN DANG MISSION. THIS BABY'S ALL MINE!
!!
WELL COUNT ME OUT! I DIDN'T SIGN UP FOR NO SUICIDE MISSION!
BESIDES, THIS WHOLE PLAN JUST REEKS OF...
OF...
OF...
SNIFF...
COOKIES?

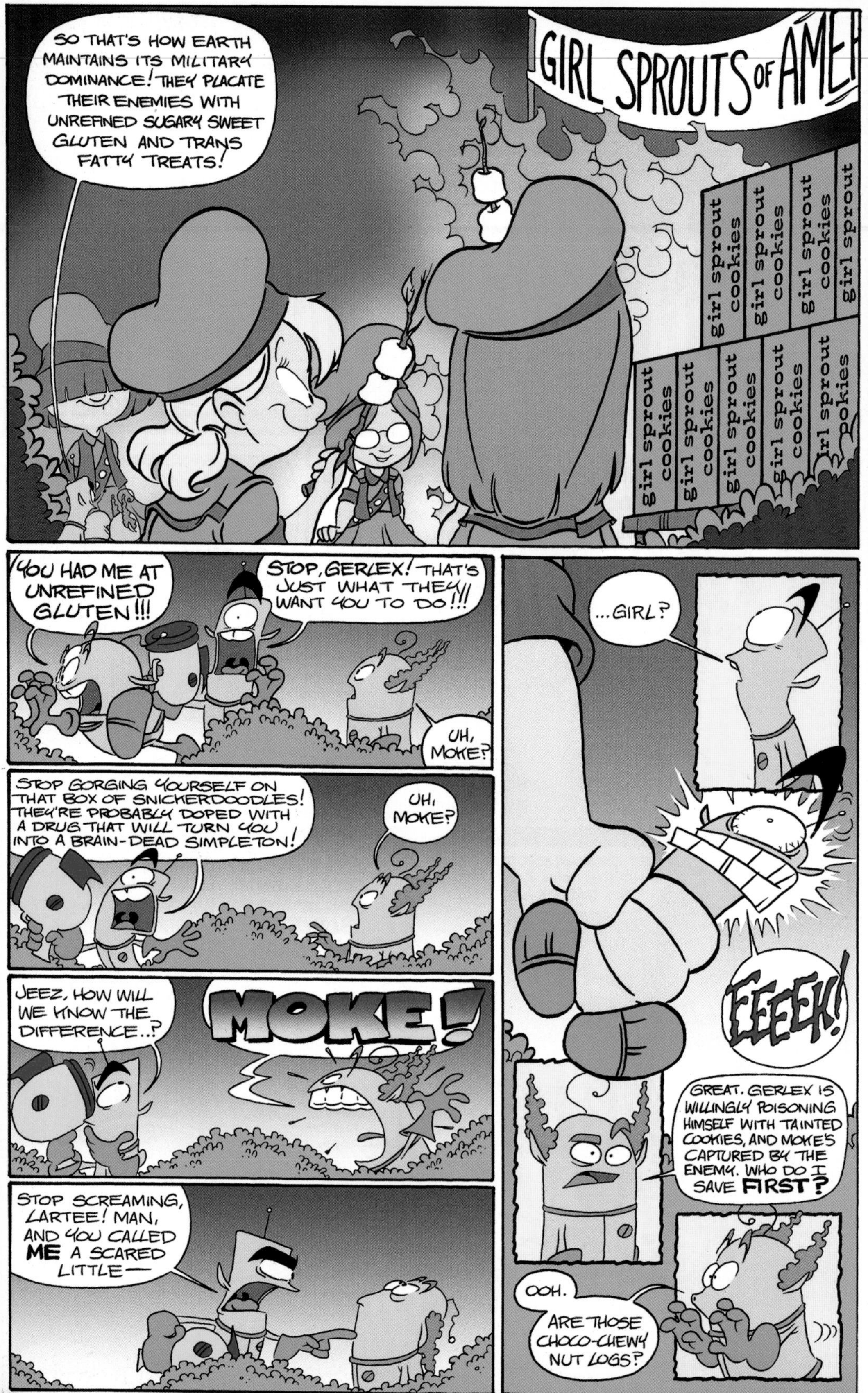
SO THAT'S HOW EARTH MAINTAINS ITS MILITARY DOMINANCE! THEY PLACATE THEIR ENEMIES WITH UNREFINED SUGARY SWEET GLUTEN AND TRANS FATTY TREATS!
GIRL SPROUTS OF AME
girl sprout cookies
YOU HAD ME AT UNREFINED GLUTEN!!!
STOP, GERLEX! THAT'S JUST WHAT THEY WANT YOU TO DO!!!
UH, MOKE?
STOP GORGING YOURSELF ON THAT BOX OF SNICKERDOODLES! THEY'RE PROBABLY DOPED WITH A DRUG THAT WILL TURN YOU INTO A BRAIN-DEAD SIMPLETON!
UH, MOKE?
JEEZ, HOW WILL WE KNOW THE DIFFERENCE..?
MOKE!
STOP SCREAMING, LARTEE! MAN, AND YOU CALLED ME A SCARED LITTLE—
...GIRL?
EEEEK!
GREAT. GERLEX IS WILLINGLY POISONING HIMSELF WITH TAINTED COOKIES, AND MOKE'S CAPTURED BY THE ENEMY. WHO DO I SAVE FIRST?
OOH.
ARE THOSE CHOCO-CHEWY NUT LOGS?

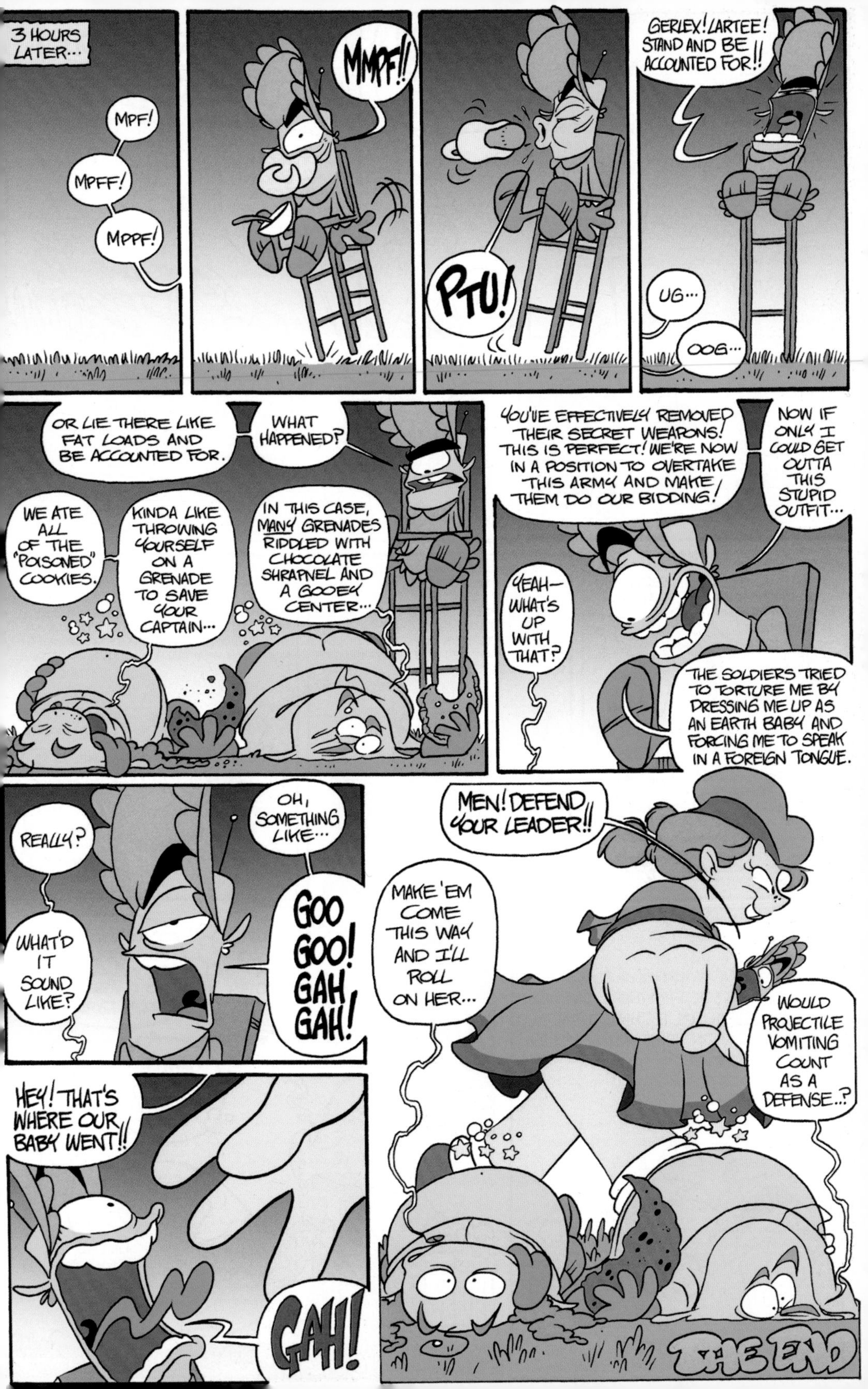
3 HOURS LATER...
MPF!
MPFF!
MPPF!
MMPF!!
PTU!
GERLEX! LARTEE! STAND AND BE ACCOUNTED FOR!!
UG...
OOG...
OR LIE THERE LIKE FAT LOADS AND BE ACCOUNTED FOR.
WHAT HAPPENED?
WE ATE ALL OF THE "POISONED" COOKIES.
KINDA LIKE THROWING YOURSELF ON A GRENADE TO SAVE YOUR CAPTAIN...
IN THIS CASE, MANY GRENADES RIDDLED WITH CHOCOLATE SHRAPNEL AND A GOOEY CENTER...
YOU'VE EFFECTIVELY REMOVED THEIR SECRET WEAPONS! THIS IS PERFECT! WE'RE NOW IN A POSITION TO OVERTAKE THIS ARMY AND MAKE THEM DO OUR BIDDING!
NOW IF ONLY I COULD GET OUTTA THIS STUPID OUTFIT...
YEAH— WHAT'S UP WITH THAT?
THE SOLDIERS TRIED TO TORTURE ME BY DRESSING ME UP AS AN EARTH BABY AND FORCING ME TO SPEAK IN A FOREIGN TONGUE.
REALLY?
WHAT'D IT SOUND LIKE?
OH, SOMETHING LIKE...
GOO GOO! GAH GAH!
HEY! THAT'S WHERE OUR BABY WENT!!
GAH!
MEN! DEFEND YOUR LEADER!!
MAKE 'EM COME THIS WAY AND I'LL ROLL ON HER...
WOULD PROJECTILE VOMITING COUNT AS A DEFENSE..?
THE END

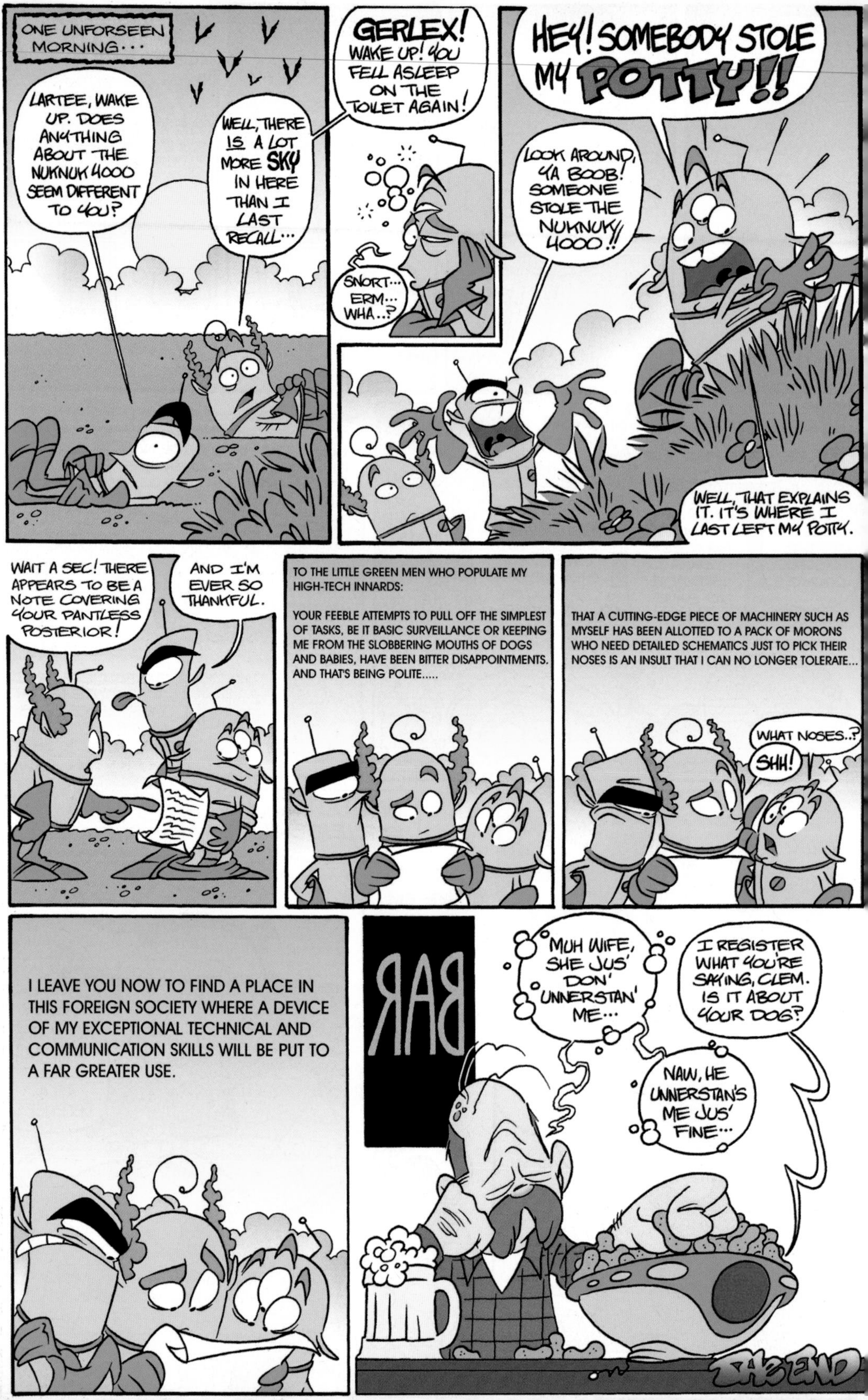

ONE UNFORSEEN MORNING...
LARTEE, WAKE UP. DOES ANYTHING ABOUT THE NUKNUK 4000 SEEM DIFFERENT TO YOU?
WELL, THERE IS A LOT MORE SKY IN HERE THAN I LAST RECALL...
GERLEX! WAKE UP! YOU FELL ASLEEP ON THE TOILET AGAIN!
SNORT... ERM... WHA..?
HEY! SOMEBODY STOLE MY POTTY!!
LOOK AROUND, YA BOOB! SOMEONE STOLE THE NUKNUK 4000!!
WELL, THAT EXPLAINS IT. IT'S WHERE I LAST LEFT MY POTTY.
WAIT A SEC! THERE APPEARS TO BE A NOTE COVERING YOUR PANTLESS POSTERIOR!
AND I'M EVER SO THANKFUL.
TO THE LITTLE GREEN MEN WHO POPULATE MY HIGH-TECH INNARDS:
YOUR FEEBLE ATTEMPTS TO PULL OFF THE SIMPLEST OF TASKS, BE IT BASIC SURVEILLANCE OR KEEPING ME FROM THE SLOBBERING MOUTHS OF DOGS AND BABIES, HAVE BEEN BITTER DISAPPOINTMENTS. AND THAT'S BEING POLITE.....
THAT A CUTTING-EDGE PIECE OF MACHINERY SUCH AS MYSELF HAS BEEN ALLOTTED TO A PACK OF MORONS WHO NEED DETAILED SCHEMATICS JUST TO PICK THEIR NOSES IS AN INSULT THAT I CAN NO LONGER TOLERATE...
WHAT NOSES..?
SHH!
I LEAVE YOU NOW TO FIND A PLACE IN THIS FOREIGN SOCIETY WHERE A DEVICE OF MY EXCEPTIONAL TECHNICAL AND COMMUNICATION SKILLS WILL BE PUT TO A FAR GREATER USE.
BAR
MUH WIFE, SHE JUS' DON' UNNERSTAN' ME...
I REGISTER WHAT YOU'RE SAYING, CLEM. IS IT ABOUT YOUR DOG?
NAW, HE UNNERSTAN'S ME JUS' FINE...
THE END

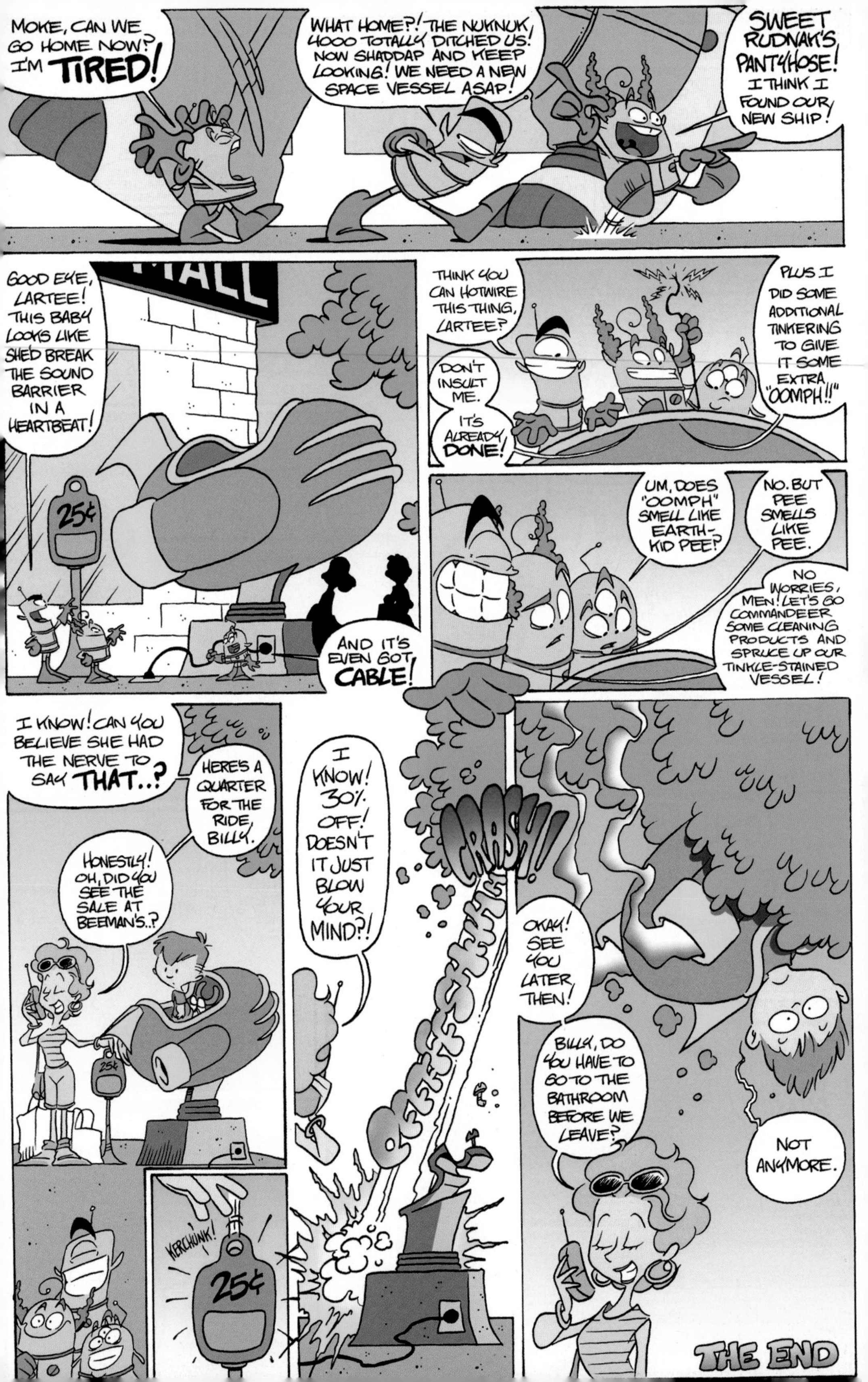

MOKE, CAN WE GO HOME NOW? I'M TIRED!
WHAT HOME?! THE NUKNUK 4000 TOTALLY DITCHED US! NOW SHADDAP AND KEEP LOOKING! WE NEED A NEW SPACE VESSEL ASAP!
SWEET RUDNAK'S PANTYHOSE! I THINK I FOUND OUR NEW SHIP!
MALL
GOOD EYE, LARTEE! THIS BABY LOOKS LIKE SHE'D BREAK THE SOUND BARRIER IN A HEARTBEAT!
25¢
AND IT'S EVEN GOT CABLE!
THINK YOU CAN HOTWIRE THIS THING, LARTEE?
DON'T INSULT ME.
IT'S ALREADY DONE!
PLUS I DID SOME ADDITIONAL TINKERING TO GIVE IT SOME EXTRA "OOMPH!!"
UM, DOES "OOMPH" SMELL LIKE EARTH-KID PEE?
NO. BUT PEE SMELLS LIKE PEE.
NO WORRIES, MEN! LET'S GO COMMANDEER SOME CLEANING PRODUCTS AND SPRUCE UP OUR TINKLE-STAINED VESSEL!
I KNOW! CAN YOU BELIEVE SHE HAD THE NERVE TO SAY THAT..?
HERE'S A QUARTER FOR THE RIDE, BILLY.
HONESTLY! OH, DID YOU SEE THE SALE AT BEEMAN'S..?
25¢
I KNOW! 30% OFF! DOESN'T IT JUST BLOW YOUR MIND?!
KERCHUNK!
25¢
CRASH!!
OKAY! SEE YOU LATER, THEN!
BILLY, DO YOU HAVE TO GO TO THE BATHROOM BEFORE WE LEAVE?
NOT ANYMORE.
THE END

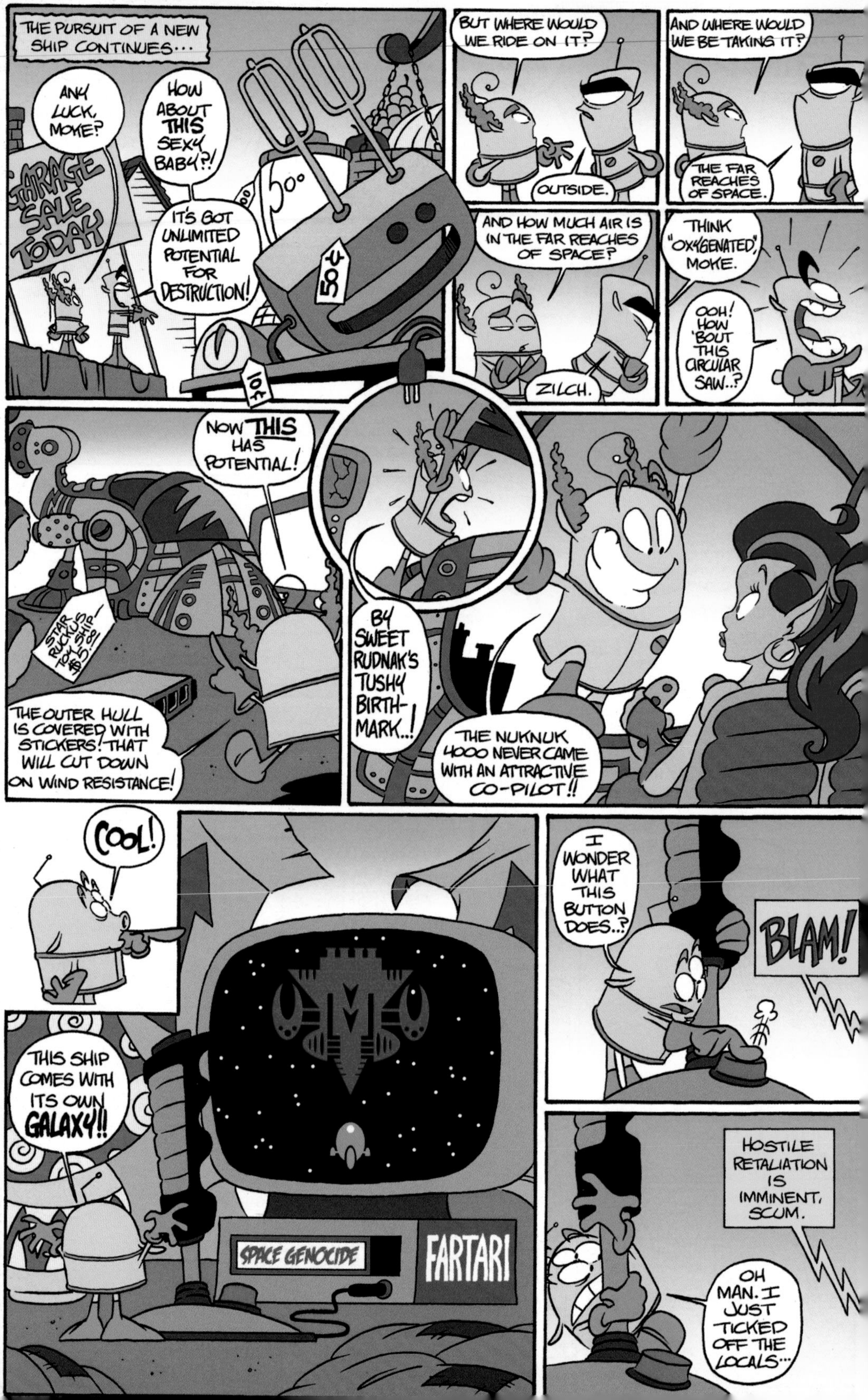
THE PURSUIT OF A NEW SHIP CONTINUES...
ANY LUCK, MOKE?
HOW ABOUT THIS SEXY BABY?!
GARAGE SALE TODAY
IT'S GOT UNLIMITED POTENTIAL FOR DESTRUCTION!
50¢
10¢
BUT WHERE WOULD WE RIDE ON IT?
OUTSIDE.
AND WHERE WOULD WE BE TAKING IT?
THE FAR REACHES OF SPACE.
AND HOW MUCH AIR IS IN THE FAR REACHES OF SPACE?
ZILCH.
THINK "OXYGENATED," MOKE.
OOH! HOW 'BOUT THIS CIRCULAR SAW..?
NOW THIS HAS POTENTIAL!
STAR RUCKUS TOY SHIP $5.00
THE OUTER HULL IS COVERED WITH STICKERS! THAT WILL CUT DOWN ON WIND RESISTANCE!
BY SWEET RUDNAK'S TUSHY BIRTH-MARK..!
THE NUKNUK 4000 NEVER CAME WITH AN ATTRACTIVE CO-PILOT!!
COOL!
THIS SHIP COMES WITH ITS OWN GALAXY!!
SPACE GENOCIDE
FARTARI
I WONDER WHAT THIS BUTTON DOES..?
BLAM!
HOSTILE RETALIATION IS IMMINENT, SCUM.
OH MAN. I JUST TICKED OFF THE LOCALS...

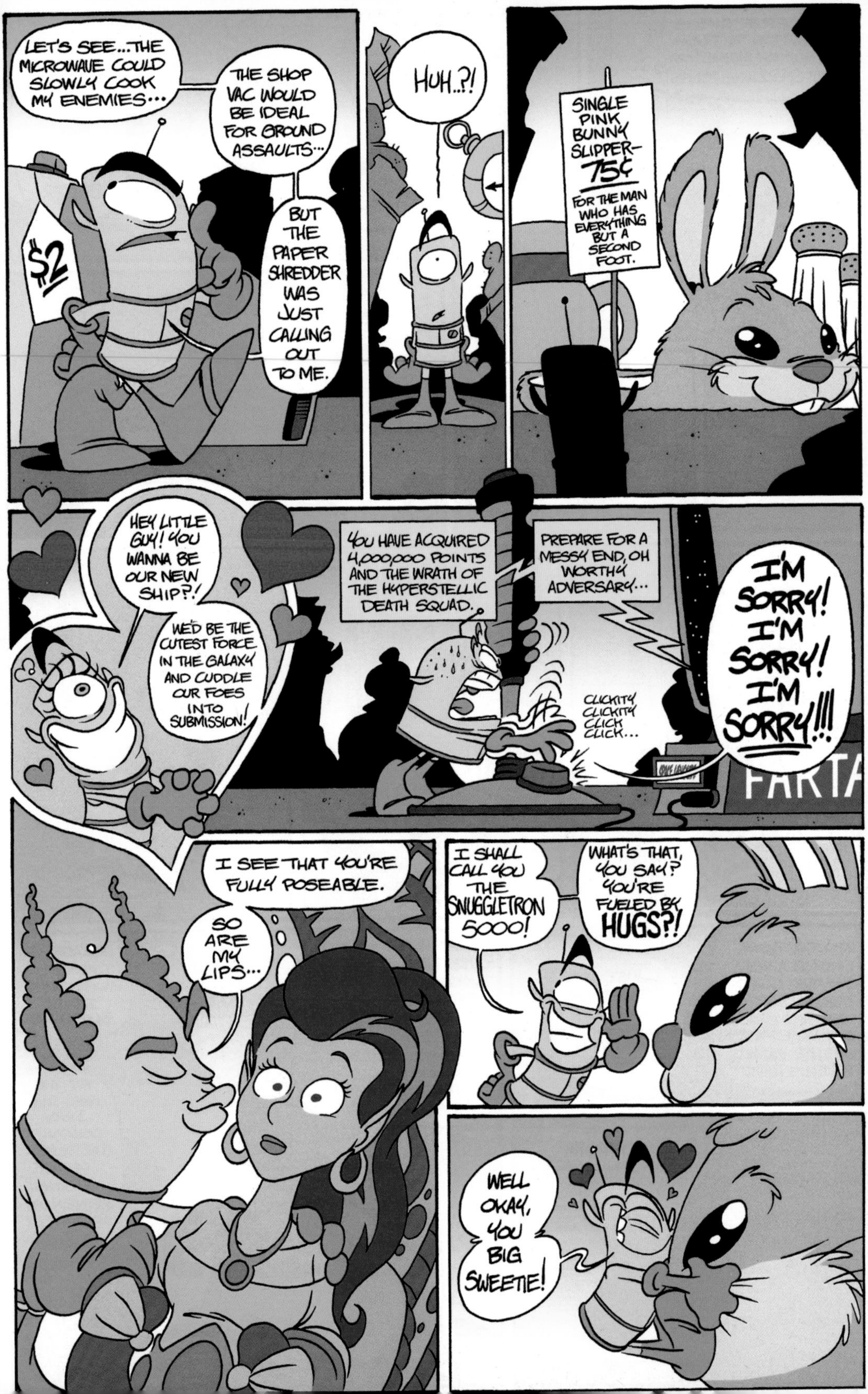
LET'S SEE...THE MICROWAVE COULD SLOWLY COOK MY ENEMIES...
THE SHOP VAC WOULD BE IDEAL FOR GROUND ASSAULTS...
BUT THE PAPER SHREDDER WAS JUST CALLING OUT TO ME.
$2
HUH..?!
SINGLE PINK BUNNY SLIPPER— 75¢ FOR THE MAN WHO HAS EVERYTHING BUT A SECOND FOOT.
HEY LITTLE GUY! YOU WANNA BE OUR NEW SHIP?!
WE'D BE THE CUTEST FORCE IN THE GALAXY AND CUDDLE OUR FOES INTO SUBMISSION!
YOU HAVE ACQUIRED 4,000,000 POINTS AND THE WRATH OF THE HYPERSTELLIC DEATH SQUAD.
PREPARE FOR A MESSY END, OH WORTHY ADVERSARY...
I'M SORRY! I'M SORRY! I'M SORRY!!!
CLICKITY CLICKITY CLICK CLICK...
FARTA
I SEE THAT YOU'RE FULLY POSEABLE.
SO ARE MY LIPS...
I SHALL CALL YOU THE SNUGGLETRON 5000!
WHAT'S THAT, YOU SAY? YOU'RE FUELED BY HUGS?!
WELL OKAY, YOU BIG SWEETIE!

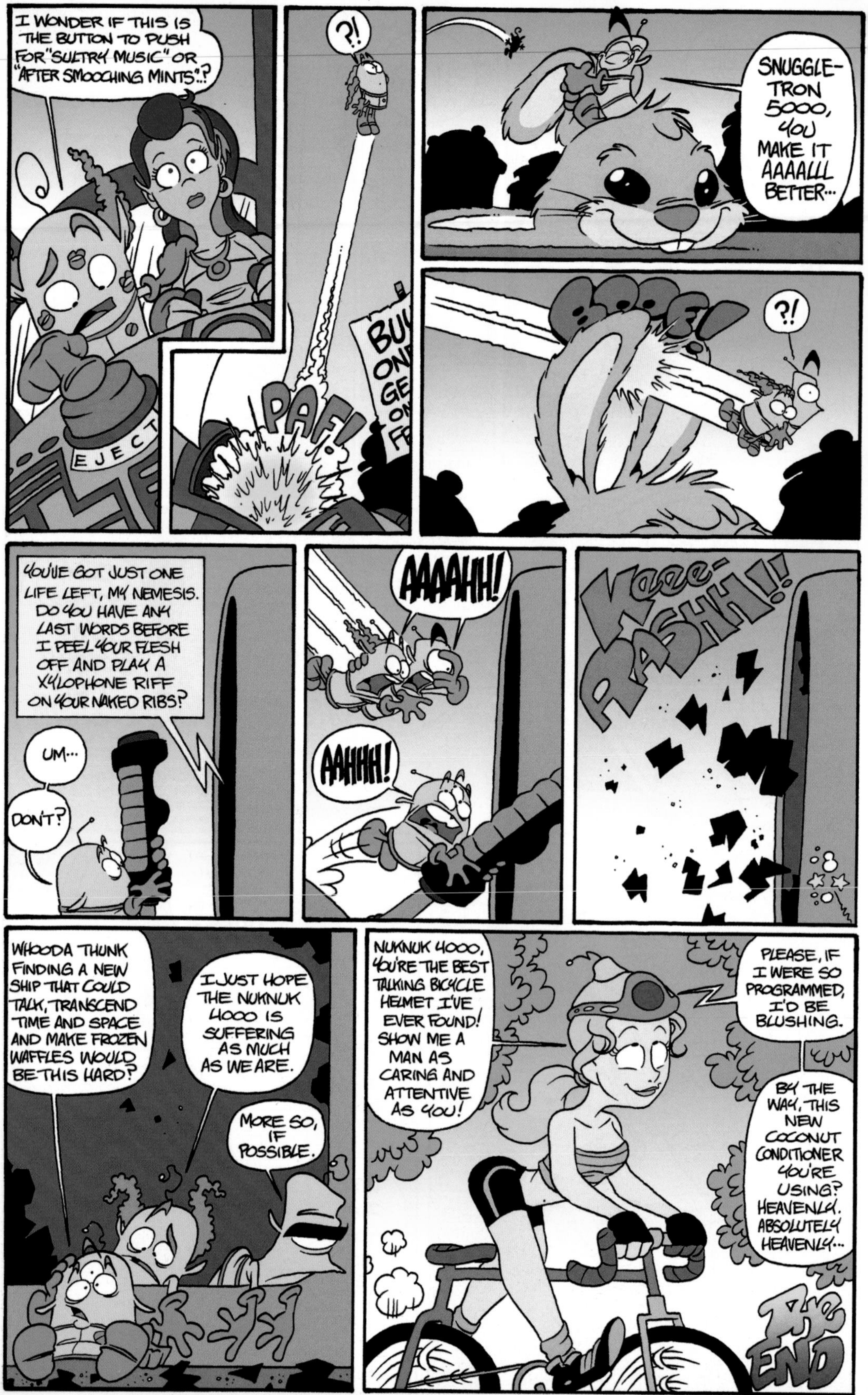

I WONDER IF THIS IS THE BUTTON TO PUSH FOR "SULTRY MUSIC" OR "AFTER SMOOCHING MINTS"..?
EJECT
?!
PAF!
SNUGGLE-TRON 5000, YOU MAKE IT AAAALLL BETTER...
?!
YOU'VE GOT JUST ONE LIFE LEFT, MY NEMESIS. DO YOU HAVE ANY LAST WORDS BEFORE I PEEL YOUR FLESH OFF AND PLAY A XYLOPHONE RIFF ON YOUR NAKED RIBS?
UM...
DON'T?
AAAAHH!
AAHHH!
Kaee-RASHH!!
WHOODA THUNK FINDING A NEW SHIP THAT COULD TALK, TRANSCEND TIME AND SPACE AND MAKE FROZEN WAFFLES WOULD BE THIS HARD?
I JUST HOPE THE NUKNUK 4000 IS SUFFERING AS MUCH AS WE ARE.
MORE SO, IF POSSIBLE.
NUKNUK 4000, YOU'RE THE BEST TALKING BICYCLE HELMET I'VE EVER FOUND! SHOW ME A MAN AS CARING AND ATTENTIVE AS YOU!
PLEASE, IF I WERE SO PROGRAMMED, I'D BE BLUSHING.
BY THE WAY, THIS NEW COCONUT CONDITIONER YOU'RE USING? HEAVENLY. ABSOLUTELY HEAVENLY...
THE END

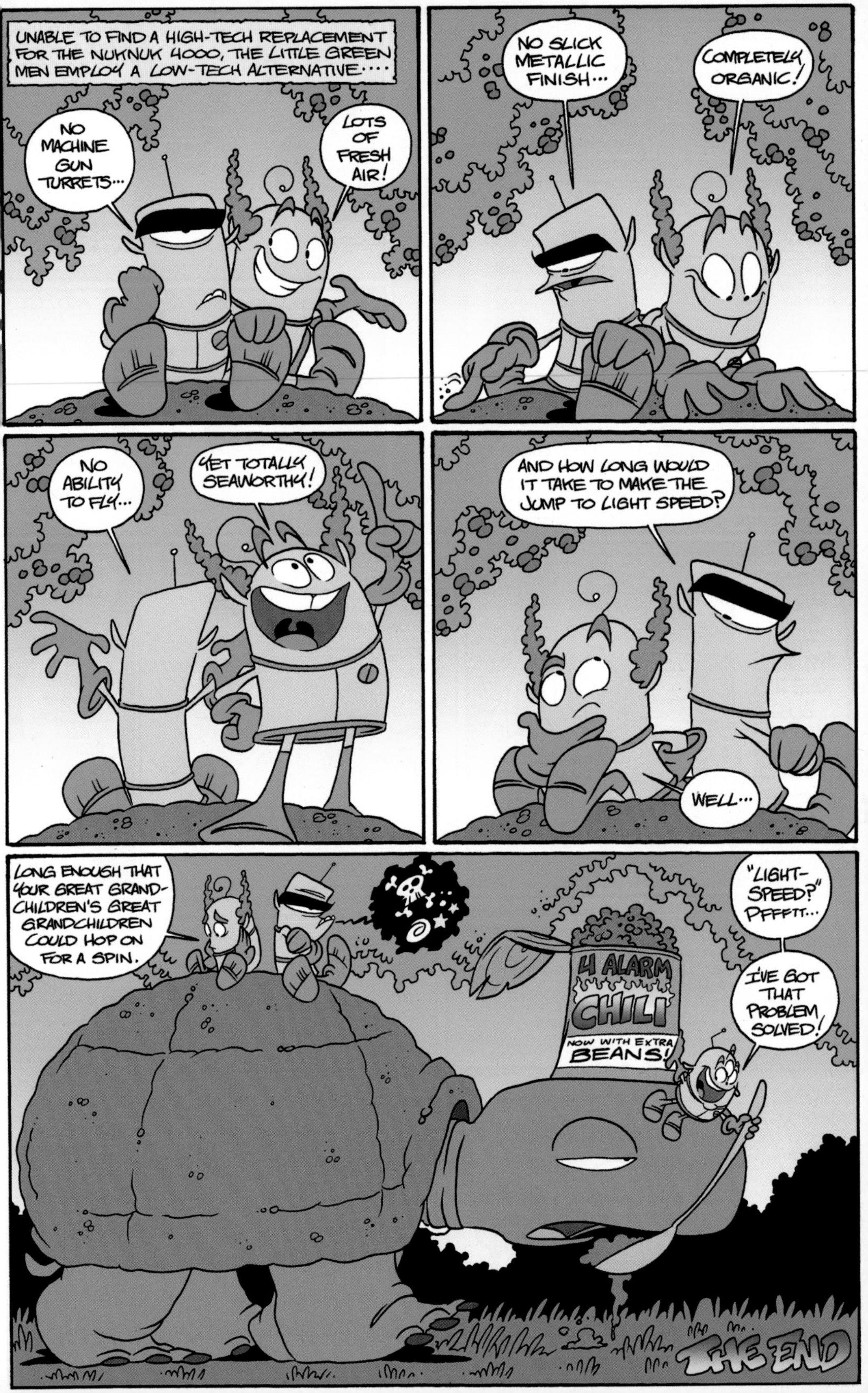
UNABLE TO FIND A HIGH-TECH REPLACEMENT FOR THE NUKNUK 4000, THE LITTLE GREEN MEN EMPLOY A LOW-TECH ALTERNATIVE....
NO MACHINE GUN TURRETS...
LOTS OF FRESH AIR!
NO SLICK METALLIC FINISH...
COMPLETELY ORGANIC!
NO ABILITY TO FLY...
YET TOTALLY SEAWORTHY!
AND HOW LONG WOULD IT TAKE TO MAKE THE JUMP TO LIGHT SPEED?
WELL...
LONG ENOUGH THAT YOUR GREAT GRAND-CHILDREN'S GREAT GRANDCHILDREN COULD HOP ON FOR A SPIN.
"LIGHT-SPEED?" PFFFTT...
I'VE GOT THAT PROBLEM SOLVED!
4 ALARM CHILI
NOW WITH EXTRA BEANS!
THE END

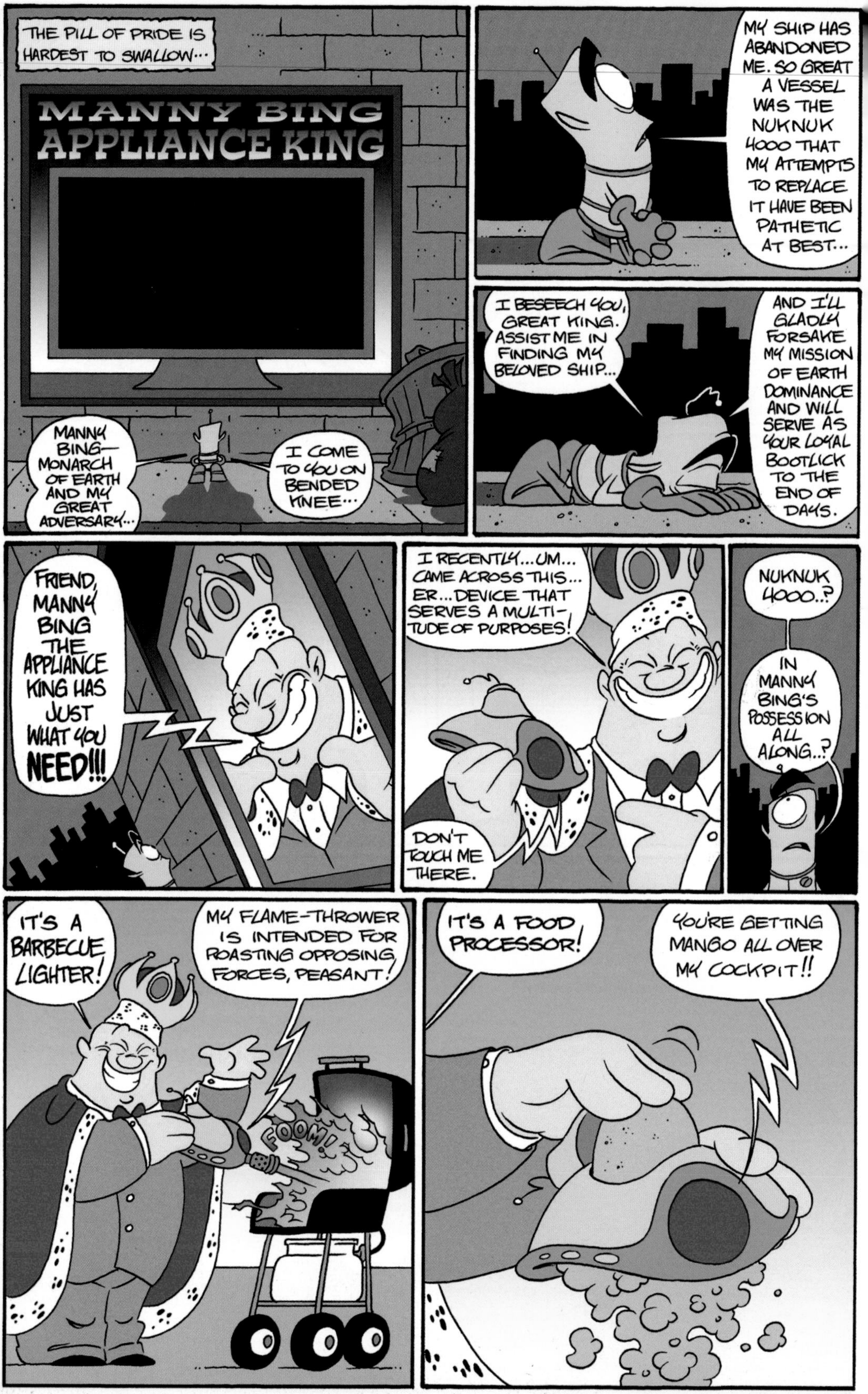
THE PILL OF PRIDE IS HARDEST TO SWALLOW...
MANNY BING APPLIANCE KING
MANNY BING—MONARCH OF EARTH AND MY GREAT ADVERSARY...
I COME TO YOU ON BENDED KNEE...
MY SHIP HAS ABANDONED ME. SO GREAT A VESSEL WAS THE NUKNUK 4000 THAT MY ATTEMPTS TO REPLACE IT HAVE BEEN PATHETIC AT BEST...
I BESEECH YOU, GREAT KING. ASSIST ME IN FINDING MY BELOVED SHIP...
AND I'LL GLADLY FORSAKE MY MISSION OF EARTH DOMINANCE AND WILL SERVE AS YOUR LOYAL BOOTLICK TO THE END OF DAYS.
FRIEND, MANNY BING THE APPLIANCE KING HAS JUST WHAT YOU NEED!!!
I RECENTLY...UM... CAME ACROSS THIS... ER...DEVICE THAT SERVES A MULTI-TUDE OF PURPOSES!
DON'T TOUCH ME THERE.
NUKNUK 4000..?
IN MANNY BING'S POSSESSION ALL ALONG..?
IT'S A BARBECUE LIGHTER!
MY FLAME-THROWER IS INTENDED FOR ROASTING OPPOSING FORCES, PEASANT!
FOOM!
IT'S A FOOD PROCESSOR!
YOU'RE GETTING MANGO ALL OVER MY COCKPIT!!

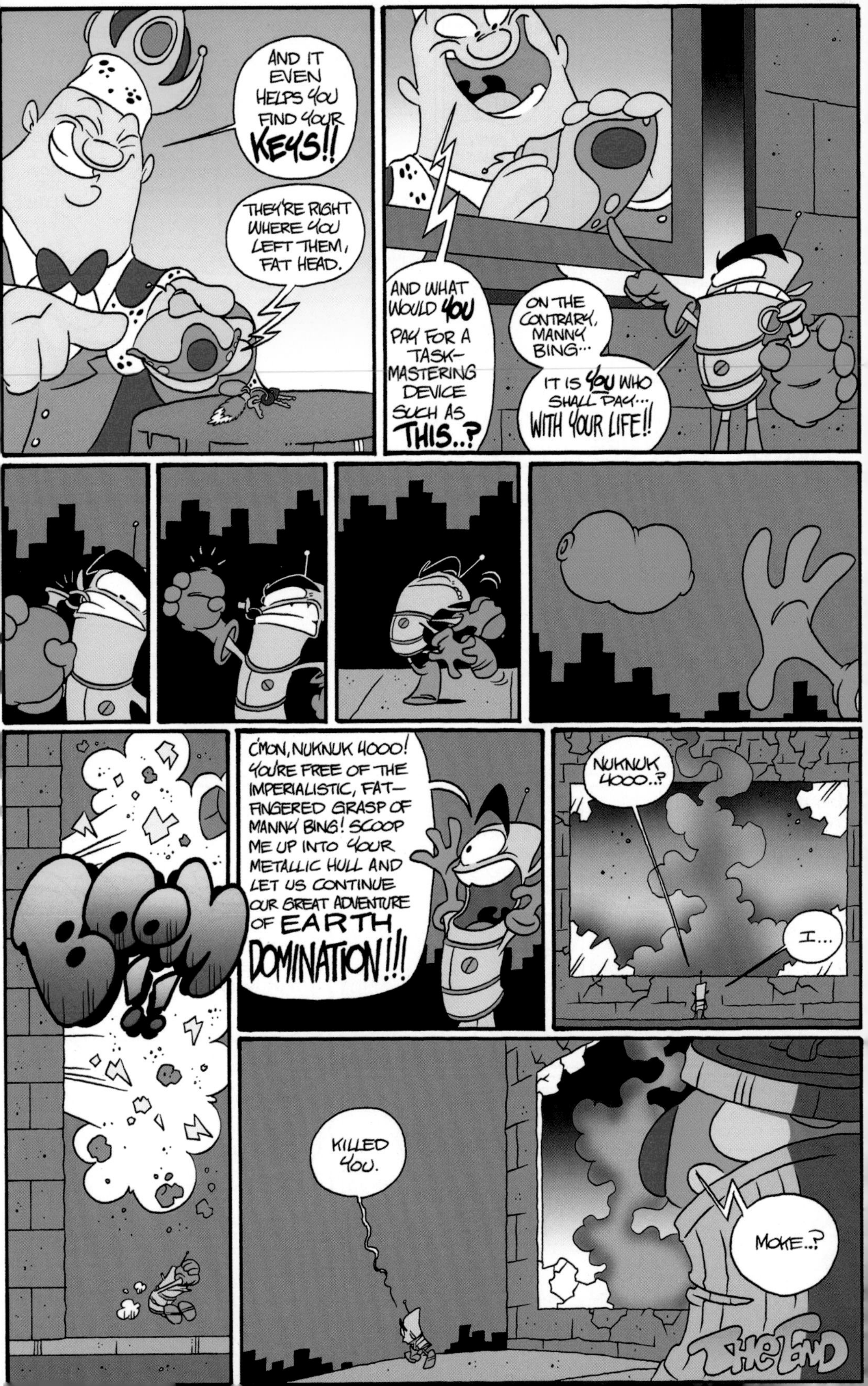

AND IT EVEN HELPS YOU FIND YOUR KEYS!!
THEY'RE RIGHT WHERE YOU LEFT THEM, FAT HEAD.
AND WHAT WOULD YOU PAY FOR A TASK-MASTERING DEVICE SUCH AS THIS..?
ON THE CONTRARY, MANNY BING...
IT IS YOU WHO SHALL PAY... WITH YOUR LIFE!!
BOOM
C'MON, NUKNUK 4000! YOU'RE FREE OF THE IMPERIALISTIC, FAT-FINGERED GRASP OF MANNY BING! SCOOP ME UP INTO YOUR METALLIC HULL AND LET US CONTINUE OUR GREAT ADVENTURE OF EARTH DOMINATION!!!
NUKNUK 4000..?
I...
KILLED YOU.
MOKE..?
THE END

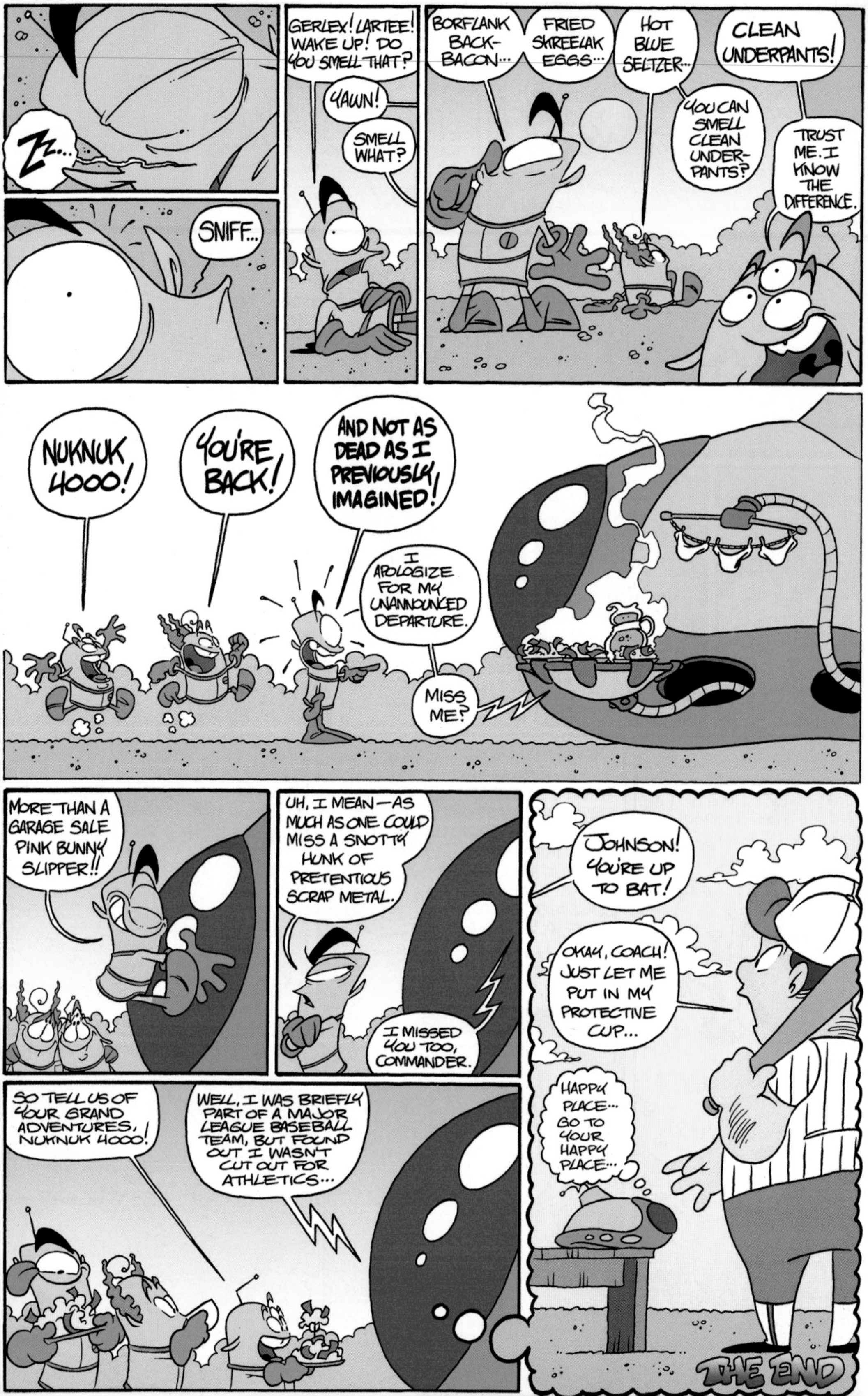

ZZ...
SNIFF...
GERLEX! LARTEE! WAKE UP! DO YOU SMELL THAT?
YAWN!
SMELL WHAT?
BORFLANK BACK-BACON...
FRIED SKREELAK EGGS...
HOT BLUE SELTZER...
CLEAN UNDERPANTS!
YOU CAN SMELL CLEAN UNDER-PANTS?
TRUST ME. I KNOW THE DIFFERENCE.
NUKNUK 4000!
YOU'RE BACK!
AND NOT AS DEAD AS I PREVIOUSLY IMAGINED!
I APOLOGIZE FOR MY UNANNOUNCED DEPARTURE.
MISS ME?
MORE THAN A GARAGE SALE PINK BUNNY SLIPPER!!
UH, I MEAN—AS MUCH AS ONE COULD MISS A SNOTTY HUNK OF PRETENTIOUS SCRAP METAL.
I MISSED YOU TOO, COMMANDER.
SO TELL US OF YOUR GRAND ADVENTURES, NUKNUK 4000!
WELL, I WAS BRIEFLY PART OF A MAJOR LEAGUE BASEBALL TEAM, BUT FOUND OUT I WASN'T CUT OUT FOR ATHLETICS...
JOHNSON! YOU'RE UP TO BAT!
OKAY, COACH! JUST LET ME PUT IN MY PROTECTIVE CUP...
HAPPY PLACE... GO TO YOUR HAPPY PLACE...
THE END

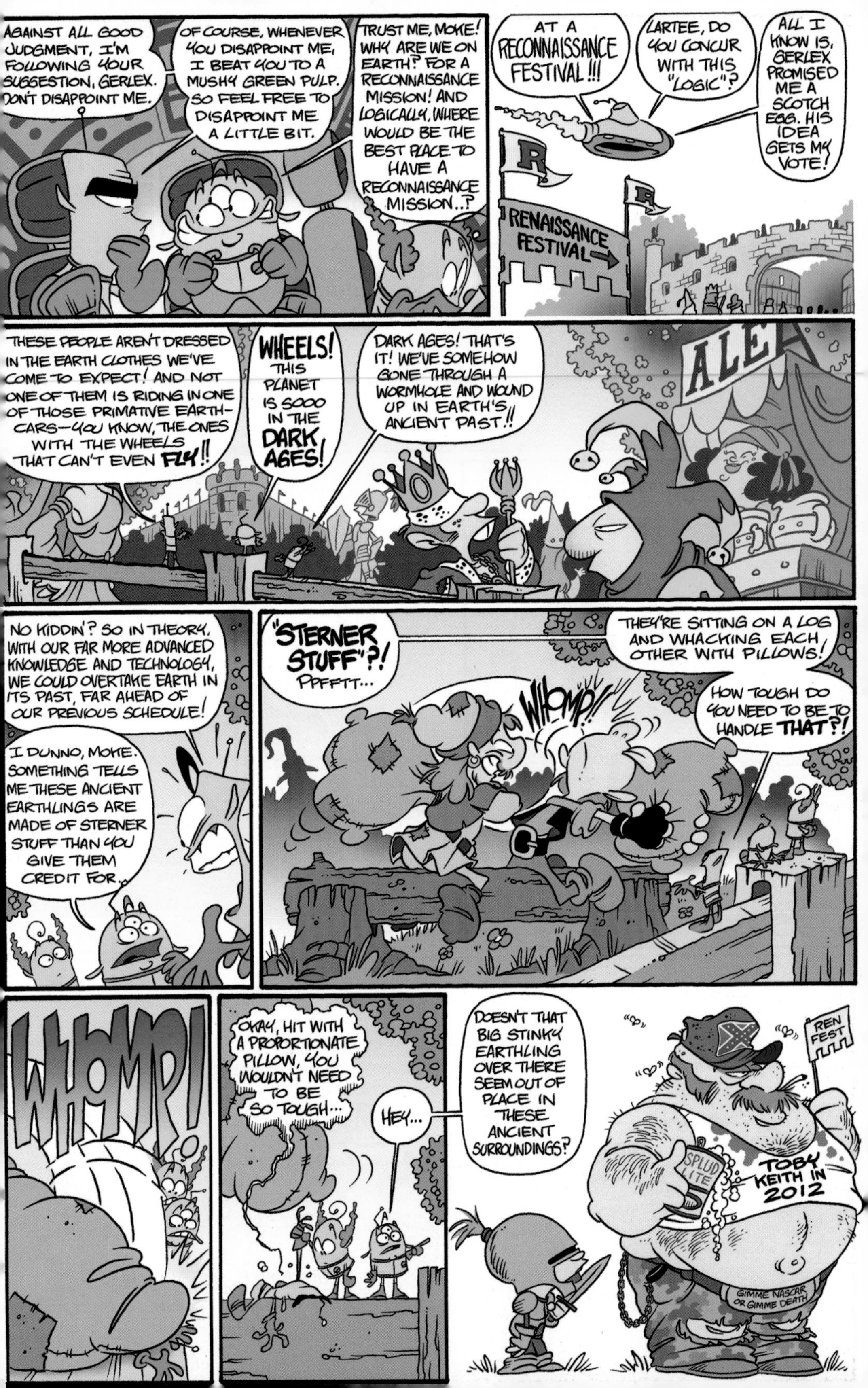
AGAINST ALL GOOD JUDGMENT, I'M FOLLOWING YOUR SUGGESTION, GERLEX. DON'T DISAPPOINT ME.
OF COURSE, WHENEVER YOU DISAPPOINT ME, I BEAT YOU TO A MUSHY GREEN PULP. SO FEEL FREE TO DISAPPOINT ME A LITTLE BIT.
TRUST ME, MOKE! WHY ARE WE ON EARTH? FOR A RECONNAISSANCE MISSION! AND LOGICALLY, WHERE WOULD BE THE BEST PLACE TO HAVE A RECONNAISSANCE MISSION..?
AT A RECONNAISSANCE FESTIVAL!!!
LARTEE, DO YOU CONCUR WITH THIS "LOGIC"?
ALL I KNOW IS, GERLEX PROMISED ME A SCOTCH EGG. HIS IDEA GETS MY VOTE!
RENAISSANCE FESTIVAL
THESE PEOPLE AREN'T DRESSED IN THE EARTH CLOTHES WE'VE COME TO EXPECT! AND NOT ONE OF THEM IS RIDING IN ONE OF THOSE PRIMATIVE EARTH-CARS—YOU KNOW, THE ONES WITH THE WHEELS THAT CAN'T EVEN FLY!!
WHEELS! THIS PLANET IS SOOO IN THE DARK AGES!
DARK AGES! THAT'S IT! WE'VE SOMEHOW GONE THROUGH A WORMHOLE AND WOUND UP IN EARTH'S ANCIENT PAST!!
ALE
NO KIDDIN'? SO IN THEORY, WITH OUR FAR MORE ADVANCED KNOWLEDGE AND TECHNOLOGY, WE COULD OVERTAKE EARTH IN ITS PAST, FAR AHEAD OF OUR PREVIOUS SCHEDULE!
I DUNNO, MOKE. SOMETHING TELLS ME THESE ANCIENT EARTHLINGS ARE MADE OF STERNER STUFF THAN YOU GIVE THEM CREDIT FOR...
"STERNER STUFF"?! PPFFTT...
THEY'RE SITTING ON A LOG AND WHACKING EACH OTHER WITH PILLOWS!
WHOMP!!
HOW TOUGH DO YOU NEED TO BE TO HANDLE THAT?!
WHOMP!
OKAY, HIT WITH A PROPORTIONATE PILLOW, YOU WOULDN'T NEED TO BE SO TOUGH...
HEY...
DOESN'T THAT BIG STINKY EARTHLING OVER THERE SEEM OUT OF PLACE IN THESE ANCIENT SURROUNDINGS?
REN FEST
SPLUD LITE
TOBY KEITH IN 2012
GIMME NASCAR OR GIMME DEATH

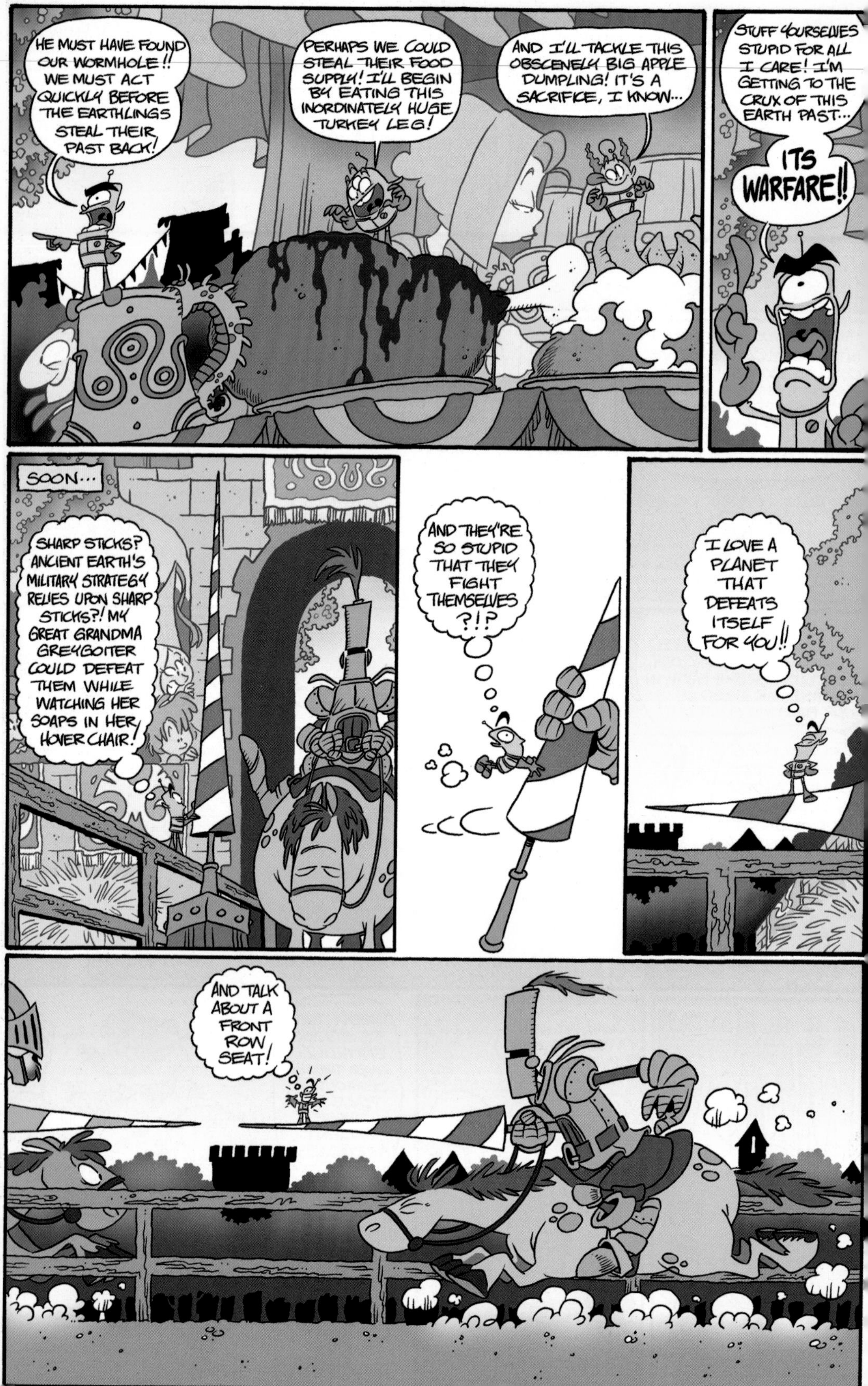
HE MUST HAVE FOUND OUR WORMHOLE!! WE MUST ACT QUICKLY BEFORE THE EARTHLINGS STEAL THEIR PAST BACK!
PERHAPS WE COULD STEAL THEIR FOOD SUPPLY! I'LL BEGIN BY EATING THIS INORDINATELY HUGE TURKEY LEG!
AND I'LL TACKLE THIS OBSCENELY BIG APPLE DUMPLING! IT'S A SACRIFICE, I KNOW...
STUFF YOURSELVES STUPID FOR ALL I CARE! I'M GETTING TO THE CRUX OF THIS EARTH PAST...
ITS WARFARE!!
SOON...
SHARP STICKS? ANCIENT EARTH'S MILITARY STRATEGY RELIES UPON SHARP STICKS?! MY GREAT GRANDMA GREYGOITER COULD DEFEAT THEM WHILE WATCHING HER SOAPS IN HER HOVER CHAIR!
AND THEY'RE SO STUPID THAT THEY FIGHT THEMSELVES ?!?
I LOVE A PLANET THAT DEFEATS ITSELF FOR YOU!!
AND TALK ABOUT A FRONT ROW SEAT!

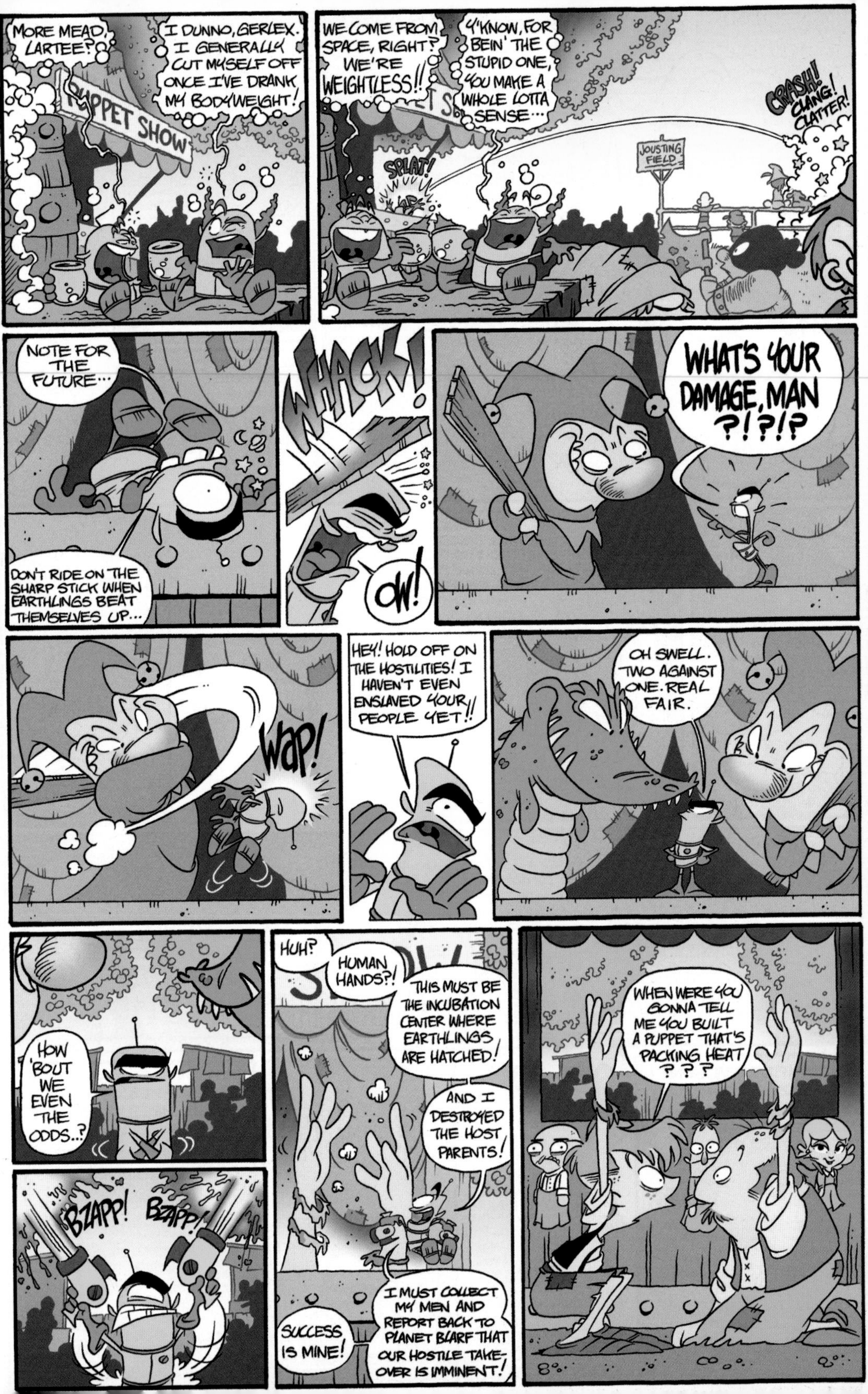
MORE MEAD, LARTEE?
I DUNNO, GERLEX. I GENERALLY CUT MYSELF OFF ONCE I'VE DRANK MY BODYWEIGHT!
PUPPET SHOW
WE COME FROM SPACE, RIGHT? WE'RE WEIGHTLESS!!
Y'KNOW, FOR BEIN' THE STUPID ONE, YOU MAKE A WHOLE LOTTA SENSE...
SPLAT!
JOUSTING FIELD
CRASH! CLANG! CLATTER!
NOTE FOR THE FUTURE...
DON'T RIDE ON THE SHARP STICK WHEN EARTHLINGS BEAT THEMSELVES UP...
WHACK!
OW!
WHAT'S YOUR DAMAGE, MAN ?!?!?
WAP!
HEY! HOLD OFF ON THE HOSTILITIES! I HAVEN'T EVEN ENSLAVED YOUR PEOPLE YET!!
OH SWELL. TWO AGAINST ONE. REAL FAIR.
HOW 'BOUT WE EVEN THE ODDS..?
BZAPP! BZAPP!
HUH?
HUMAN HANDS?!
THIS MUST BE THE INCUBATION CENTER WHERE EARTHLINGS ARE HATCHED!
AND I DESTROYED THE HOST PARENTS!
SUCCESS IS MINE!
I MUST COLLECT MY MEN AND REPORT BACK TO PLANET BLARF THAT OUR HOSTILE TAKE-OVER IS IMMINENT!
WHEN WERE YOU GONNA TELL ME YOU BUILT A PUPPET THAT'S PACKING HEAT ???

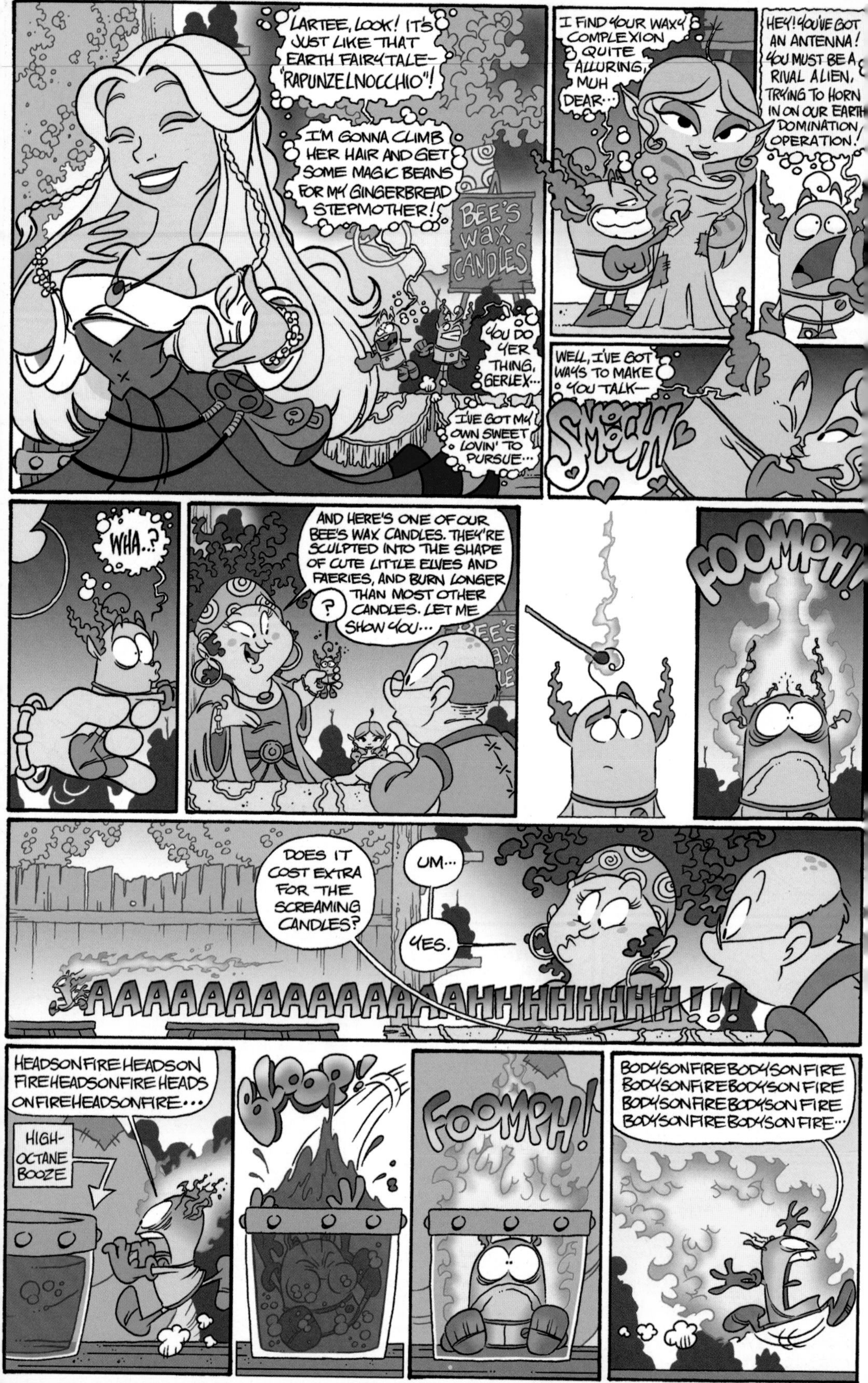
LARTEE, LOOK! IT'S JUST LIKE THAT EARTH FAIRY TALE— "RAPUNZELNOCCHIO"!
I'M GONNA CLIMB HER HAIR AND GET SOME MAGIC BEANS FOR MY GINGERBREAD STEPMOTHER!
BEE'S WAX CANDLES
YOU DO YER THING, GERLEX...
I'VE GOT MY OWN SWEET LOVIN' TO PURSUE...
I FIND YOUR WAXY COMPLEXION QUITE ALLURING, MUH DEAR...
HEY! YOU'VE GOT AN ANTENNA! YOU MUST BE A RIVAL ALIEN, TRYING TO HORN IN ON OUR EARTH DOMINATION OPERATION!
WELL, I'VE GOT WAYS TO MAKE YOU TALK—
SMOOCH
WHA..?
AND HERE'S ONE OF OUR BEE'S WAX CANDLES. THEY'RE SCULPTED INTO THE SHAPE OF CUTE LITTLE ELVES AND FAERIES, AND BURN LONGER THAN MOST OTHER CANDLES. LET ME SHOW YOU...
?
FOOMPH!
DOES IT COST EXTRA FOR THE SCREAMING CANDLES?
UM...
YES.
AAAAAAAAAAAAAAAHHHHHHHHH!!!
HEADSONFIREHEADSON FIREHEADSONFIREHEADS ONFIREHEADSONFIRE...
HIGH-OCTANE BOOZE
BLOOP!
FOOMPH!
BODYSONFIREBODYSONFIRE BODYSONFIREBODYSONFIRE BODYSONFIREBODYSONFIRE BODYSONFIREBODYSONFIRE...

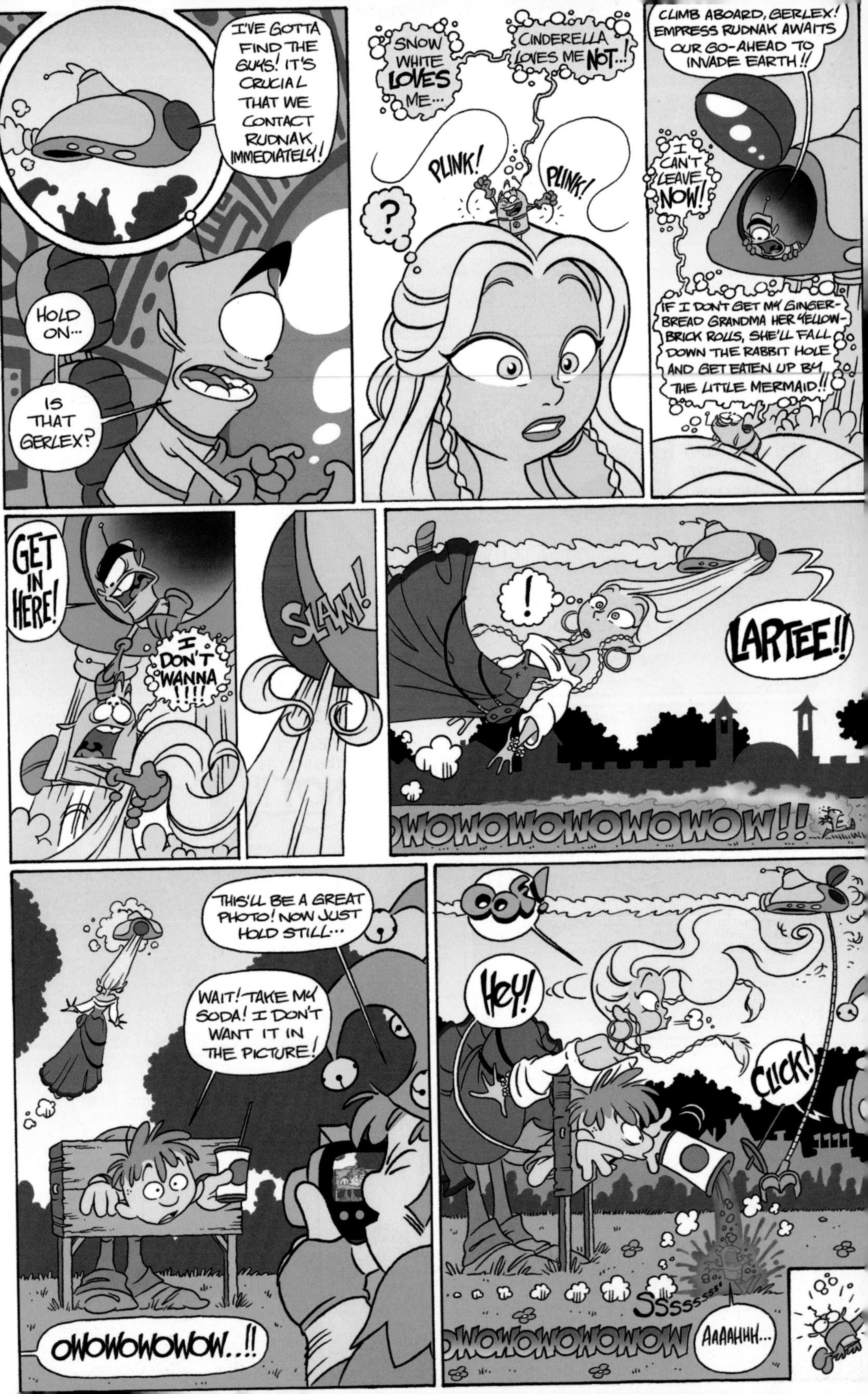
I'VE GOTTA FIND THE GUYS! IT'S CRUCIAL THAT WE CONTACT RUDNAK IMMEDIATELY!
HOLD ON...
IS THAT GERLEX?
SNOW WHITE LOVES ME...
CINDERELLA LOVES ME NOT...!
PLINK!
PLINK!
?
CLIMB ABOARD, GERLEX! EMPRESS RUDNAK AWAITS OUR GO-AHEAD TO INVADE EARTH!!
I CAN'T LEAVE NOW!
IF I DON'T GET MY GINGERBREAD GRANDMA HER YELLOW-BRICK ROLLS, SHE'LL FALL DOWN THE RABBIT HOLE AND GET EATEN UP BY THE LITTLE MERMAID!!
GET IN HERE!
I DON'T WANNA!!!!
SLAM!
!
LARTEE!!
OWOWOWOWOWOWOWOW!!
THIS'LL BE A GREAT PHOTO! NOW JUST HOLD STILL...
WAIT! TAKE MY SODA! I DON'T WANT IT IN THE PICTURE!
OWOWOWOWOW...!!
OOF!
HEY!
CLICK!
SSSSSSSS
OWOWOWOWOWOW
AAAAHHH...

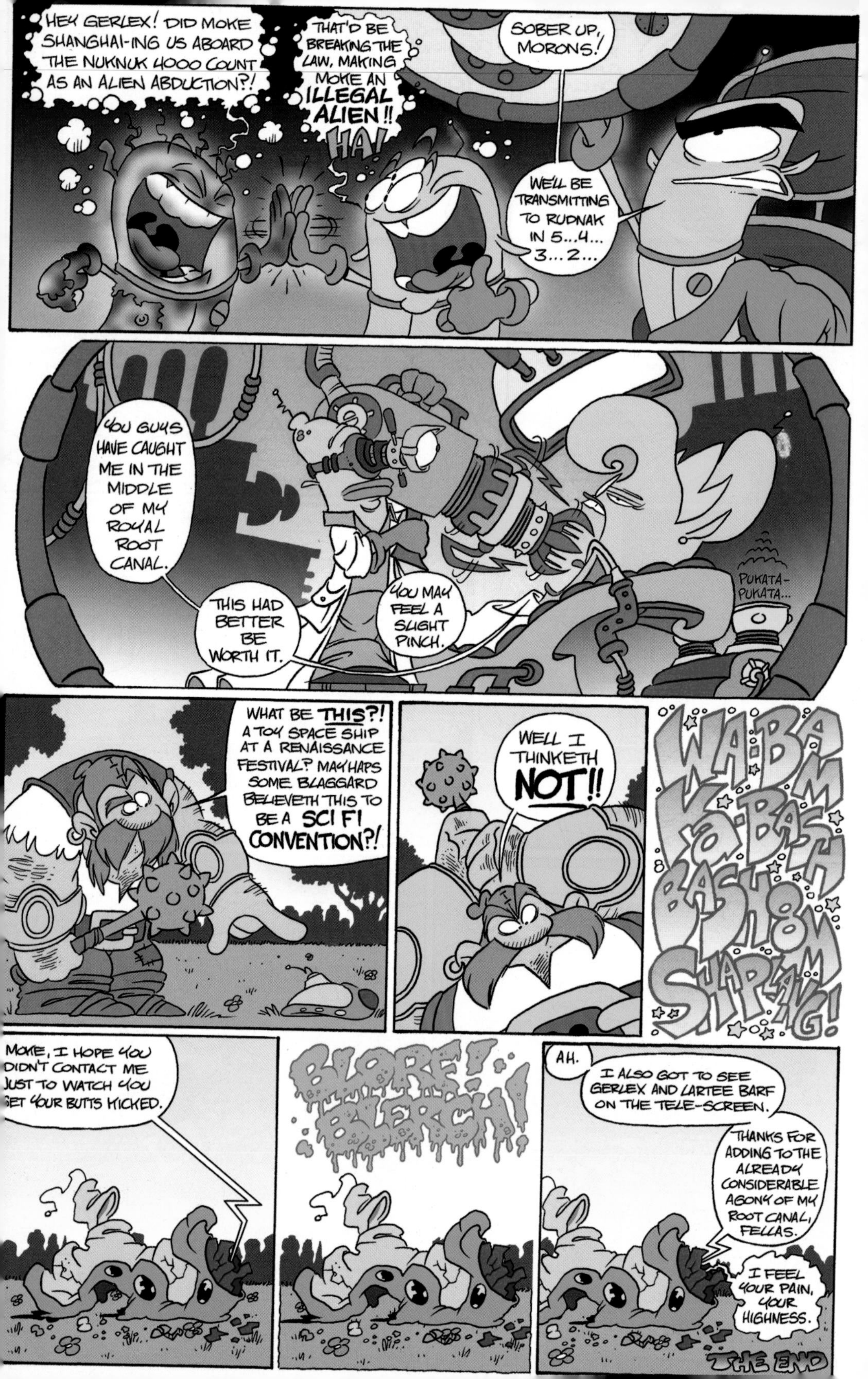

HEY GERLEX! DID MOKE SHANGHAI-ING US ABOARD THE NUKNUK 4000 COUNT AS AN ALIEN ABDUCTION?!
THAT'D BE BREAKING THE LAW, MAKING MOKE AN ILLEGAL ALIEN!! HA!
SOBER UP, MORONS!
WE'LL BE TRANSMITTING TO RUDNAK IN 5...4... 3...2...
YOU GUYS HAVE CAUGHT ME IN THE MIDDLE OF MY ROYAL ROOT CANAL.
THIS HAD BETTER BE WORTH IT.
YOU MAY FEEL A SLIGHT PINCH.
PUKATA-PUKATA...
WHAT BE THIS?! A TOY SPACE SHIP AT A RENAISSANCE FESTIVAL? MAYHAPS SOME BLAGGARD BELIEVETH THIS TO BE A SCI FI CONVENTION?!
WELL I THINKETH NOT!!
WA-BAM KA-BASH BASH BOOM SHPLANG!
MOKE, I HOPE YOU DIDN'T CONTACT ME JUST TO WATCH YOU GET YOUR BUTTS KICKED.
BLORF! BLERCH!
AH.
I ALSO GOT TO SEE GERLEX AND LARTEE BARF ON THE TELE-SCREEN.
THANKS FOR ADDING TO THE ALREADY CONSIDERABLE AGONY OF MY ROOT CANAL, FELLAS.
I FEEL YOUR PAIN, YOUR HIGHNESS.
THE END

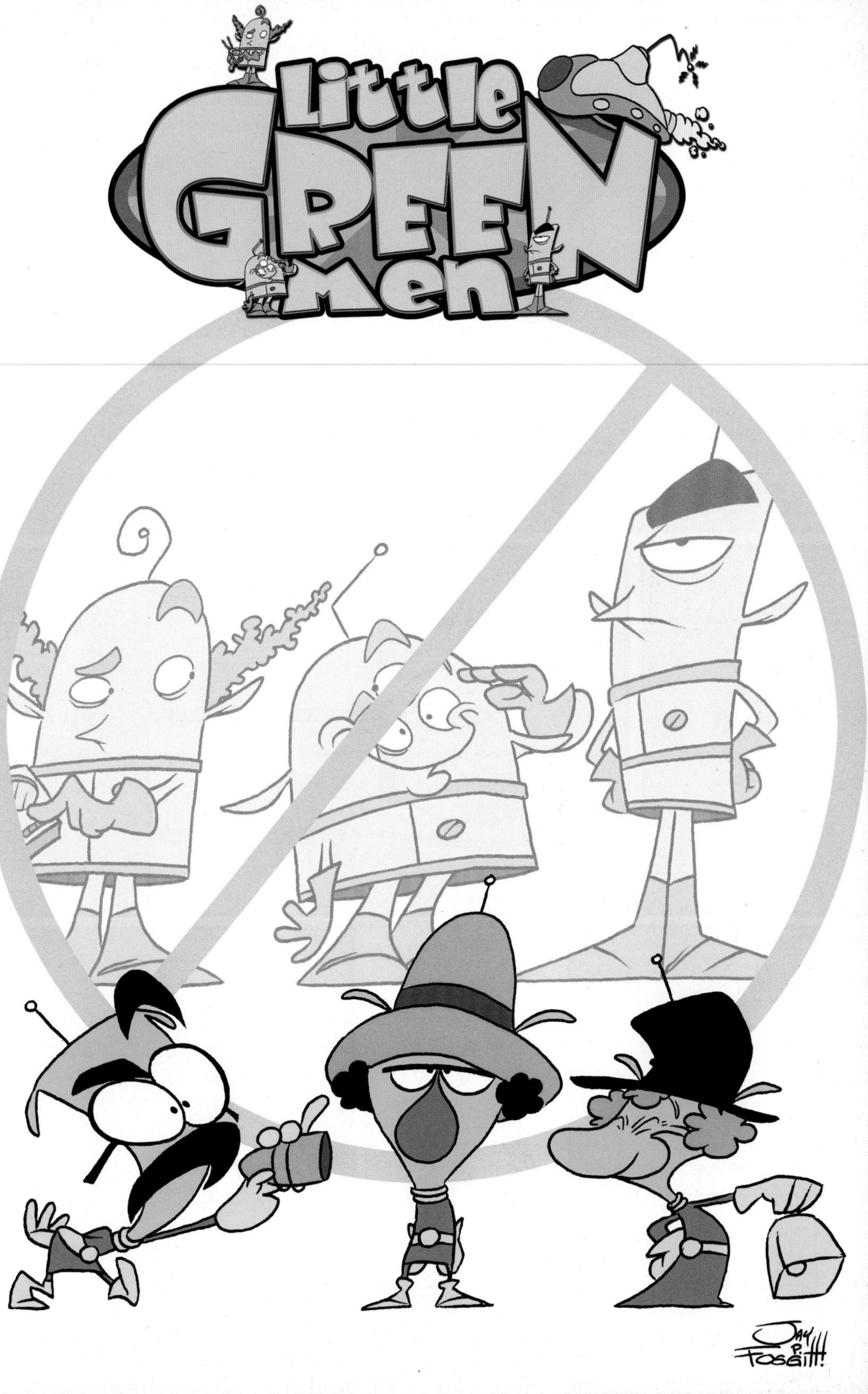
Little GREEN Men
JAY P. FOSGITT!

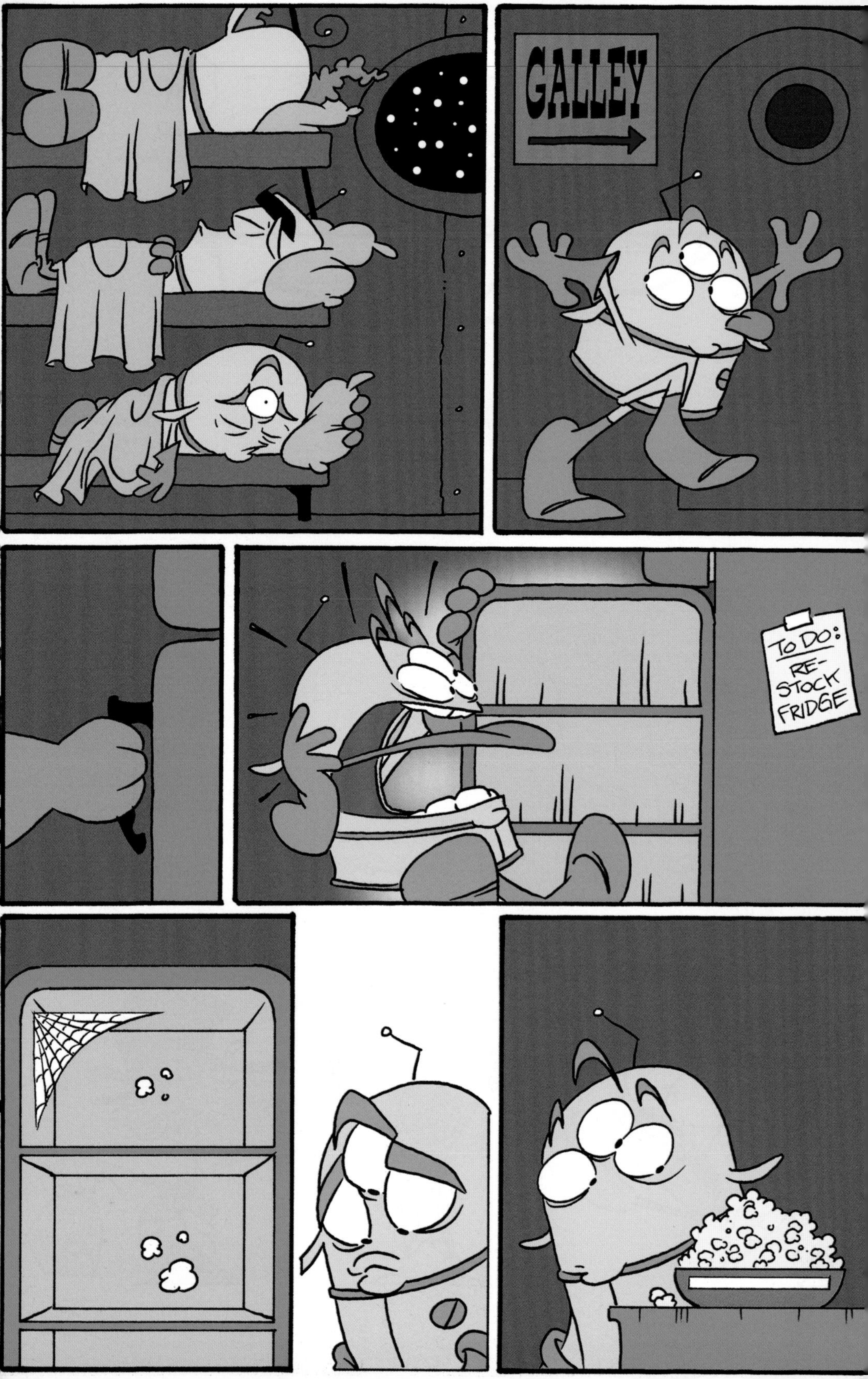
GALLEY
TO DO: RE-STOCK FRIDGE

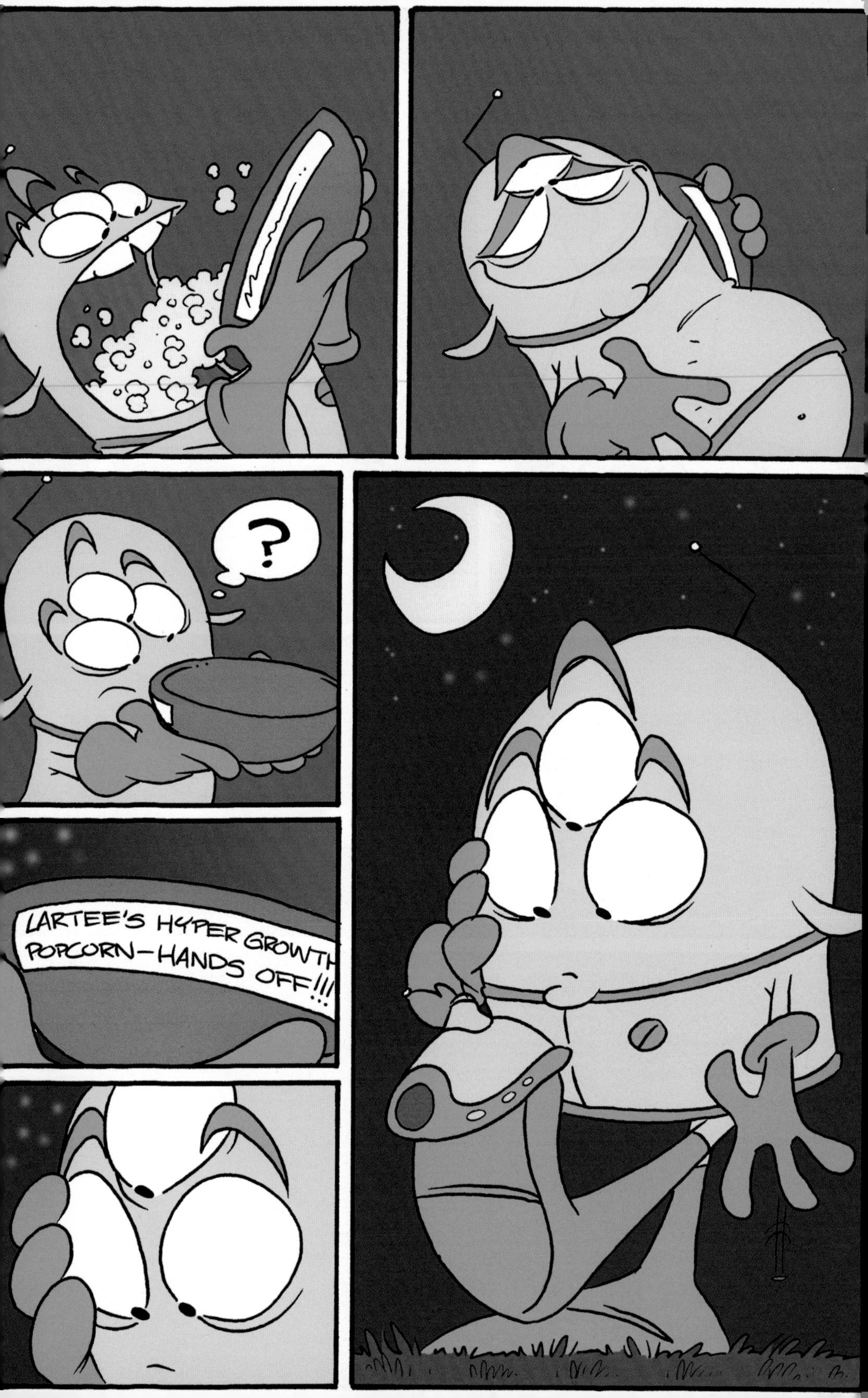
?
LARTEE'S HYPER GROWTH POPCORN—HANDS OFF!!!

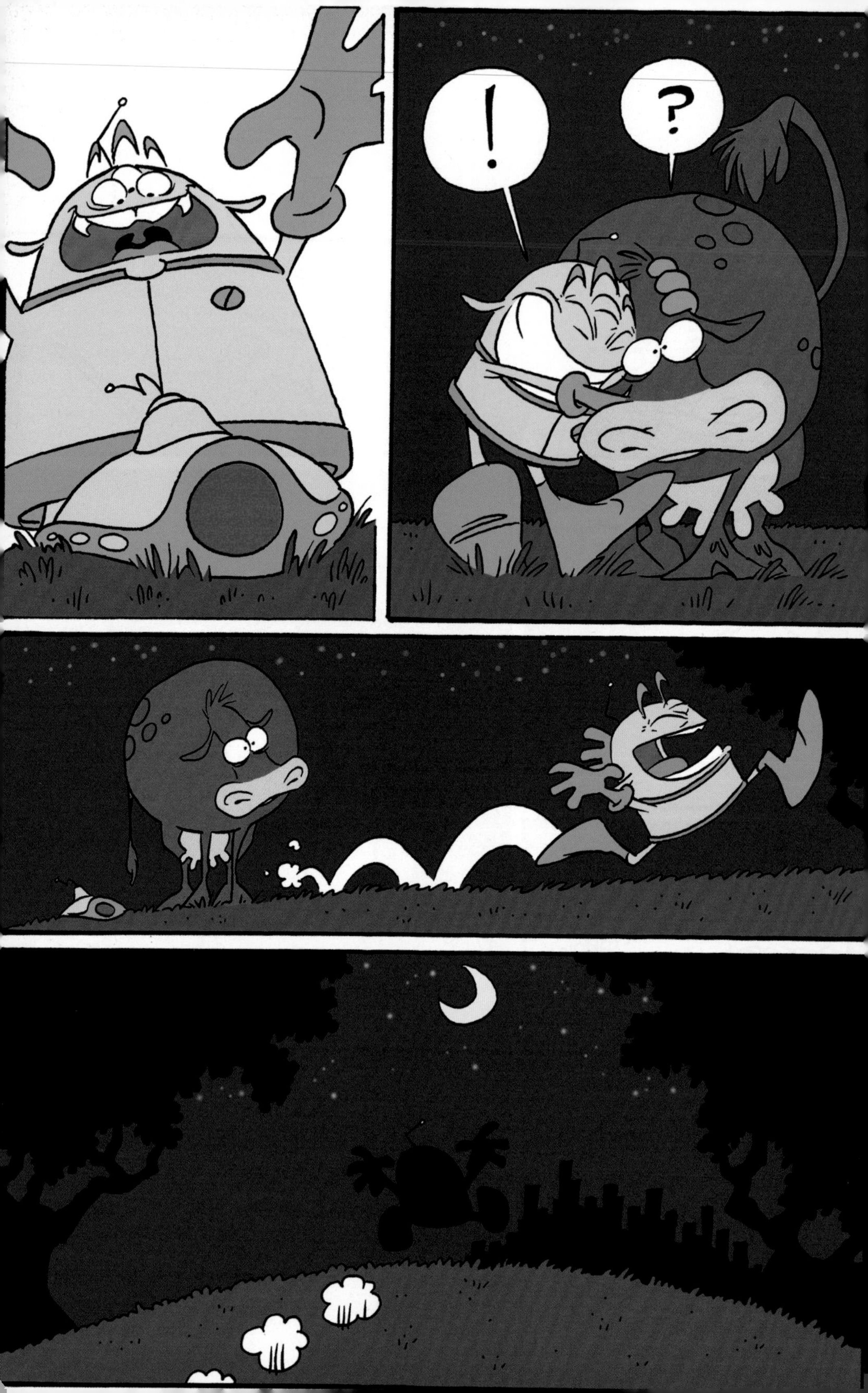
!
?

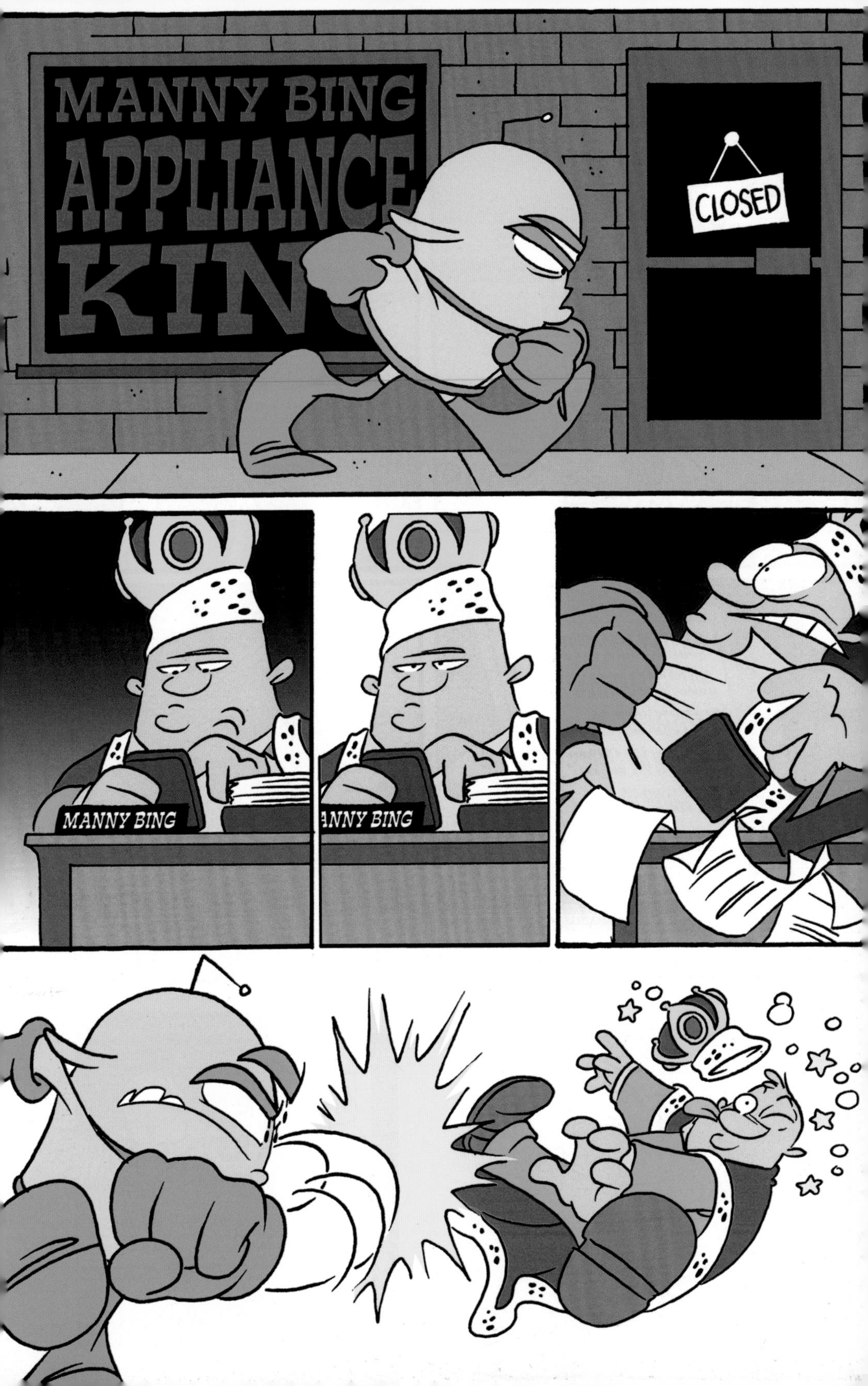
MANNY BING
APPLIANCE
KIN
CLOSED
MANNY BING
ANNY BING

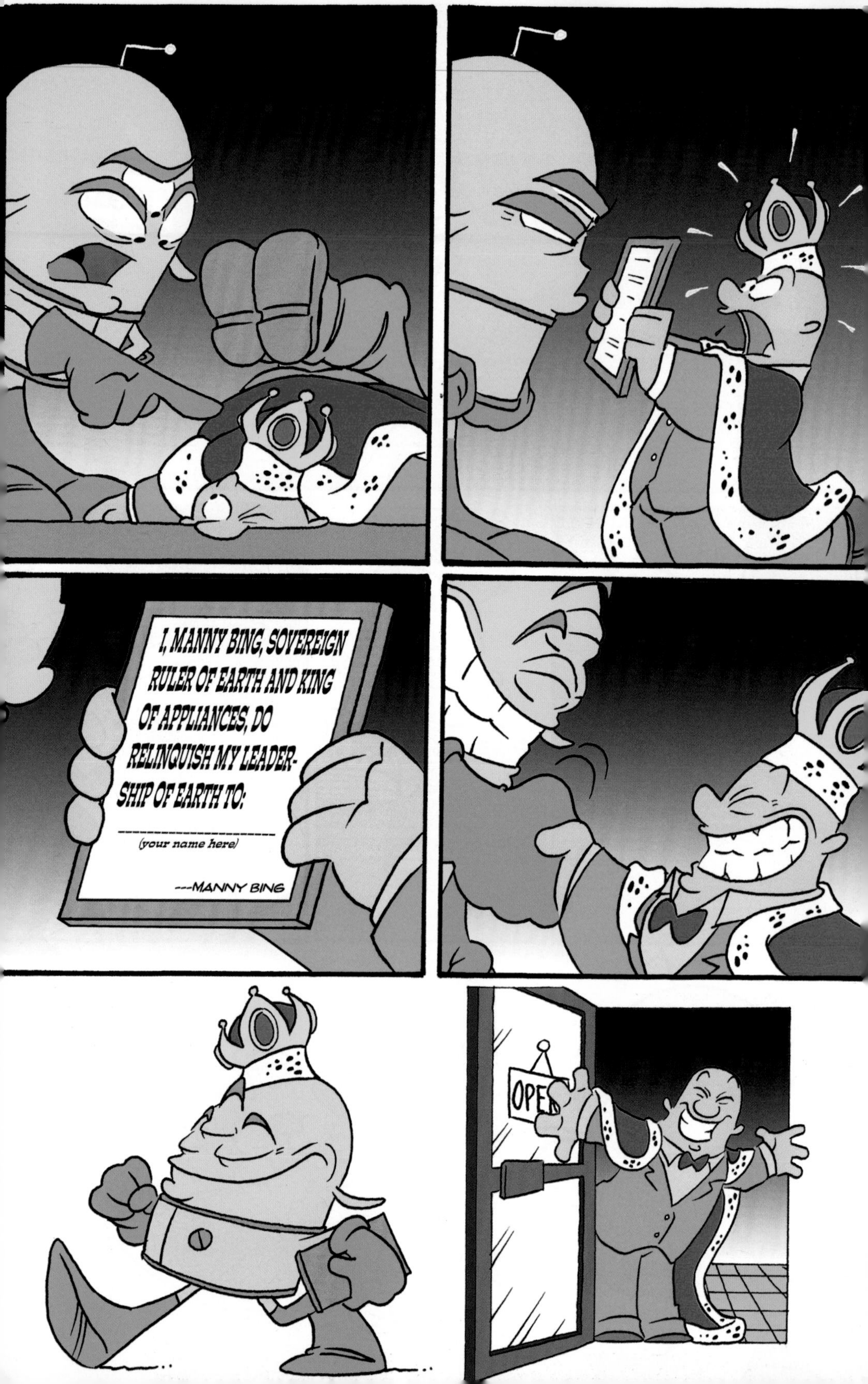
I, MANNY BING, SOVEREIGN RULER OF EARTH AND KING OF APPLIANCES, DO RELINQUISH MY LEADERSHIP OF EARTH TO:
(your name here)
---MANNY BING
OPEN

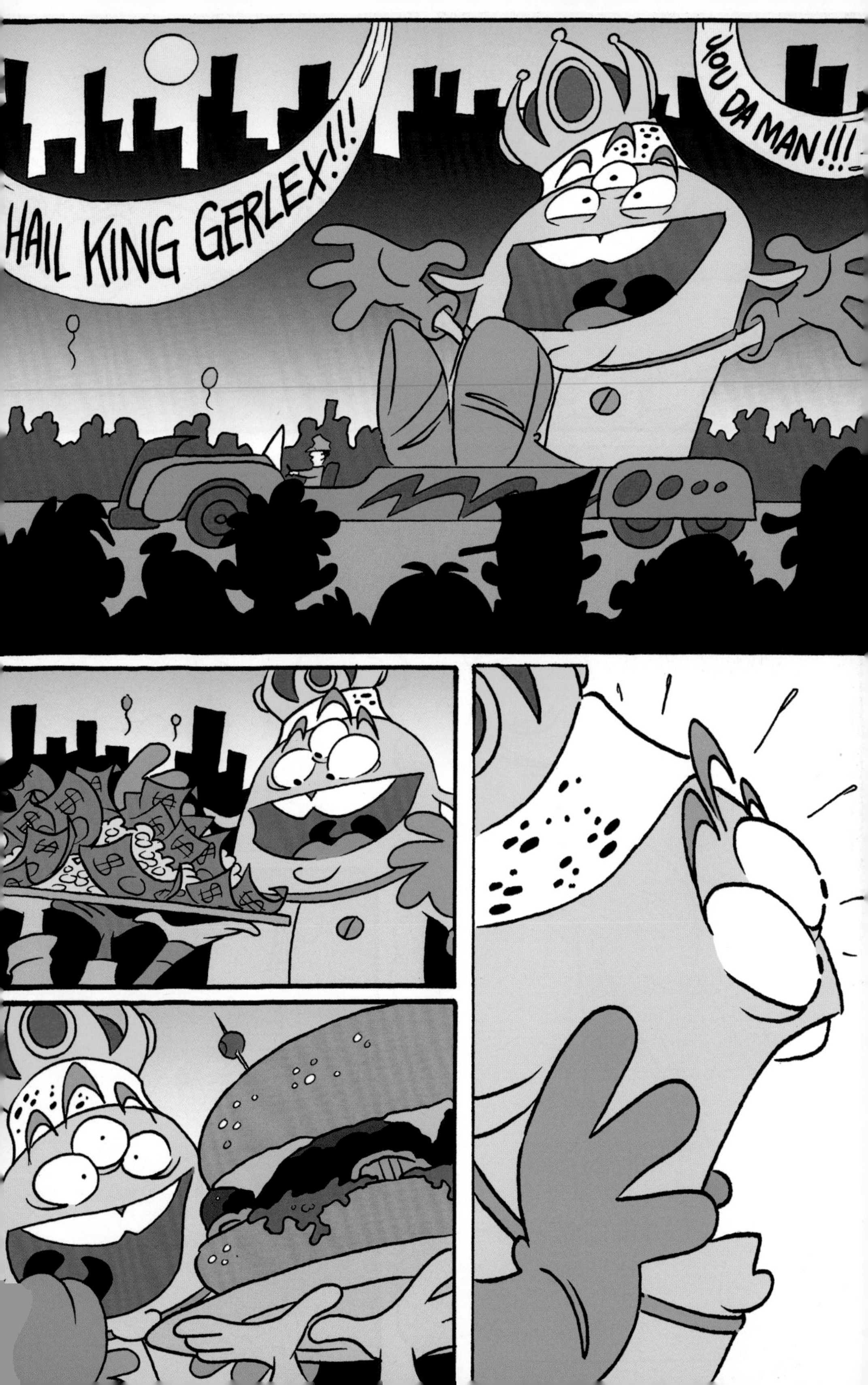
HAIL KING GERLEX!!!
YOU DA MAN!!!

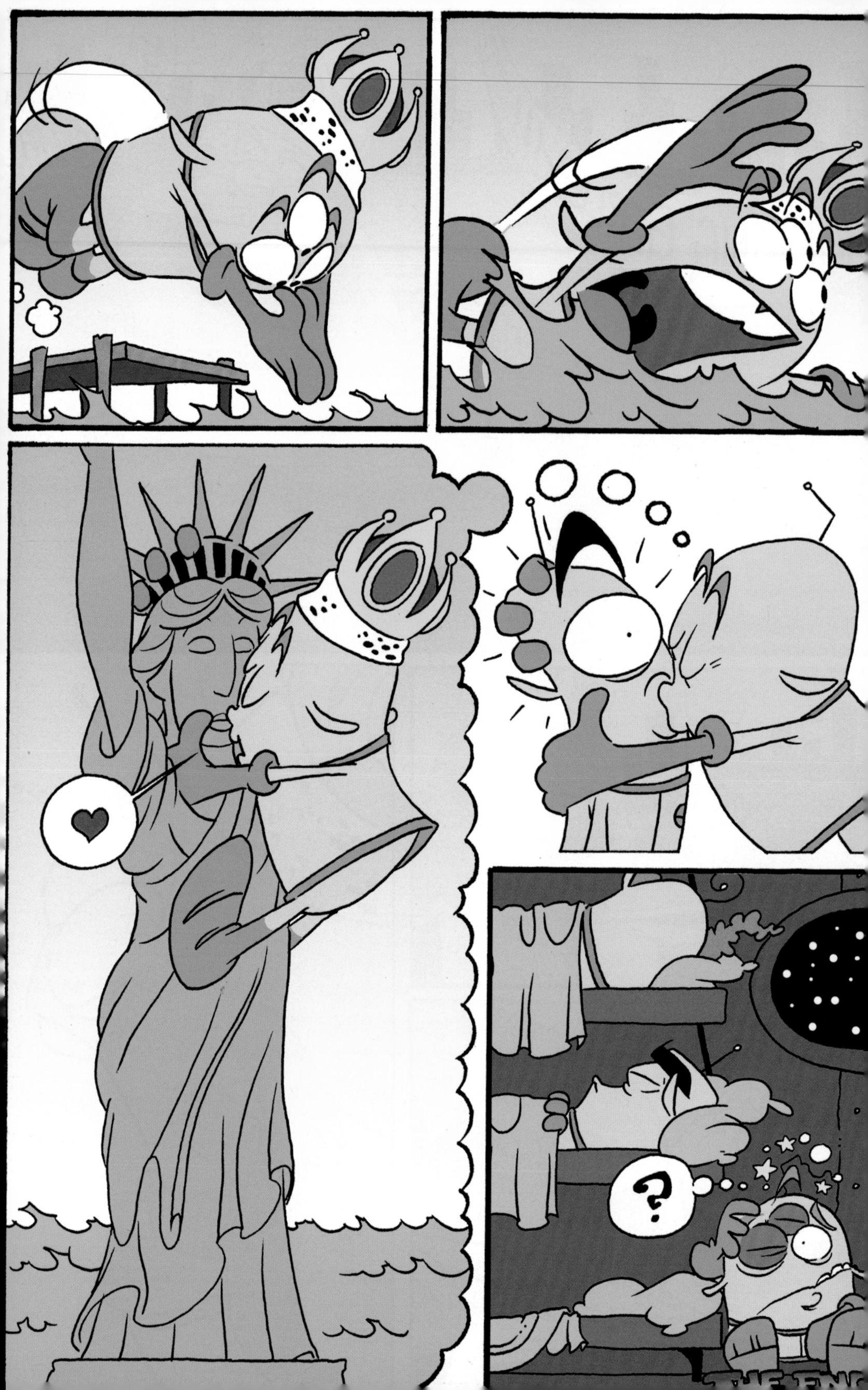
?

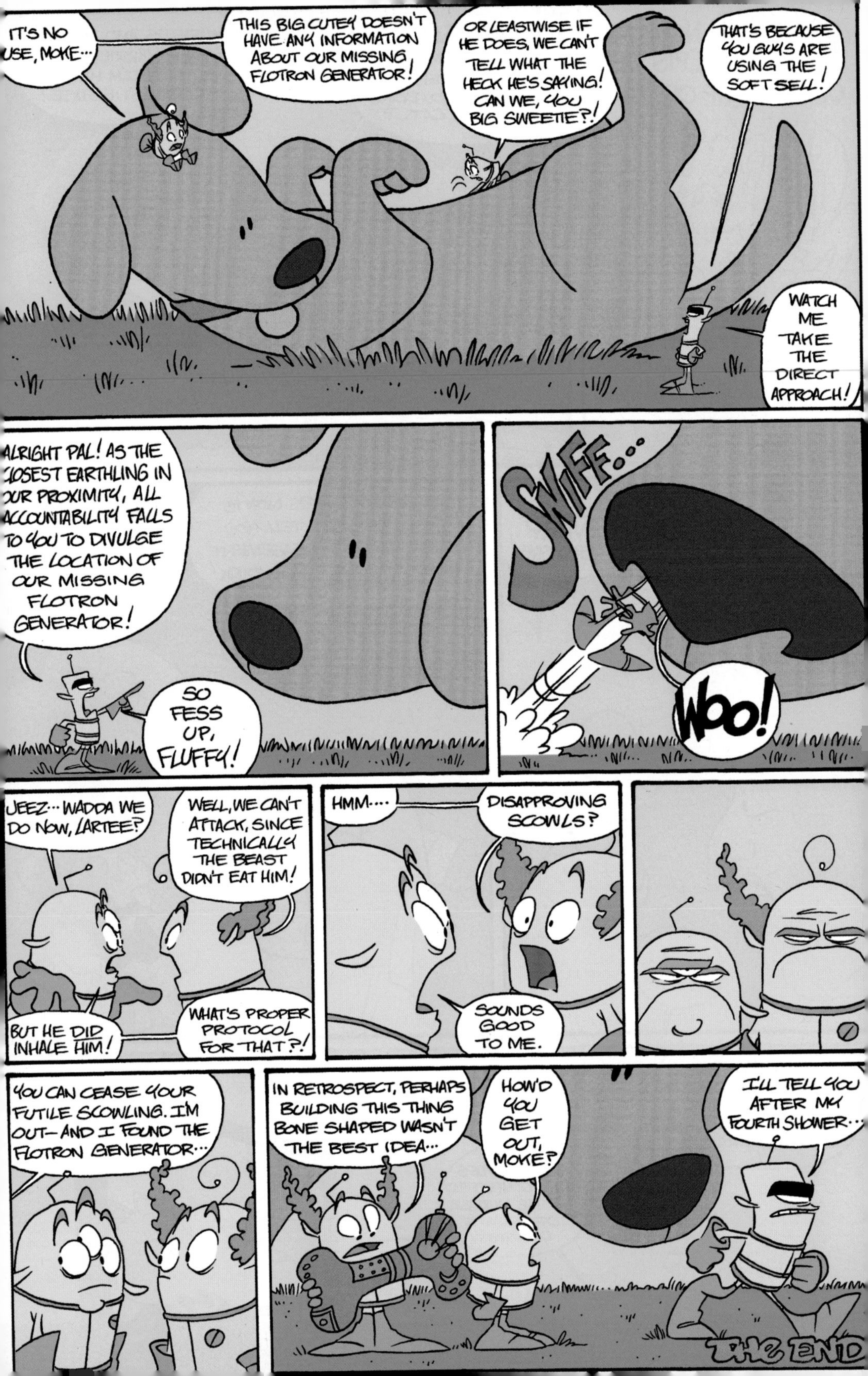
IT'S NO USE, MOKE...
THIS BIG CUTEY DOESN'T HAVE ANY INFORMATION ABOUT OUR MISSING FLOTRON GENERATOR!
OR LEASTWISE IF HE DOES, WE CAN'T TELL WHAT THE HECK HE'S SAYING! CAN WE, YOU BIG SWEETIE?!
THAT'S BECAUSE YOU GUYS ARE USING THE SOFT SELL!
WATCH ME TAKE THE DIRECT APPROACH!
ALRIGHT PAL! AS THE CLOSEST EARTHLING IN OUR PROXIMITY, ALL ACCOUNTABILITY FALLS TO YOU TO DIVULGE THE LOCATION OF OUR MISSING FLOTRON GENERATOR!
SO FESS UP, FLUFFY!
SNIFF...
WOO!
JEEZ... WADDA WE DO NOW, LARTEE?
WELL, WE CAN'T ATTACK, SINCE TECHNICALLY THE BEAST DIDN'T EAT HIM!
BUT HE DID INHALE HIM!
WHAT'S PROPER PROTOCOL FOR THAT?!
HMM....
DISAPPROVING SCOWLS?
SOUNDS GOOD TO ME.
YOU CAN CEASE YOUR FUTILE SCOWLING. I'M OUT— AND I FOUND THE FLOTRON GENERATOR...
IN RETROSPECT, PERHAPS BUILDING THIS THING BONE SHAPED WASN'T THE BEST IDEA...
HOW'D YOU GET OUT, MOKE?
I'LL TELL YOU AFTER MY FOURTH SHOWER...
THE END

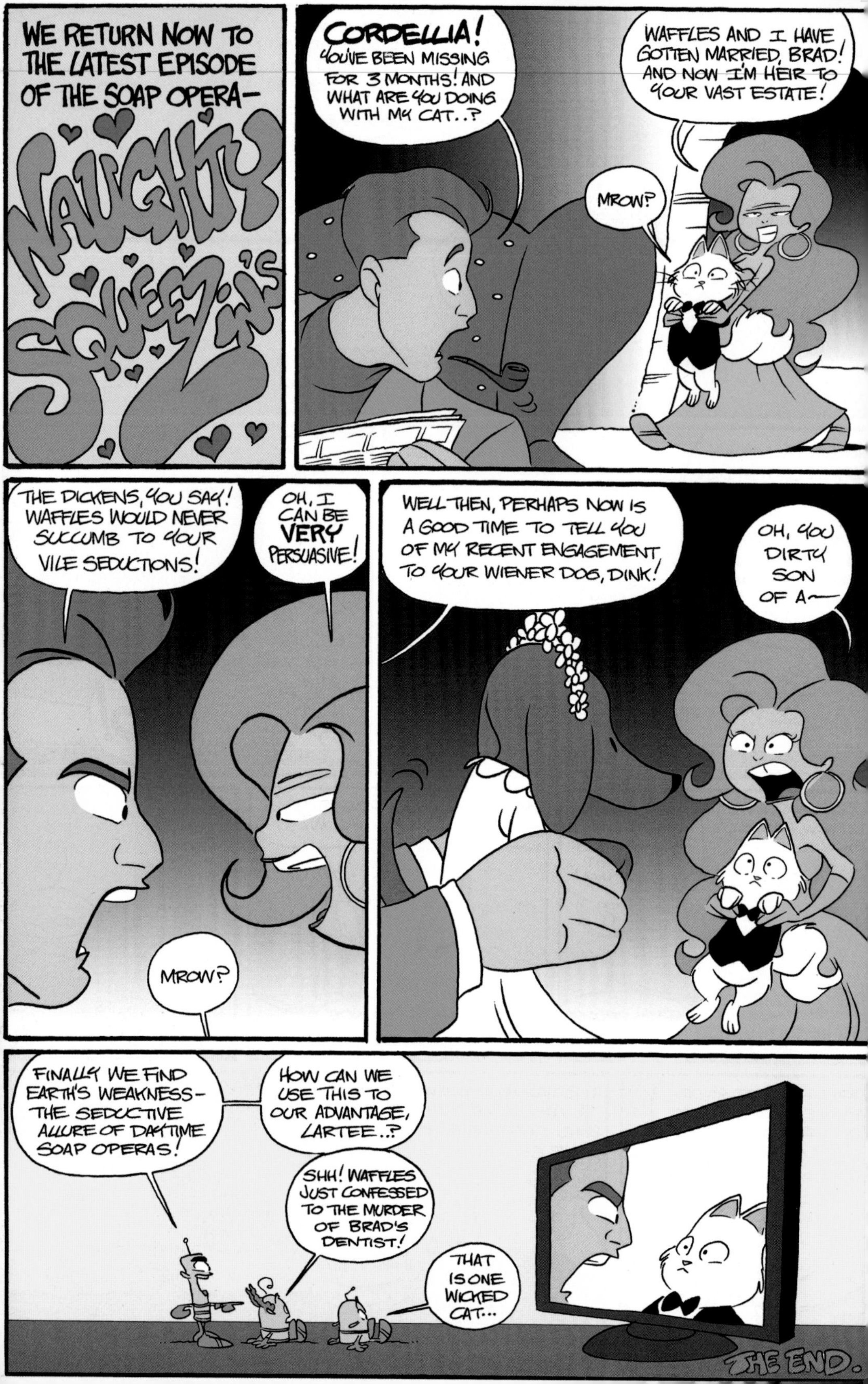
WE RETURN NOW TO THE LATEST EPISODE OF THE SOAP OPERA-
NAUGHTY SQUEEZIN'S
CORDELLIA! YOU'VE BEEN MISSING FOR 3 MONTHS! AND WHAT ARE YOU DOING WITH MY CAT..?
WAFFLES AND I HAVE GOTTEN MARRIED, BRAD! AND NOW I'M HEIR TO YOUR VAST ESTATE!
MROW?
THE DICKENS, YOU SAY! WAFFLES WOULD NEVER SUCCUMB TO YOUR VILE SEDUCTIONS!
OH, I CAN BE VERY PERSUASIVE!
MROW?
WELL THEN, PERHAPS NOW IS A GOOD TIME TO TELL YOU OF MY RECENT ENGAGEMENT TO YOUR WIENER DOG, DINK!
OH, YOU DIRTY SON OF A—
FINALLY WE FIND EARTH'S WEAKNESS- THE SEDUCTIVE ALLURE OF DAYTIME SOAP OPERAS!
HOW CAN WE USE THIS TO OUR ADVANTAGE, LARTEE..?
SHH! WAFFLES JUST CONFESSED TO THE MURDER OF BRAD'S DENTIST!
THAT IS ONE WICKED CAT...
THE END.

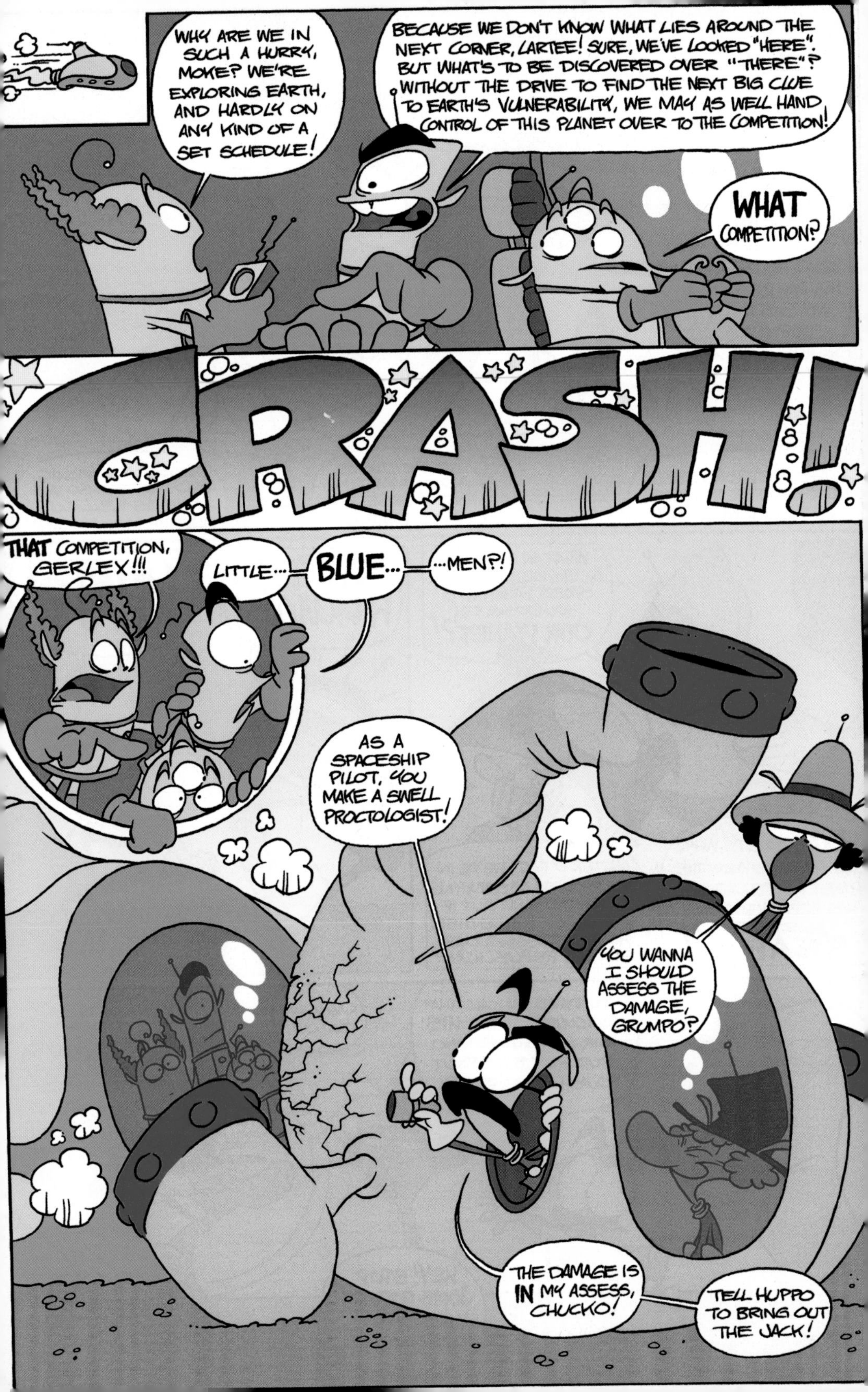
WHY ARE WE IN SUCH A HURRY, MOKE? WE'RE EXPLORING EARTH, AND HARDLY ON ANY KIND OF A SET SCHEDULE!
BECAUSE WE DON'T KNOW WHAT LIES AROUND THE NEXT CORNER, LARTEE! SURE, WE'VE LOOKED "HERE". BUT WHAT'S TO BE DISCOVERED OVER "THERE"? WITHOUT THE DRIVE TO FIND THE NEXT BIG CLUE TO EARTH'S VULNERABILITY, WE MAY AS WELL HAND CONTROL OF THIS PLANET OVER TO THE COMPETITION!
WHAT COMPETITION?
CRASH!
THAT COMPETITION, GERLEX!!!
LITTLE... BLUE... ...MEN?!
AS A SPACESHIP PILOT, YOU MAKE A SWELL PROCTOLOGIST!
YOU WANNA I SHOULD ASSESS THE DAMAGE, GRUMPO?
THE DAMAGE IS IN MY ASSESS, CHUCKO!
TELL HUPPO TO BRING OUT THE JACK!

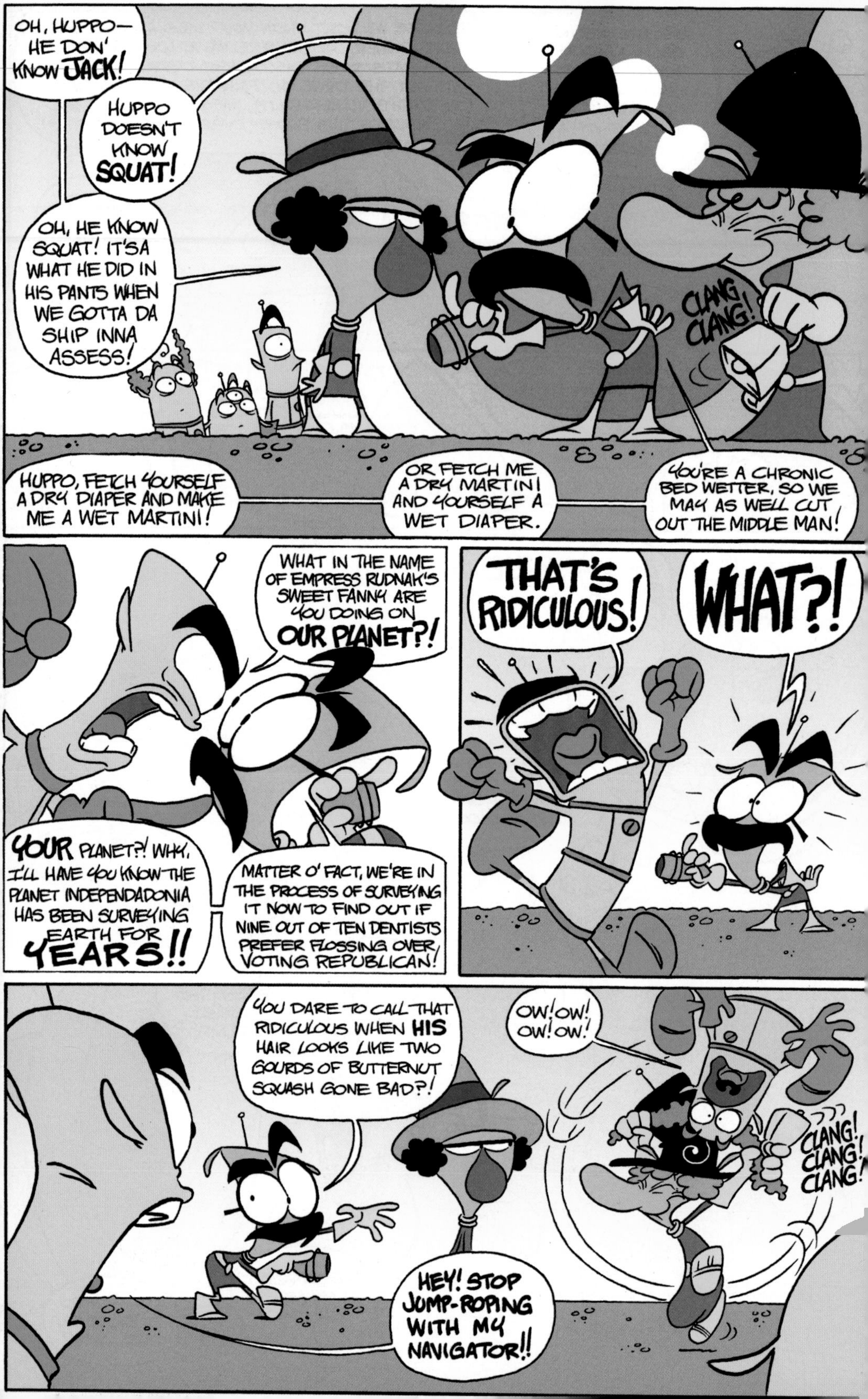
OH, HUPPO— HE DON' KNOW JACK!
HUPPO DOESN'T KNOW SQUAT!
OH, HE KNOW SQUAT! IT'SA WHAT HE DID IN HIS PANTS WHEN WE GOTTA DA SHIP INNA ASSESS!
CLANG CLANG!
HUPPO, FETCH YOURSELF A DRY DIAPER AND MAKE ME A WET MARTINI!
OR FETCH ME A DRY MARTINI AND YOURSELF A WET DIAPER.
YOU'RE A CHRONIC BED WETTER, SO WE MAY AS WELL CUT OUT THE MIDDLE MAN!
WHAT IN THE NAME OF EMPRESS RUDNAK'S SWEET FANNY ARE YOU DOING ON OUR PLANET?!
YOUR PLANET?! WHY, I'LL HAVE YOU KNOW THE PLANET INDEPENDADONIA HAS BEEN SURVEYING EARTH FOR YEARS!!
MATTER O' FACT, WE'RE IN THE PROCESS OF SURVEYING IT NOW TO FIND OUT IF NINE OUT OF TEN DENTISTS PREFER FLOSSING OVER VOTING REPUBLICAN!
THAT'S RIDICULOUS!
WHAT?!
YOU DARE TO CALL THAT RIDICULOUS WHEN HIS HAIR LOOKS LIKE TWO GOURDS OF BUTTERNUT SQUASH GONE BAD?!
OW! OW! OW! OW!
CLANG! CLANG! CLANG!
HEY! STOP JUMP-ROPING WITH MY NAVIGATOR!!

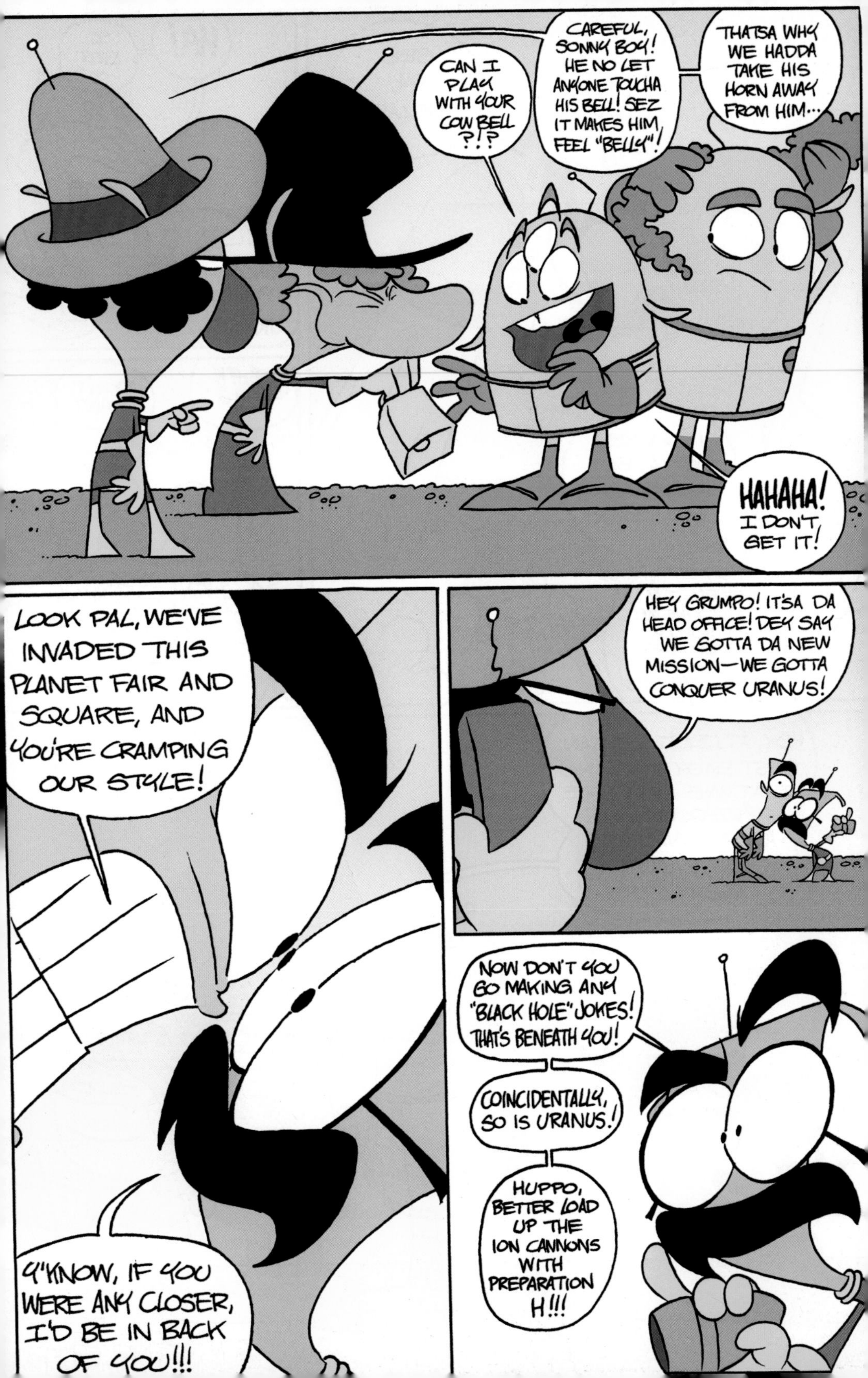
CAN I PLAY WITH YOUR COW BELL ?!?
CAREFUL, SONNY BOY! HE NO LET ANYONE TOUCHA HIS BELL! SEZ IT MAKES HIM FEEL "BELLY"!
THATSA WHY WE HADDA TAKE HIS HORN AWAY FROM HIM...
HAHAHA! I DON'T GET IT!
LOOK PAL, WE'VE INVADED THIS PLANET FAIR AND SQUARE, AND YOU'RE CRAMPING OUR STYLE!
HEY GRUMPO! IT'SA DA HEAD OFFICE! DEY SAY WE GOTTA DA NEW MISSION—WE GOTTA CONQUER URANUS!
NOW DON'T YOU GO MAKING ANY "BLACK HOLE" JOKES! THAT'S BENEATH YOU!
COINCIDENTALLY, SO IS URANUS!
HUPPO, BETTER LOAD UP THE ION CANNONS WITH PREPARATION H!!!
Y'KNOW, IF YOU WERE ANY CLOSER, I'D BE IN BACK OF YOU!!!

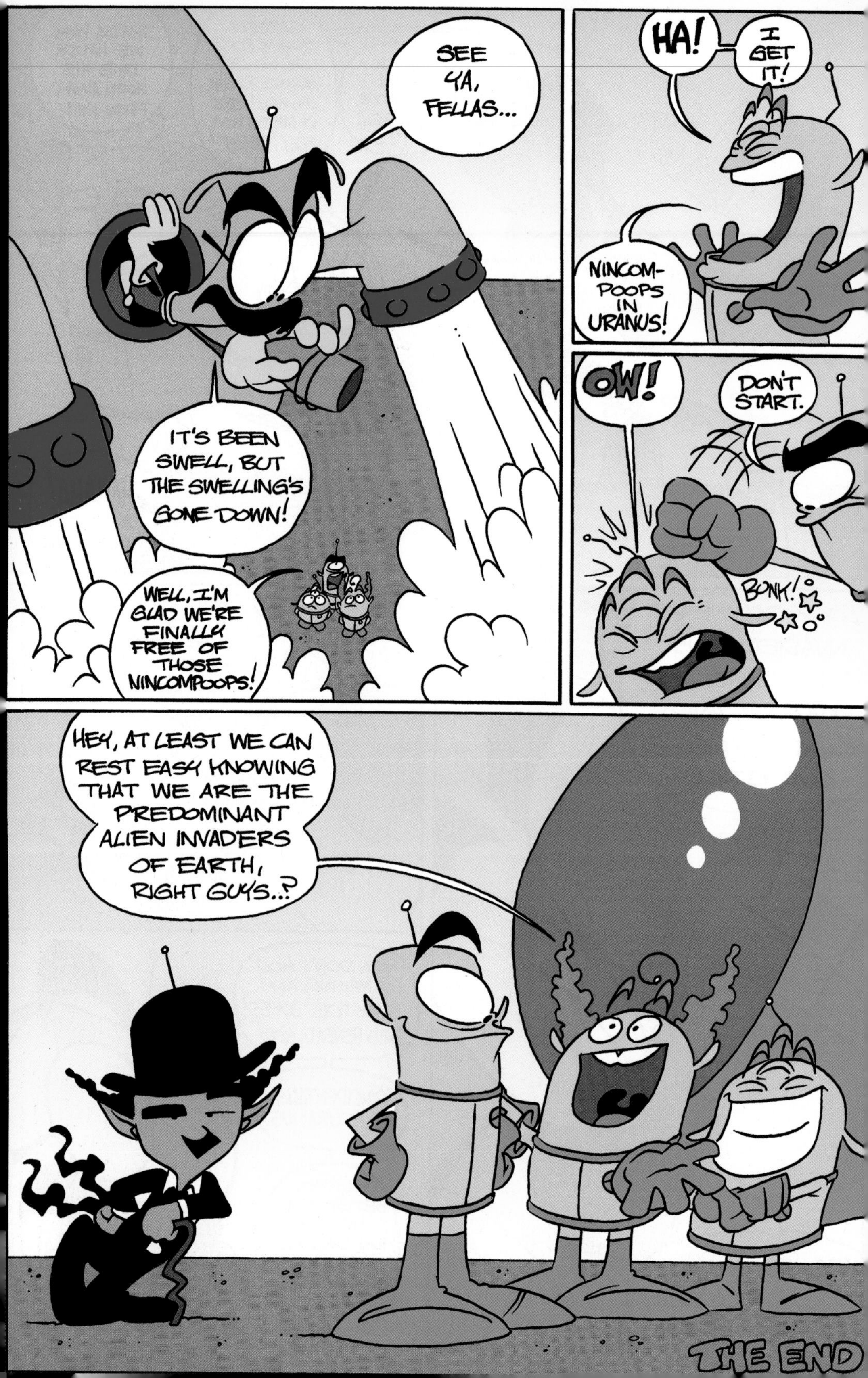
SEE YA, FELLAS...
IT'S BEEN SWELL, BUT THE SWELLING'S GONE DOWN!
WELL, I'M GLAD WE'RE FINALLY FREE OF THOSE NINCOMPOOPS!
HA!
I GET IT!
NINCOM-POOPS IN URANUS!
OW!
DON'T START.
BONK!
HEY, AT LEAST WE CAN REST EASY KNOWING THAT WE ARE THE PREDOMINANT ALIEN INVADERS OF EARTH, RIGHT GUYS..?
THE END

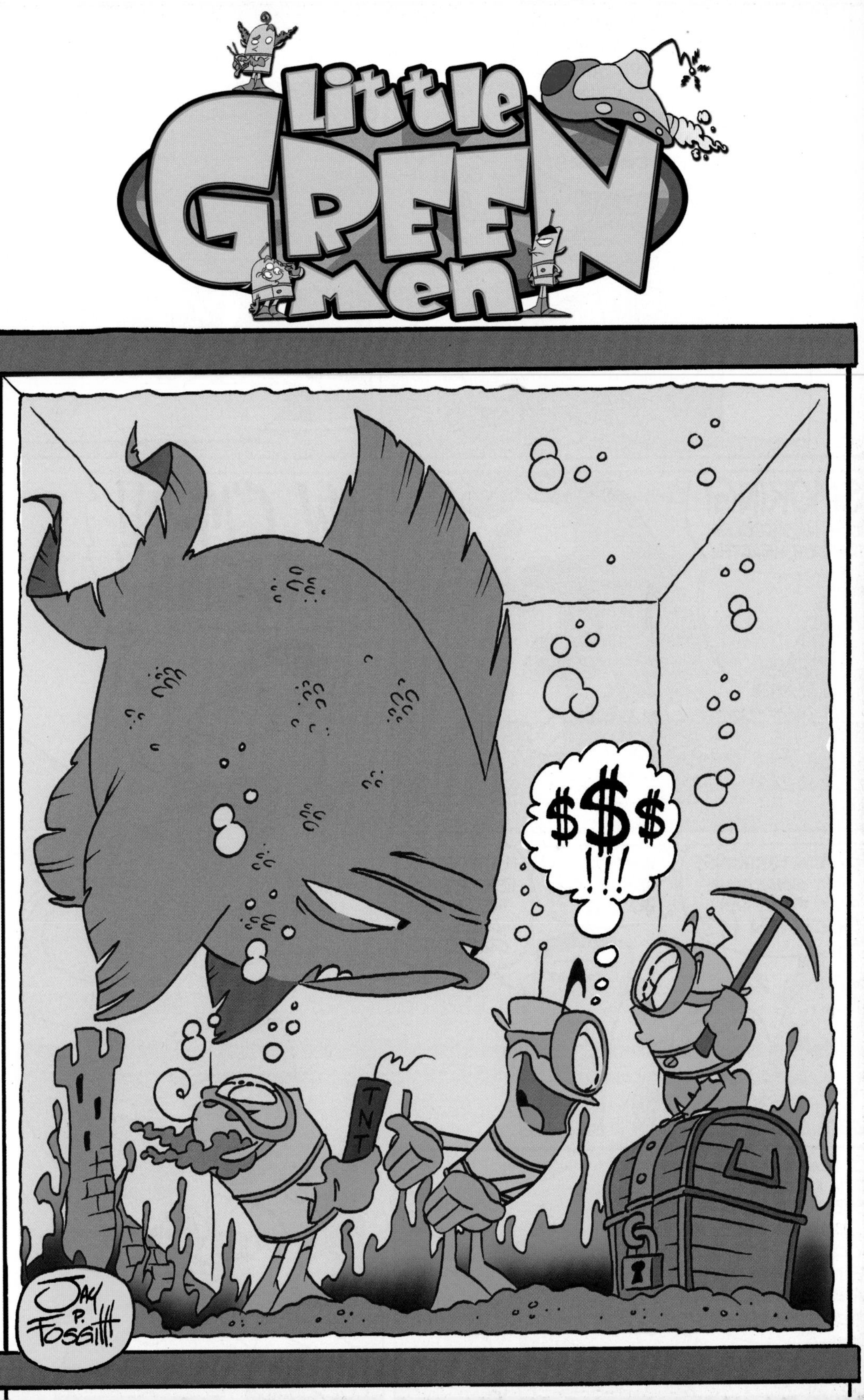
Little GREEN Men
$$$!!!
TNT
JAY P. FOSGITT!

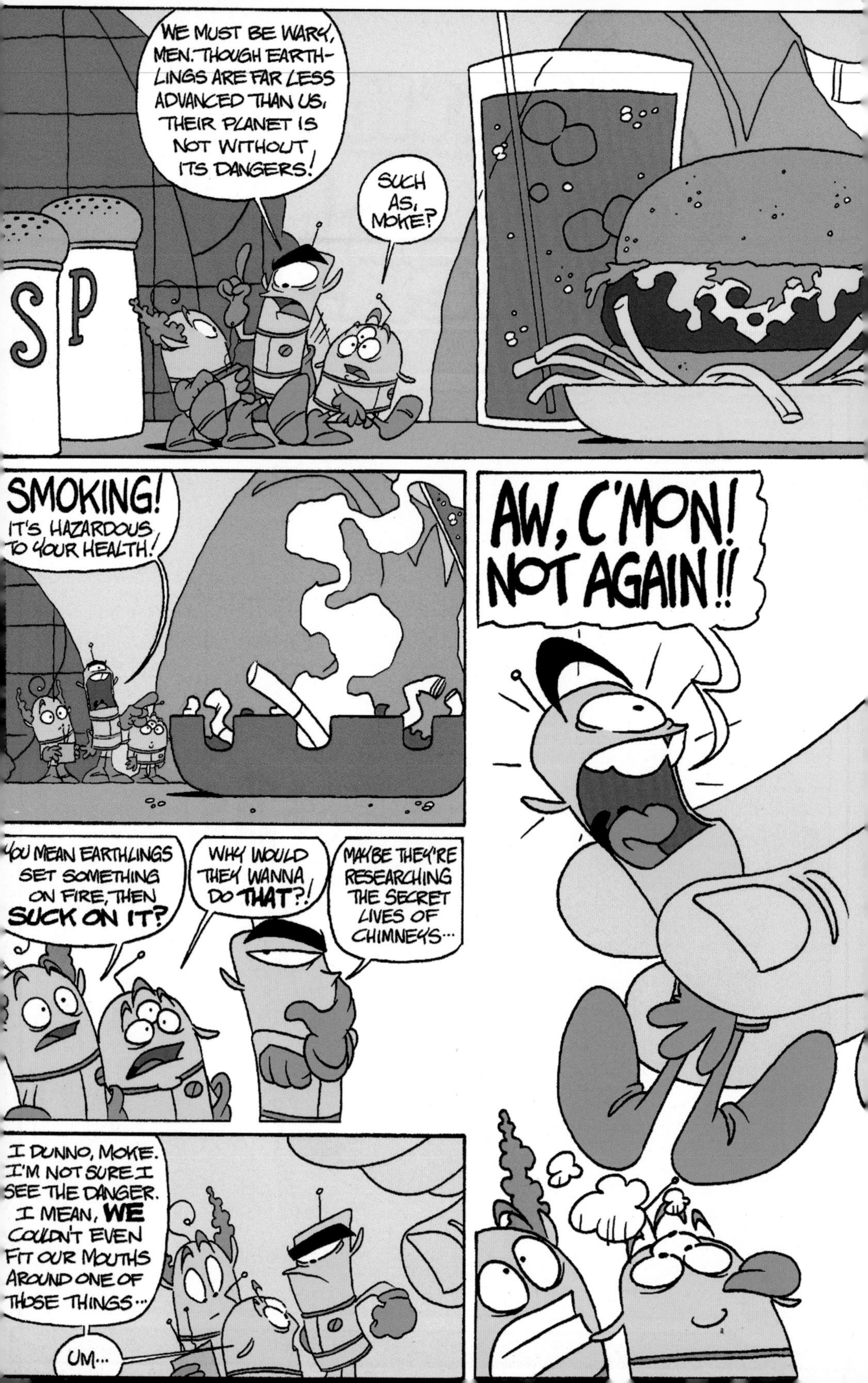

WE MUST BE WARY, MEN. THOUGH EARTHLINGS ARE FAR LESS ADVANCED THAN US, THEIR PLANET IS NOT WITHOUT ITS DANGERS!
SUCH AS, MOKE?
S
P
SMOKING! IT'S HAZARDOUS TO YOUR HEALTH!
YOU MEAN EARTHLINGS SET SOMETHING ON FIRE, THEN SUCK ON IT?
WHY WOULD THEY WANNA DO THAT?!
MAYBE THEY'RE RESEARCHING THE SECRET LIVES OF CHIMNEYS...
I DUNNO, MOKE. I'M NOT SURE I SEE THE DANGER. I MEAN, WE COULDN'T EVEN FIT OUR MOUTHS AROUND ONE OF THOSE THINGS...
UM...
AW, C'MON! NOT AGAIN!!

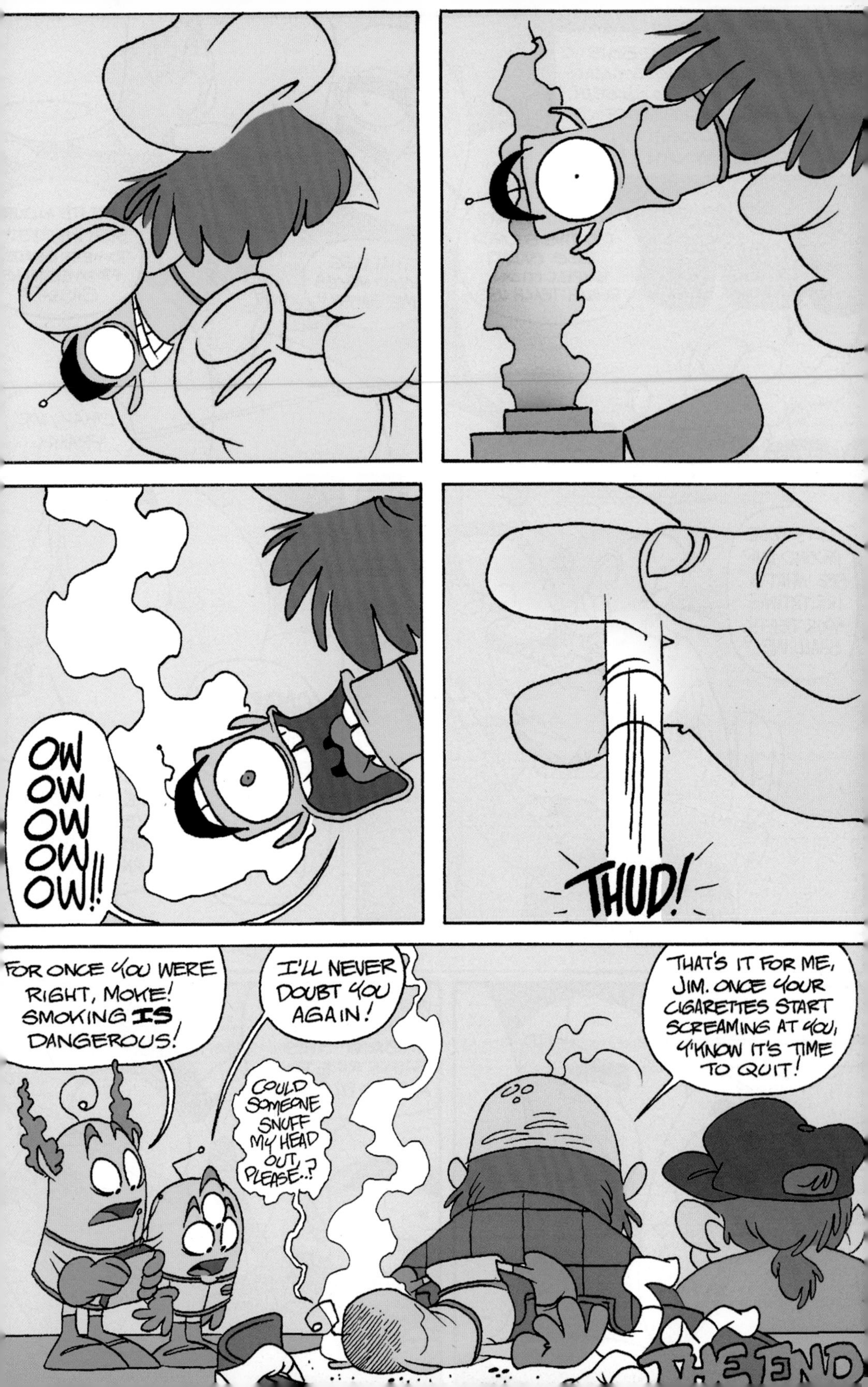
OWOWOWOWOW!!
THUD!
FOR ONCE YOU WERE RIGHT, MOKE! SMOKING IS DANGEROUS!
I'LL NEVER DOUBT YOU AGAIN!
COULD SOMEONE SNUFF MY HEAD OUT, PLEASE..?
THAT'S IT FOR ME, JIM. ONCE YOUR CIGARETTES START SCREAMING AT YOU, Y'KNOW IT'S TIME TO QUIT!
THE END

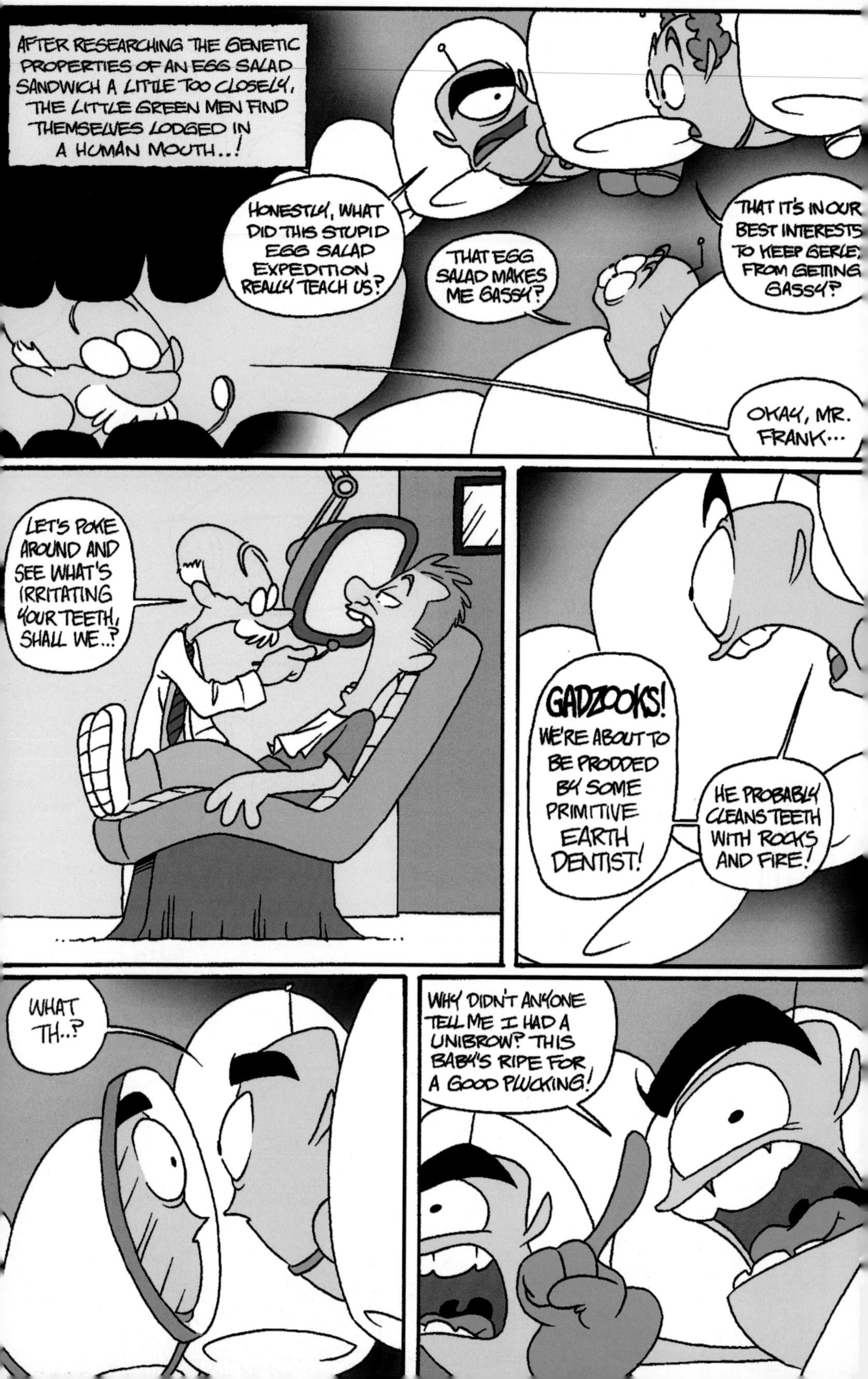
AFTER RESEARCHING THE GENETIC PROPERTIES OF AN EGG SALAD SANDWICH A LITTLE TOO CLOSELY, THE LITTLE GREEN MEN FIND THEMSELVES LODGED IN A HUMAN MOUTH...!
HONESTLY, WHAT DID THIS STUPID EGG SALAD EXPEDITION REALLY TEACH US?
THAT EGG SALAD MAKES ME GASSY?
THAT IT'S IN OUR BEST INTERESTS TO KEEP GERLE FROM GETTING GASSY?
OKAY, MR. FRANK...
LET'S POKE AROUND AND SEE WHAT'S IRRITATING YOUR TEETH, SHALL WE..?
GADZOOKS! WE'RE ABOUT TO BE PRODDED BY SOME PRIMITIVE EARTH DENTIST!
HE PROBABLY CLEANS TEETH WITH ROCKS AND FIRE!
WHAT TH..?
WHY DIDN'T ANYONE TELL ME I HAD A UNIBROW? THIS BABY'S RIPE FOR A GOOD PLUCKING!

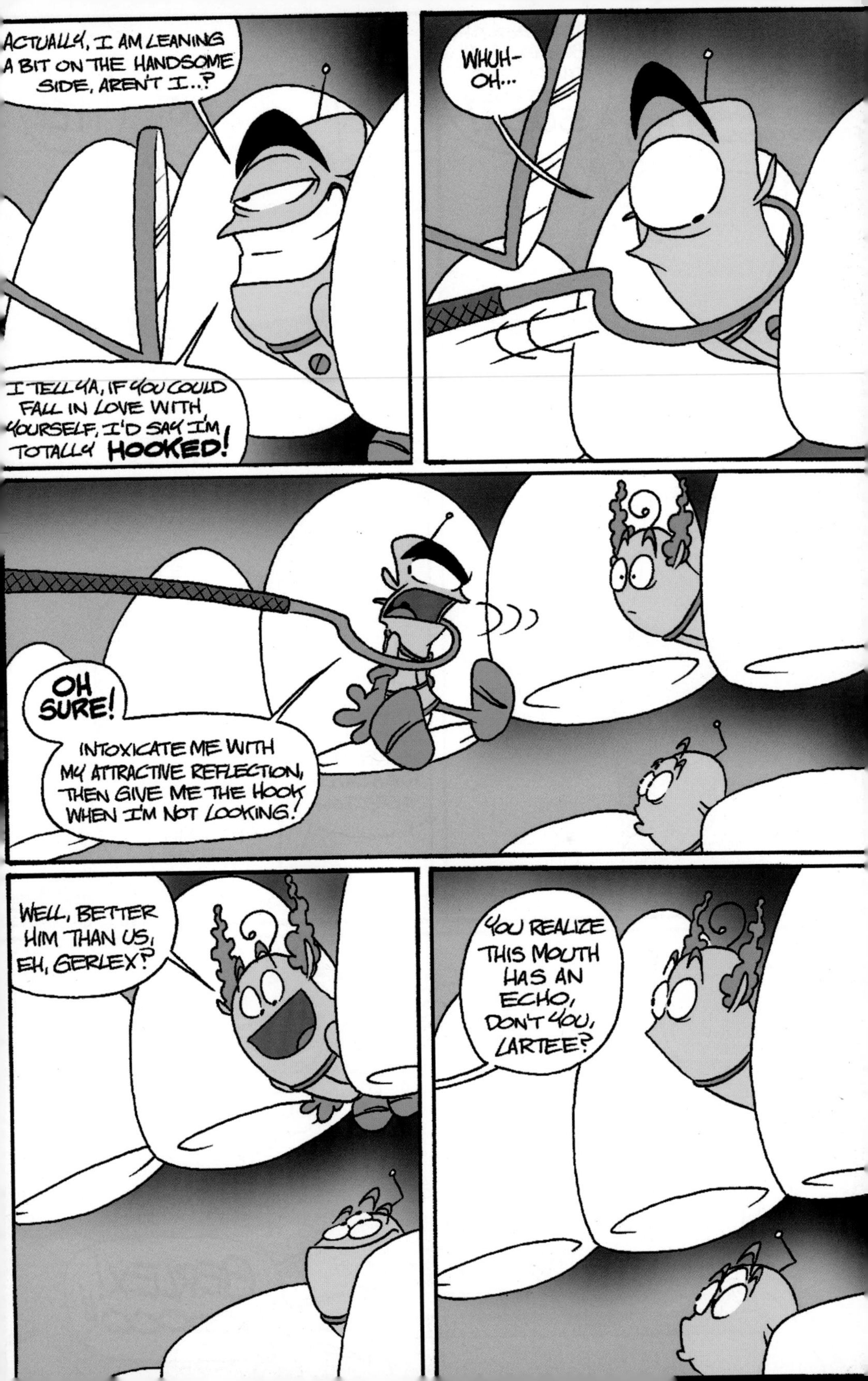
ACTUALLY, I AM LEANING A BIT ON THE HANDSOME SIDE, AREN'T I...?
I TELL YA, IF YOU COULD FALL IN LOVE WITH YOURSELF, I'D SAY I'M TOTALLY HOOKED!
WHUH-OH...
OH SURE!
INTOXICATE ME WITH MY ATTRACTIVE REFLECTION, THEN GIVE ME THE HOOK WHEN I'M NOT LOOKING!
WELL, BETTER HIM THAN US, EH, GERLEX?
YOU REALIZE THIS MOUTH HAS AN ECHO, DON'T YOU, LARTEE?

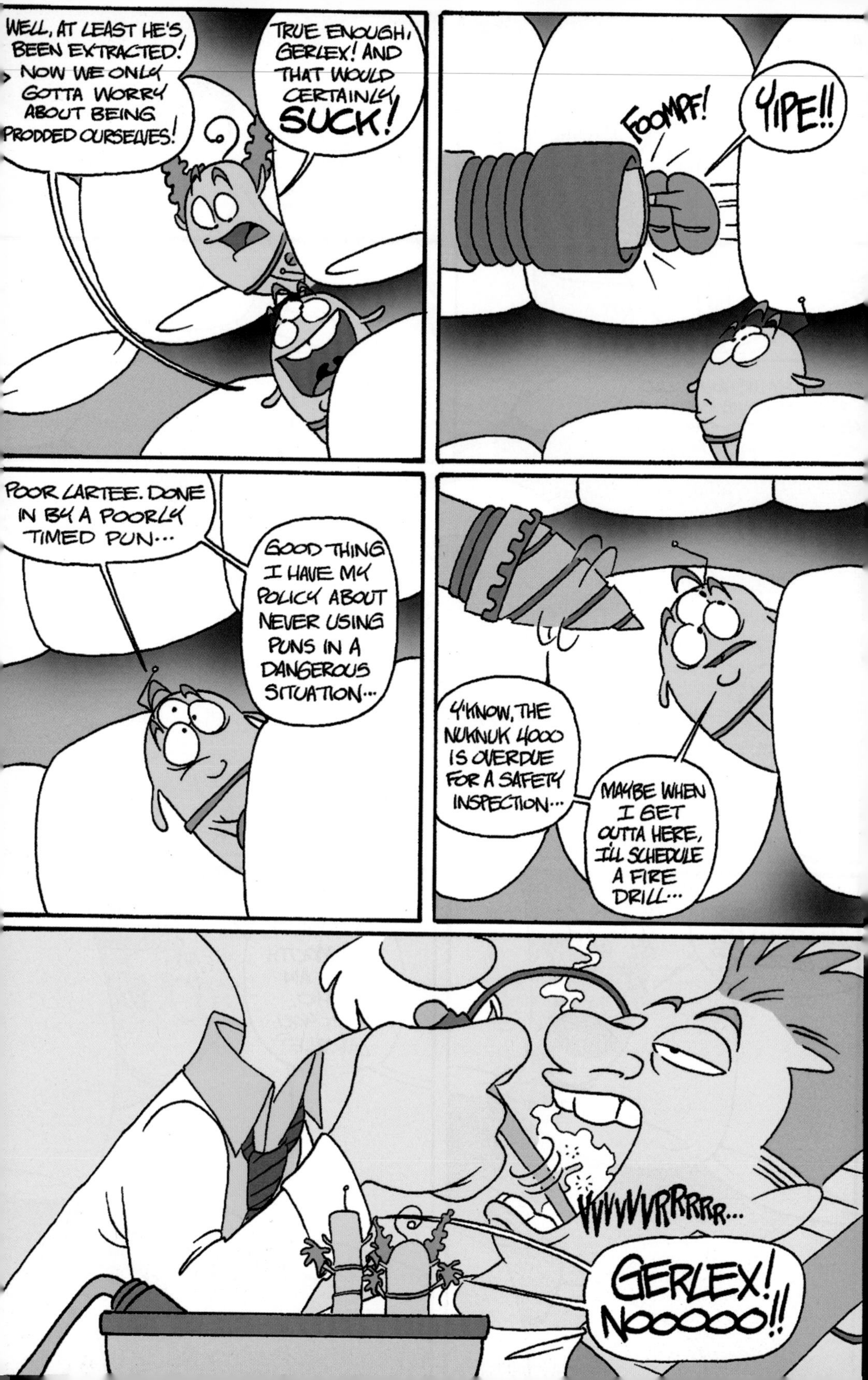

WELL, AT LEAST HE'S BEEN EXTRACTED! NOW WE ONLY GOTTA WORRY ABOUT BEING PRODDED OURSELVES!
TRUE ENOUGH, GERLEX! AND THAT WOULD CERTAINLY SUCK!
FOOMPF!
YIPE!!
POOR LARTEE. DONE IN BY A POORLY TIMED PUN...
GOOD THING I HAVE MY POLICY ABOUT NEVER USING PUNS IN A DANGEROUS SITUATION...
Y'KNOW, THE NUKNUK 4000 IS OVERDUE FOR A SAFETY INSPECTION...
MAYBE WHEN I GET OUTTA HERE, I'LL SCHEDULE A FIRE DRILL...
VVVVVVRRRRR...
GERLEX! NOOOOOO!!

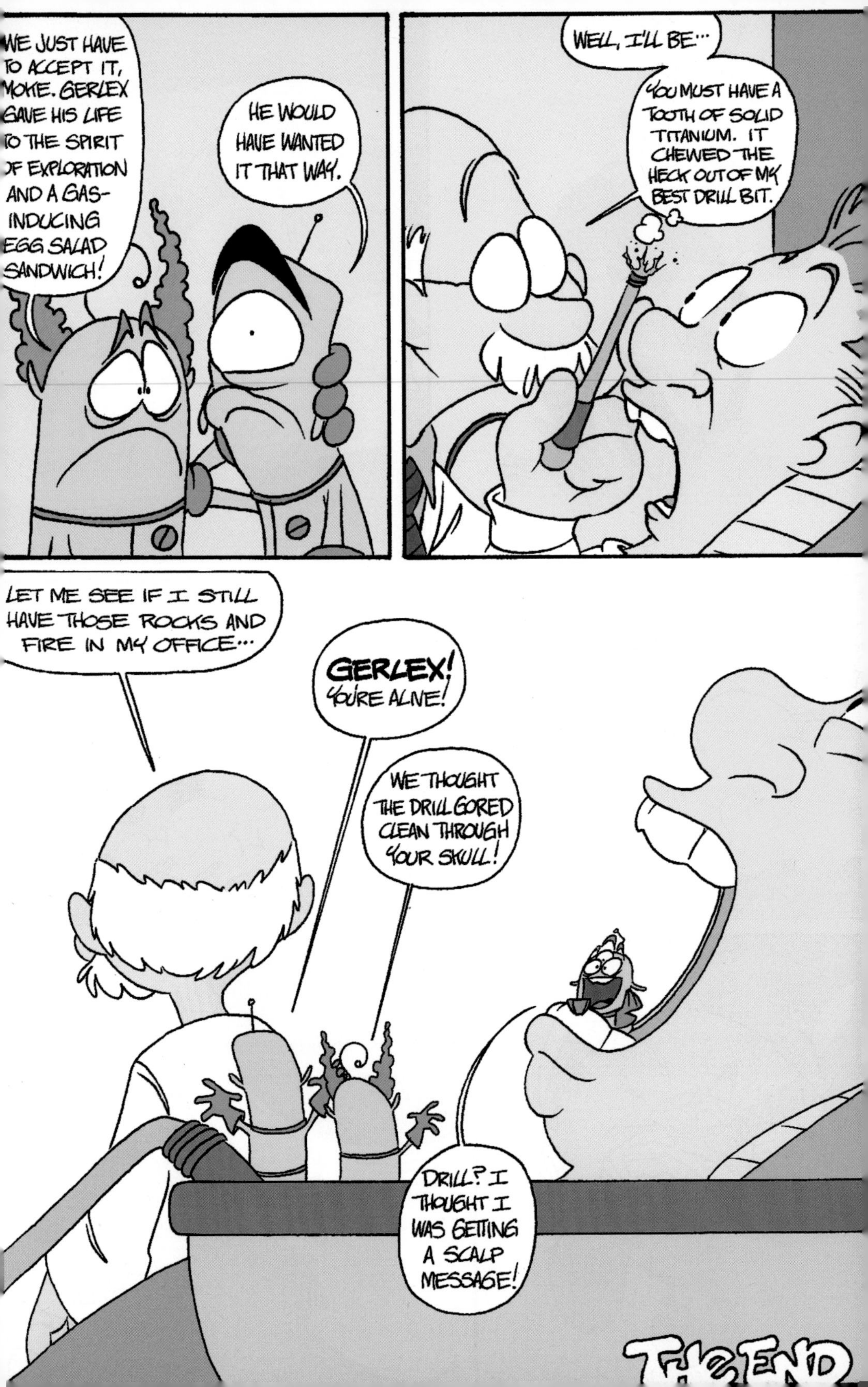
WE JUST HAVE TO ACCEPT IT, MOKE. GERLEX GAVE HIS LIFE TO THE SPIRIT OF EXPLORATION AND A GAS-INDUCING EGG SALAD SANDWICH!
HE WOULD HAVE WANTED IT THAT WAY.
WELL, I'LL BE...
YOU MUST HAVE A TOOTH OF SOLID TITANIUM. IT CHEWED THE HECK OUT OF MY BEST DRILL BIT.
LET ME SEE IF I STILL HAVE THOSE ROCKS AND FIRE IN MY OFFICE...
GERLEX! YOU'RE ALIVE!
WE THOUGHT THE DRILL GORED CLEAN THROUGH YOUR SKULL!
DRILL? I THOUGHT I WAS GETTING A SCALP MESSAGE!
THE END

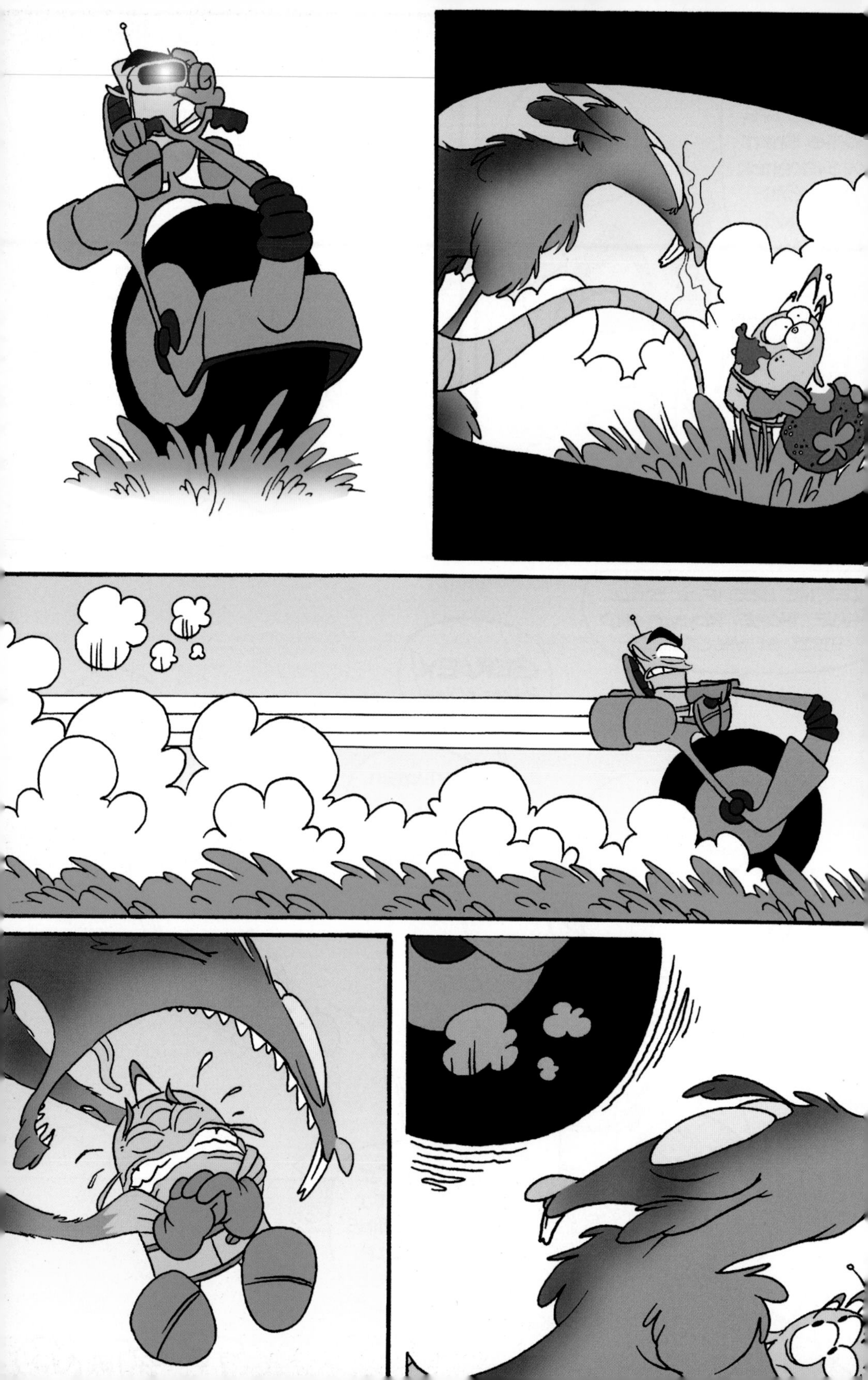

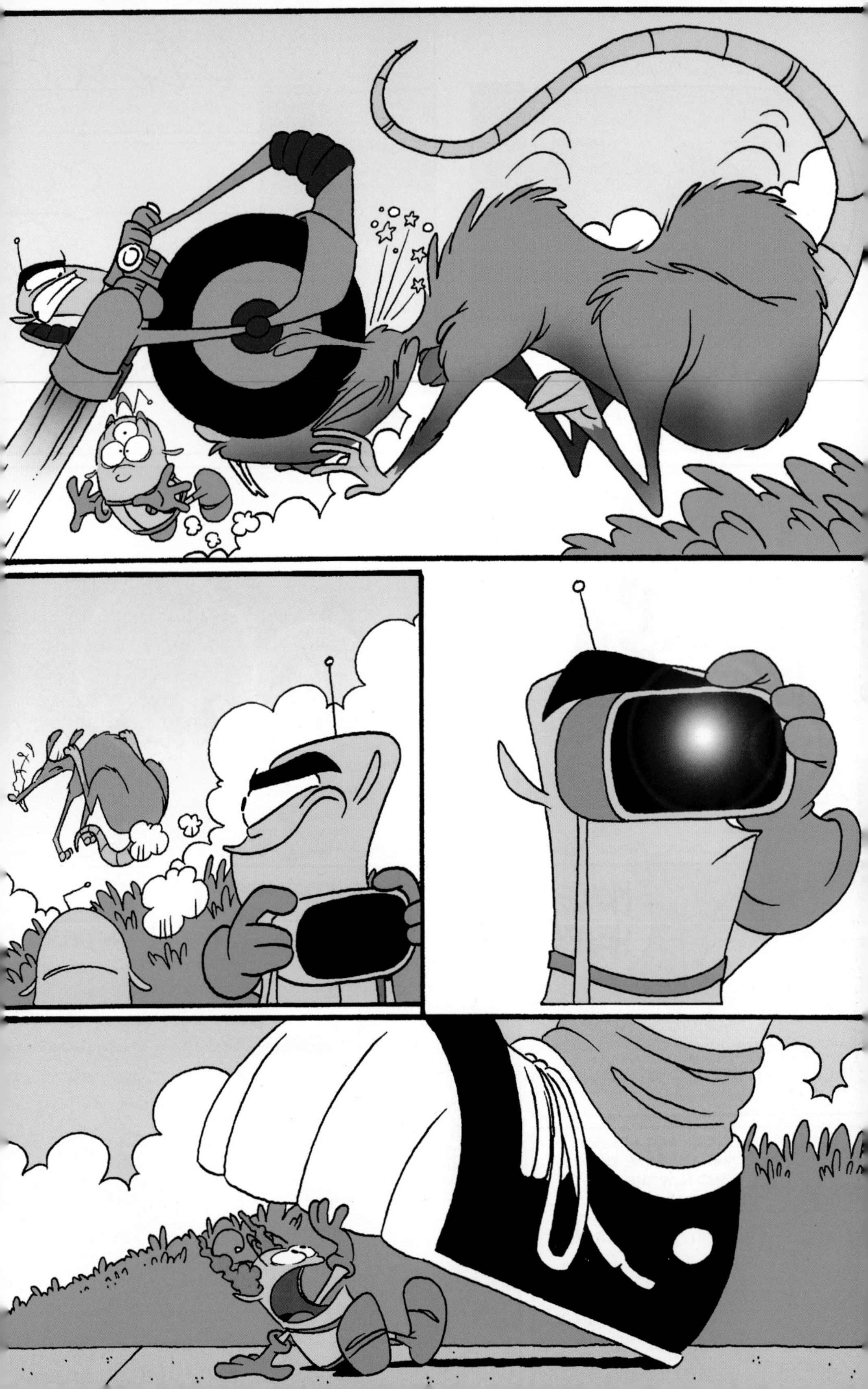

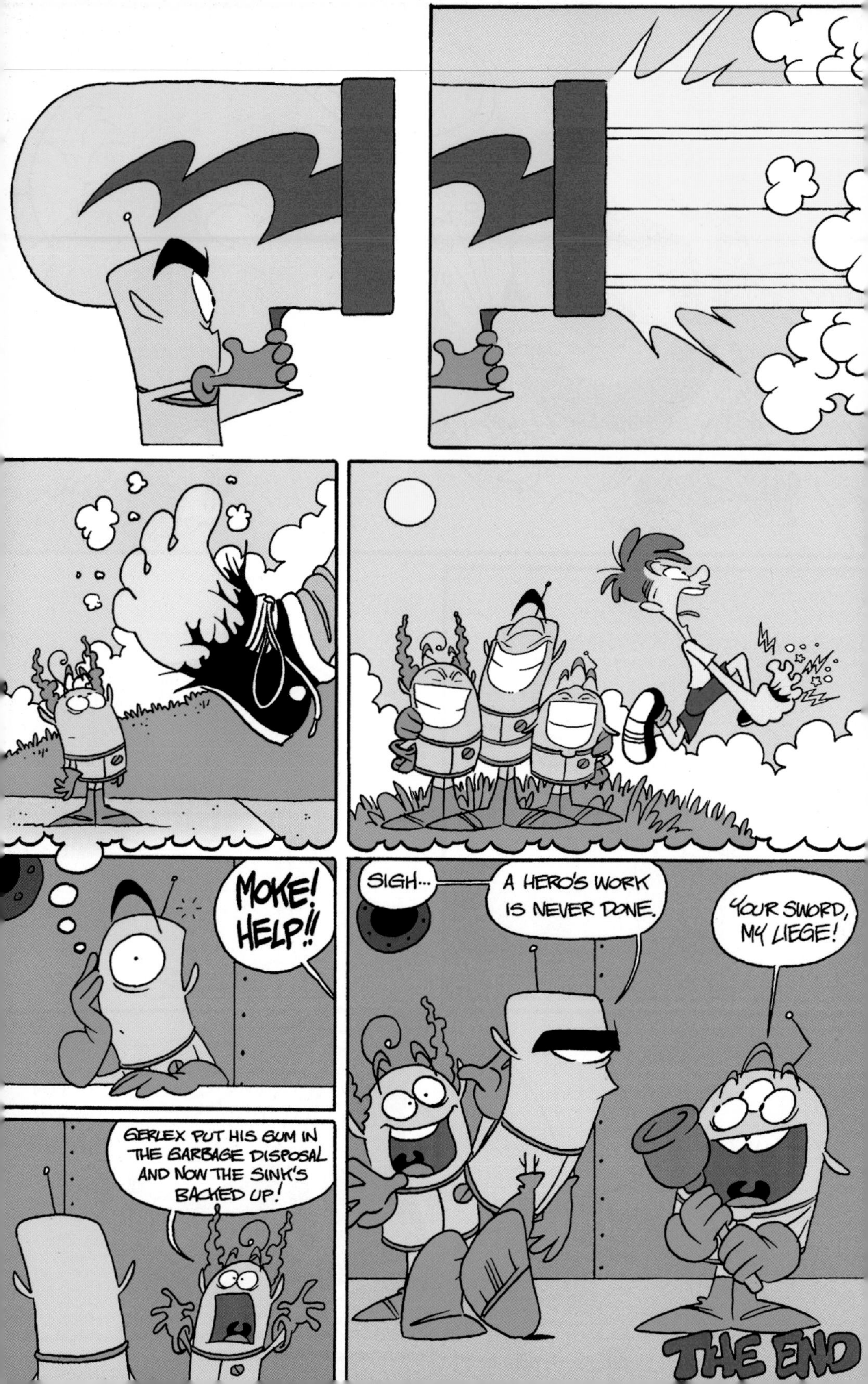
MOKE! HELP!!
GERLEX PUT HIS GUM IN THE GARBAGE DISPOSAL AND NOW THE SINK'S BACKED UP!
SIGH...
A HERO'S WORK IS NEVER DONE.
YOUR SWORD, MY LIEGE!
THE END

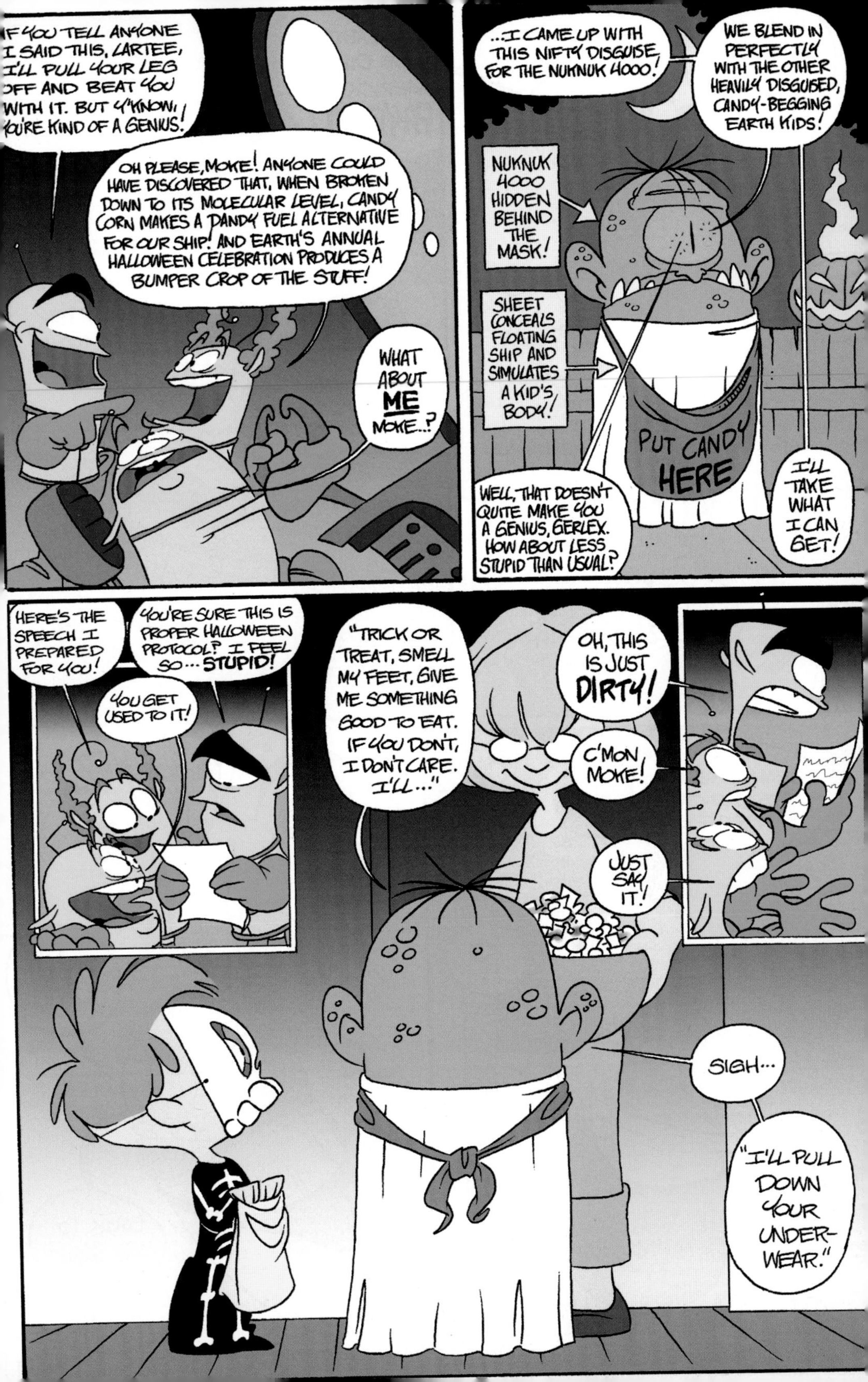
IF YOU TELL ANYONE I SAID THIS, LARTEE, I'LL PULL YOUR LEG OFF AND BEAT YOU WITH IT. BUT Y'KNOW, YOU'RE KIND OF A GENIUS!
OH PLEASE, MOKE! ANYONE COULD HAVE DISCOVERED THAT, WHEN BROKEN DOWN TO ITS MOLECULAR LEVEL, CANDY CORN MAKES A DANDY FUEL ALTERNATIVE FOR OUR SHIP! AND EARTH'S ANNUAL HALLOWEEN CELEBRATION PRODUCES A BUMPER CROP OF THE STUFF!
WHAT ABOUT ME MOKE..?
...I CAME UP WITH THIS NIFTY DISGUISE FOR THE NUKNUK 4000!
WE BLEND IN PERFECTLY WITH THE OTHER HEAVILY DISGUISED, CANDY-BEGGING EARTH KIDS!
NUKNUK 4000 HIDDEN BEHIND THE MASK!
SHEET CONCEALS FLOATING SHIP AND SIMULATES A KID'S BODY!
PUT CANDY HERE
WELL, THAT DOESN'T QUITE MAKE YOU A GENIUS, GERLEX. HOW ABOUT LESS STUPID THAN USUAL?
I'LL TAKE WHAT I CAN GET!
HERE'S THE SPEECH I PREPARED FOR YOU!
YOU'RE SURE THIS IS PROPER HALLOWEEN PROTOCOL? I FEEL SO... STUPID!
YOU GET USED TO IT!
"TRICK OR TREAT, SMELL MY FEET, GIVE ME SOMETHING GOOD TO EAT. IF YOU DON'T, I DON'T CARE. I'LL..."
OH, THIS IS JUST DIRTY!
C'MON MOKE!
JUST SAY IT!
SIGH...
"I'LL PULL DOWN YOUR UNDER-WEAR."

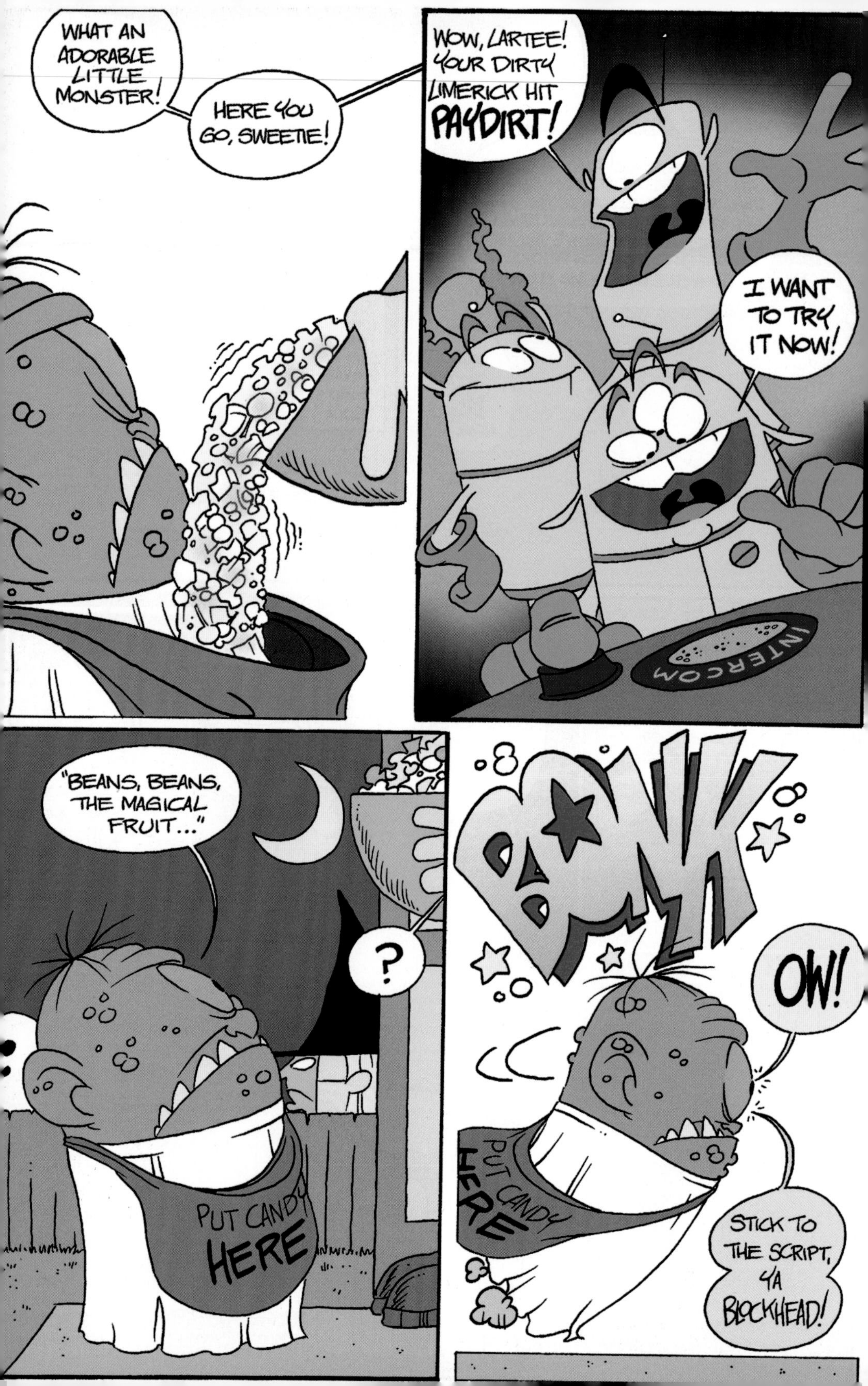
WHAT AN ADORABLE LITTLE MONSTER!
HERE YOU GO, SWEETIE!
WOW, LARTEE! YOUR DIRTY LIMERICK HIT PAYDIRT!
I WANT TO TRY IT NOW!
INTERCOM
"BEANS, BEANS, THE MAGICAL FRUIT..."
?
PUT CANDY HERE
BONK
OW!
PUT CANDY HERE
STICK TO THE SCRIPT, YA BLOCKHEAD!

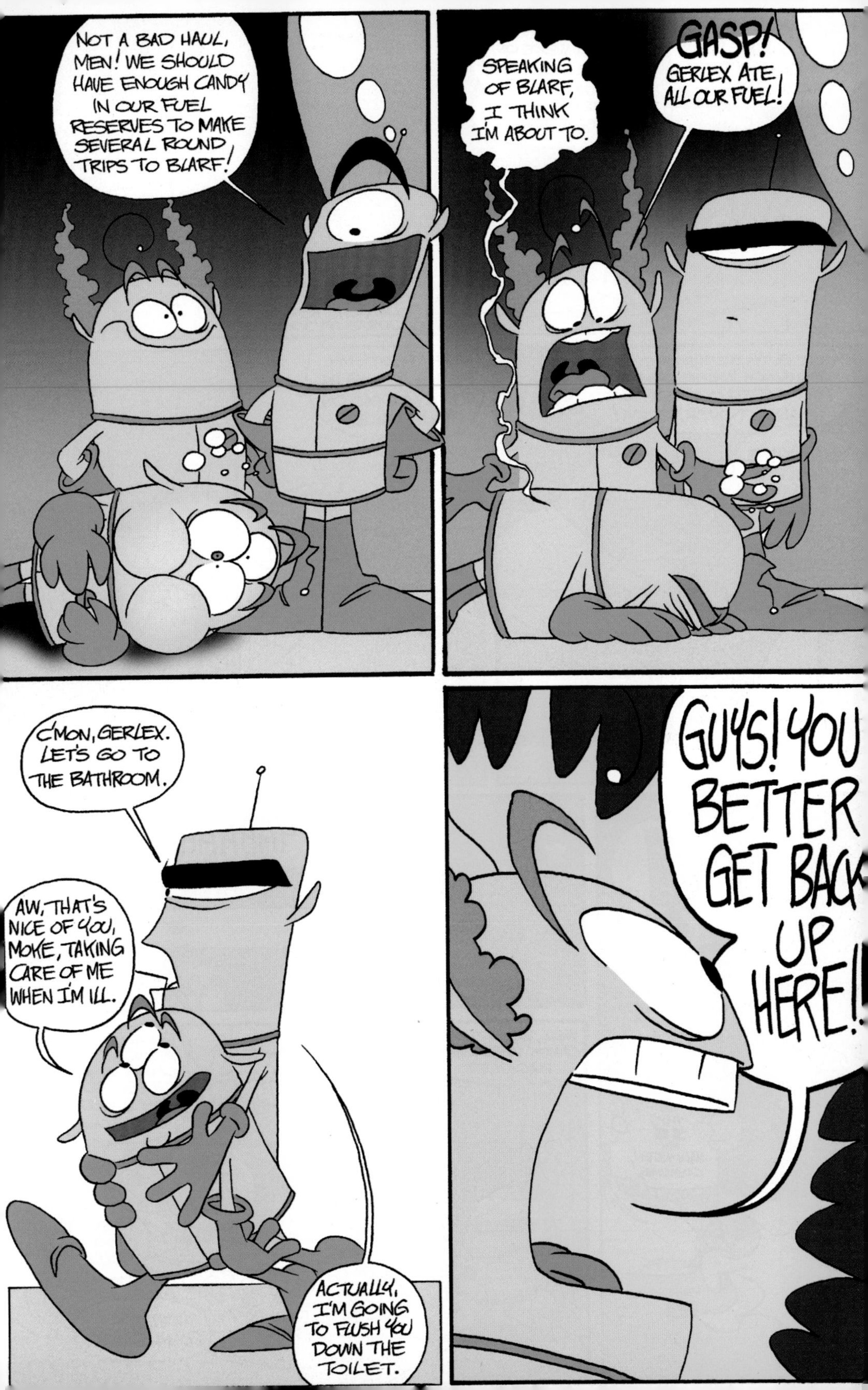
NOT A BAD HAUL, MEN! WE SHOULD HAVE ENOUGH CANDY IN OUR FUEL RESERVES TO MAKE SEVERAL ROUND TRIPS TO BLARF!
SPEAKING OF BLARF, I THINK I'M ABOUT TO.
GASP! GERLEX ATE ALL OUR FUEL!
C'MON, GERLEX. LET'S GO TO THE BATHROOM.
AW, THAT'S NICE OF YOU, MOKE, TAKING CARE OF ME WHEN I'M ILL.
ACTUALLY, I'M GOING TO FLUSH YOU DOWN THE TOILET.
GUYS! YOU BETTER GET BACK UP HERE!!

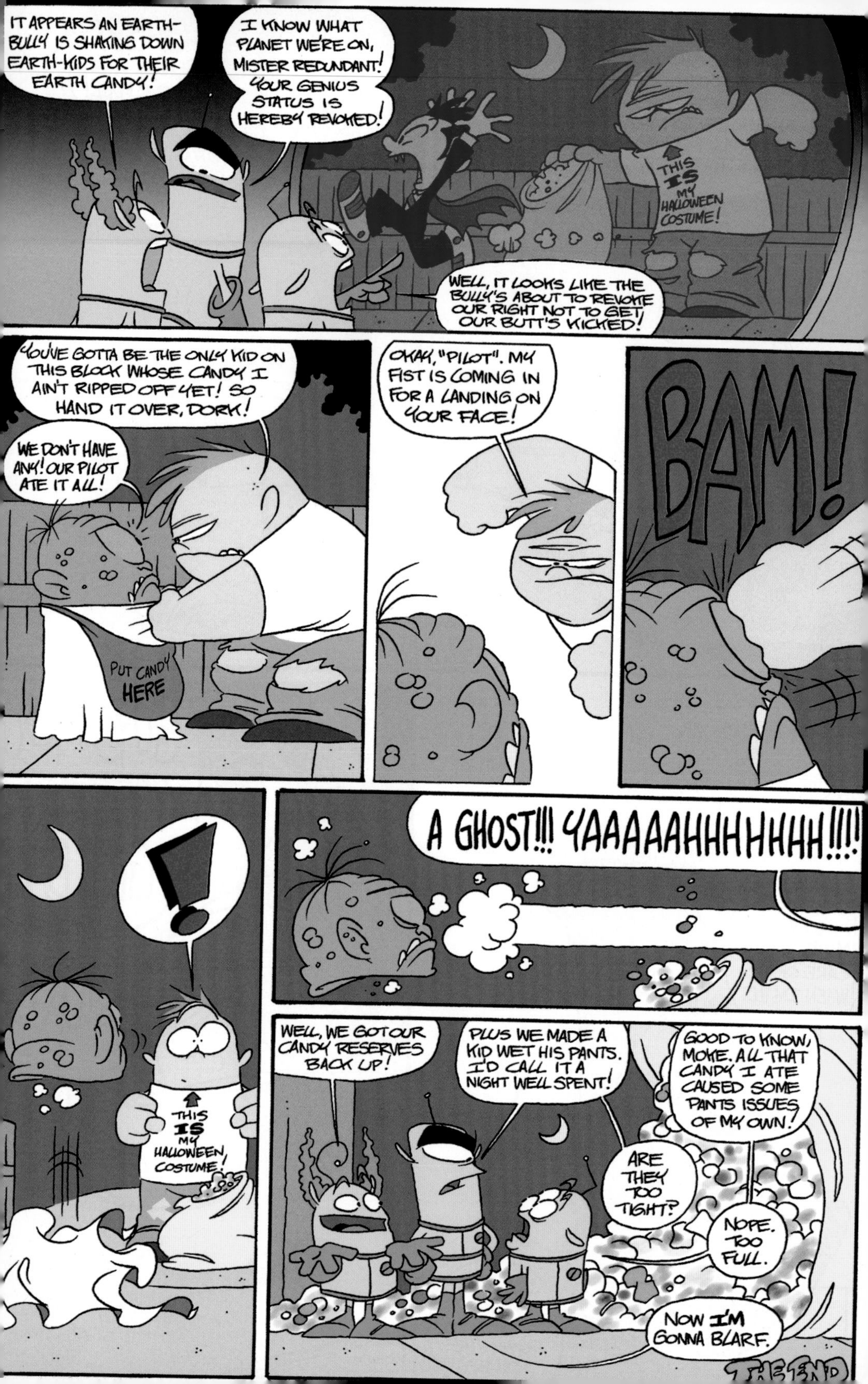
IT APPEARS AN EARTH-BULLY IS SHAKING DOWN EARTH-KIDS FOR THEIR EARTH CANDY!
I KNOW WHAT PLANET WE'RE ON, MISTER REDUNDANT! YOUR GENIUS STATUS IS HEREBY REVOKED!
THIS IS MY HALLOWEEN COSTUME!
WELL, IT LOOKS LIKE THE BULLY'S ABOUT TO REVOKE OUR RIGHT NOT TO GET OUR BUTT'S KICKED!
YOU'VE GOTTA BE THE ONLY KID ON THIS BLOCK WHOSE CANDY I AIN'T RIPPED OFF YET! SO HAND IT OVER, DORK!
WE DON'T HAVE ANY! OUR PILOT ATE IT ALL!
PUT CANDY HERE
OKAY, "PILOT". MY FIST IS COMING IN FOR A LANDING ON YOUR FACE!
BAM!
!
THIS IS MY HALLOWEEN COSTUME!
A GHOST!!! YAAAAAHHHHHHH!!!!
WELL, WE GOT OUR CANDY RESERVES BACK UP!
PLUS WE MADE A KID WET HIS PANTS. I'D CALL IT A NIGHT WELL SPENT!
GOOD TO KNOW, MOKE. ALL THAT CANDY I ATE CAUSED SOME PANTS ISSUES OF MY OWN!
ARE THEY TOO TIGHT?
NOPE. TOO FULL.
NOW I'M GONNA BLARF.
THE END

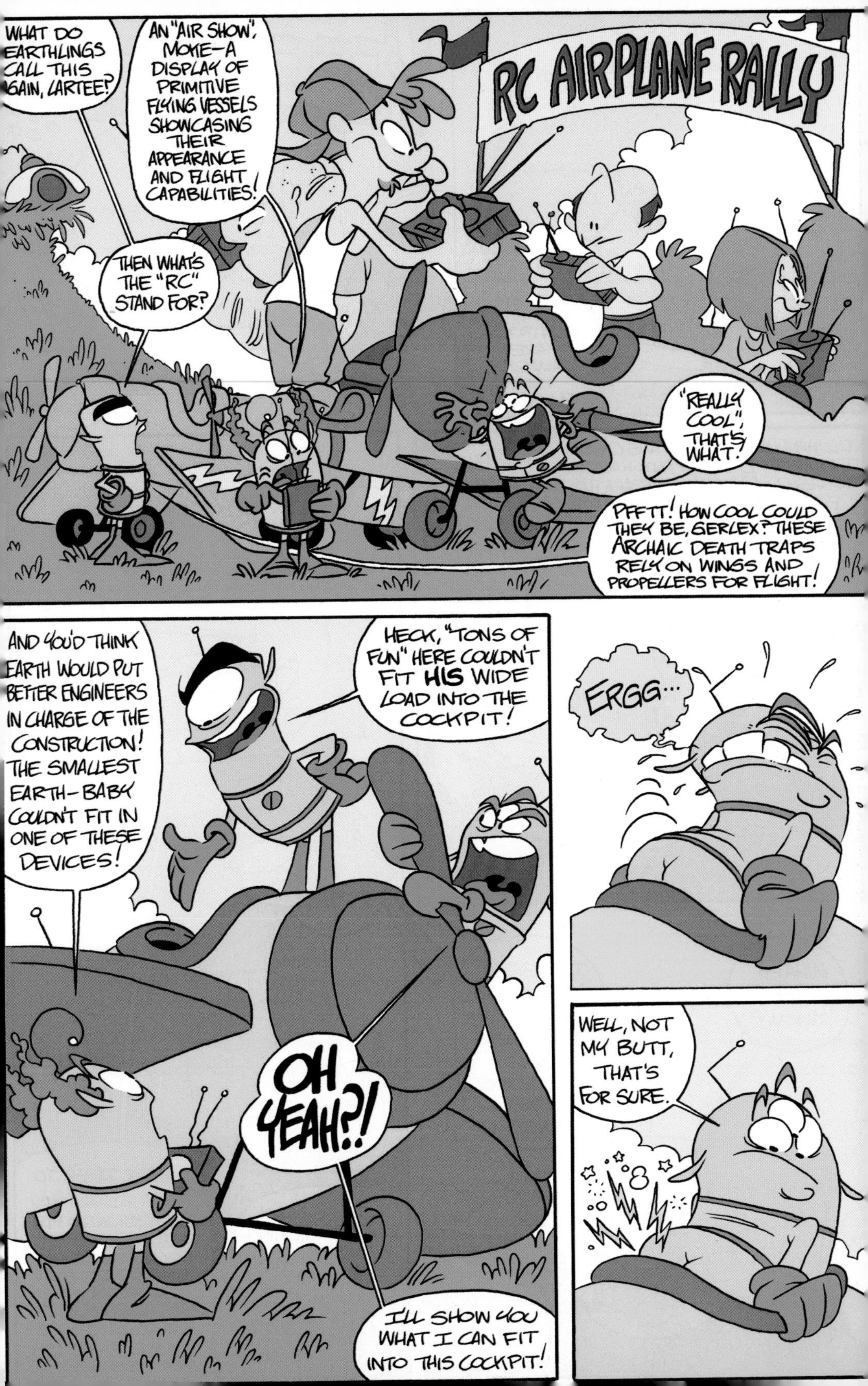
RC AIRPLANE RALLY
WHAT DO EARTHLINGS CALL THIS AGAIN, LARTEE?
AN "AIR SHOW", MOKE—A DISPLAY OF PRIMITIVE FLYING VESSELS SHOWCASING THEIR APPEARANCE AND FLIGHT CAPABILITIES!
THEN WHAT'S THE "RC" STAND FOR?
"REALLY COOL", THAT'S WHAT.
PFFTT! HOW COOL COULD THEY BE, GERLEX? THESE ARCHAIC DEATH TRAPS RELY ON WINGS AND PROPELLERS FOR FLIGHT!
AND YOU'D THINK EARTH WOULD PUT BETTER ENGINEERS IN CHARGE OF THE CONSTRUCTION! THE SMALLEST EARTH-BABY COULDN'T FIT IN ONE OF THESE DEVICES!
HECK, "TONS OF FUN" HERE COULDN'T FIT HIS WIDE LOAD INTO THE COCKPIT!
OH YEAH?!
I'LL SHOW YOU WHAT I CAN FIT INTO THIS COCKPIT!
ERGG...
WELL, NOT MY BUTT, THAT'S FOR SURE.

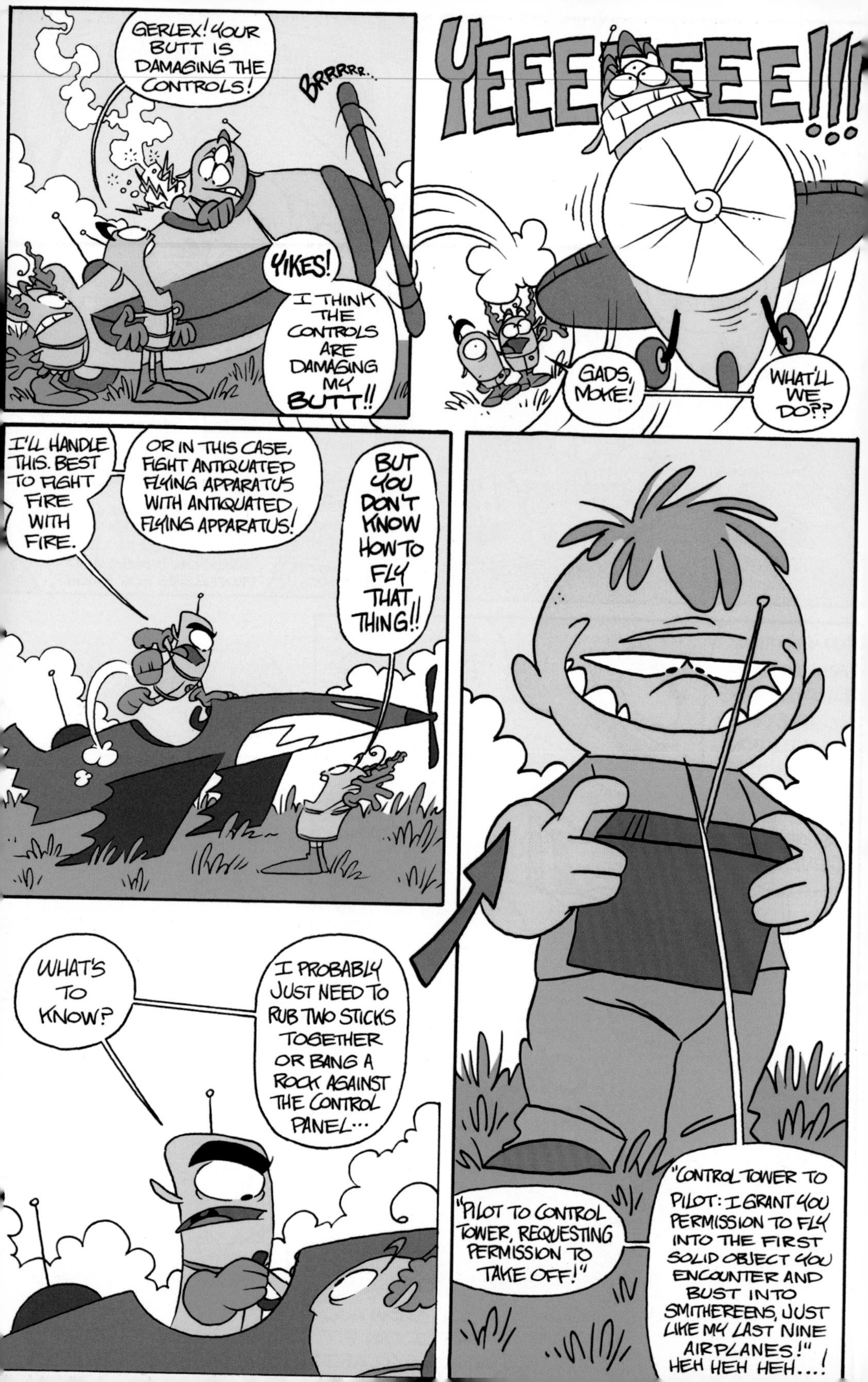

GERLEX! YOUR BUTT IS DAMAGING THE CONTROLS!
BRRRRR...
YIKES!
I THINK THE CONTROLS ARE DAMAGING MY BUTT!!
YEEEEEEE!!!
GADS, MOKE!
WHAT'LL WE DO??
I'LL HANDLE THIS. BEST TO FIGHT FIRE WITH FIRE.
OR IN THIS CASE, FIGHT ANTIQUATED FLYING APPARATUS WITH ANTIQUATED FLYING APPARATUS!
BUT YOU DON'T KNOW HOW TO FLY THAT THING!!
WHAT'S TO KNOW?
I PROBABLY JUST NEED TO RUB TWO STICKS TOGETHER OR BANG A ROCK AGAINST THE CONTROL PANEL...
"PILOT TO CONTROL TOWER, REQUESTING PERMISSION TO TAKE OFF!"
"CONTROL TOWER TO PILOT: I GRANT YOU PERMISSION TO FLY INTO THE FIRST SOLID OBJECT YOU ENCOUNTER AND BUST INTO SMITHEREENS, JUST LIKE MY LAST NINE AIRPLANES!" HEH HEH HEH...!

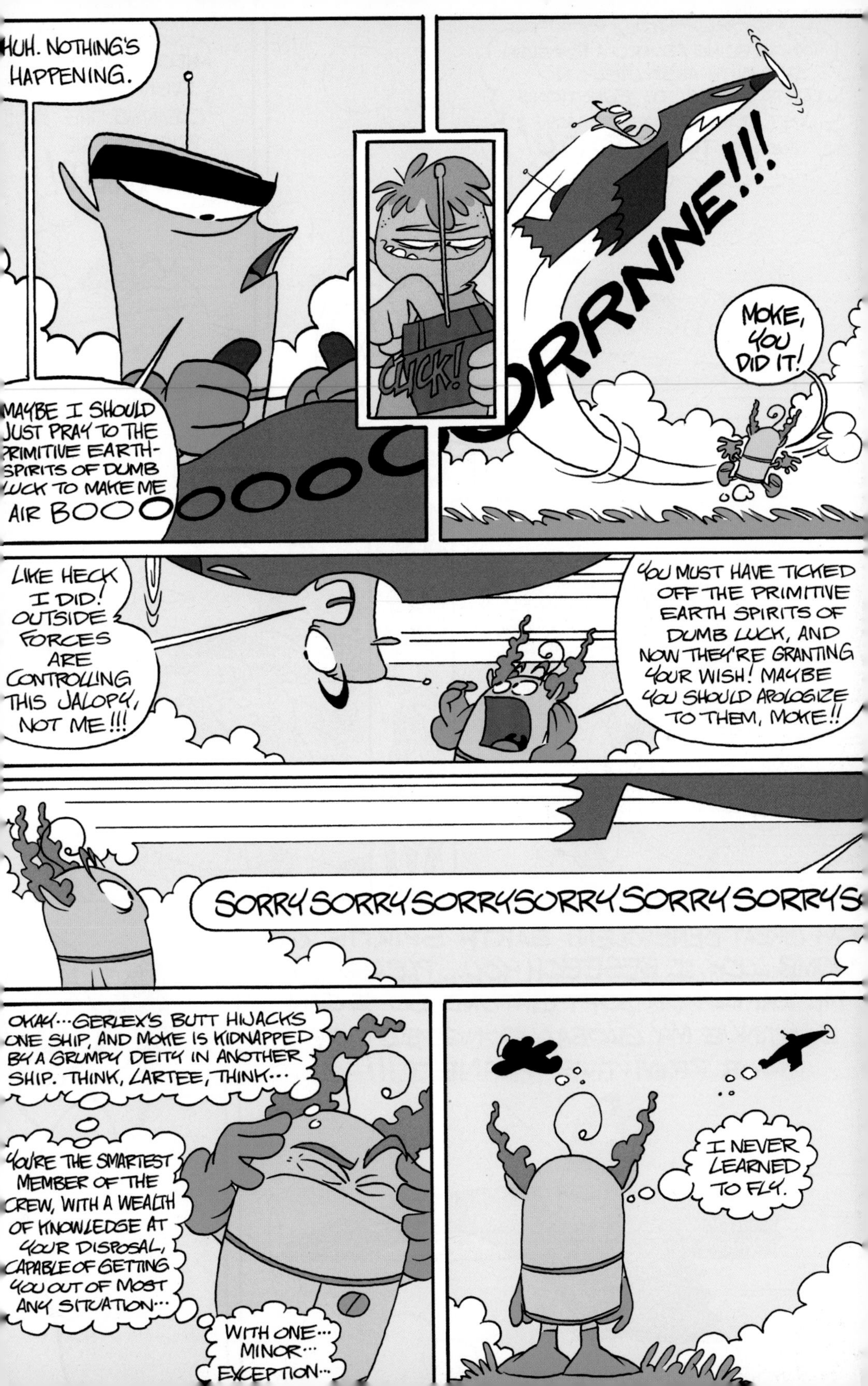
HUH. NOTHING'S HAPPENING.
MAYBE I SHOULD JUST PRAY TO THE PRIMITIVE EARTH-SPIRITS OF DUMB LUCK TO MAKE ME AIR BOOOOOOOOOOO
CLICK!
ORRRNNE!!!
MOKE, YOU DID IT!
LIKE HECK I DID! OUTSIDE FORCES ARE CONTROLLING THIS JALOPY, NOT ME!!!
YOU MUST HAVE TICKED OFF THE PRIMITIVE EARTH SPIRITS OF DUMB LUCK, AND NOW THEY'RE GRANTING YOUR WISH! MAYBE YOU SHOULD APOLOGIZE TO THEM, MOKE!!
SORRYSORRYSORRYSORRYSORRYSORRYS
OKAY... GERLEX'S BUTT HIJACKS ONE SHIP, AND MOKE IS KIDNAPPED BY A GRUMPY DEITY IN ANOTHER SHIP. THINK, LARTEE, THINK...
YOU'RE THE SMARTEST MEMBER OF THE CREW, WITH A WEALTH OF KNOWLEDGE AT YOUR DISPOSAL, CAPABLE OF GETTING YOU OUT OF MOST ANY SITUATION...
WITH ONE... MINOR... EXCEPTION...
I NEVER LEARNED TO FLY.

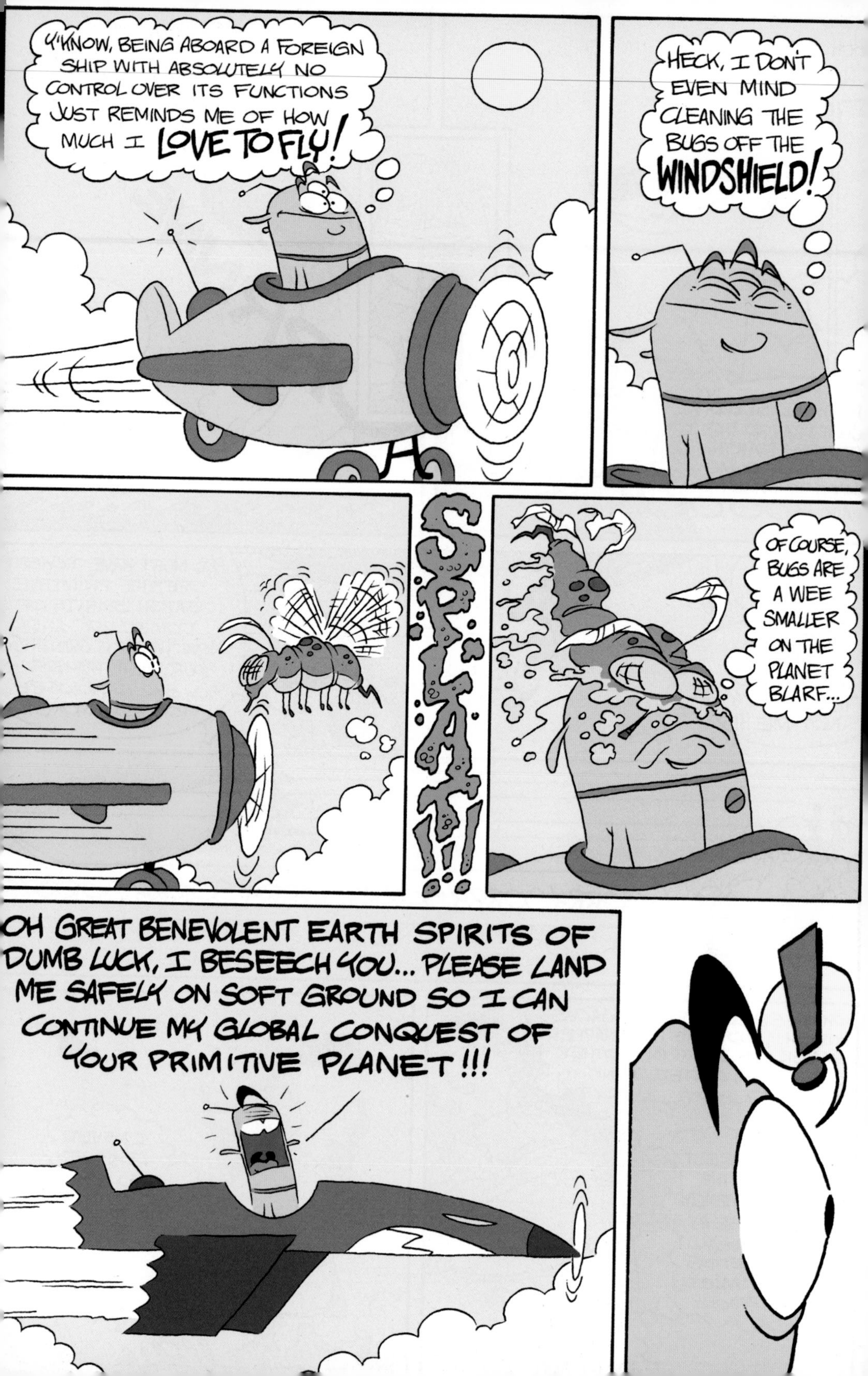
Y'KNOW, BEING ABOARD A FOREIGN SHIP WITH ABSOLUTELY NO CONTROL OVER ITS FUNCTIONS JUST REMINDS ME OF HOW MUCH I LOVE TO FLY!
HECK, I DON'T EVEN MIND CLEANING THE BUGS OFF THE WINDSHIELD!
SPLAT!!
OF COURSE, BUGS ARE A WEE SMALLER ON THE PLANET BLARF...
OH GREAT BENEVOLENT EARTH SPIRITS OF DUMB LUCK, I BESEECH YOU... PLEASE LAND ME SAFELY ON SOFT GROUND SO I CAN CONTINUE MY GLOBAL CONQUEST OF YOUR PRIMITIVE PLANET!!!
!

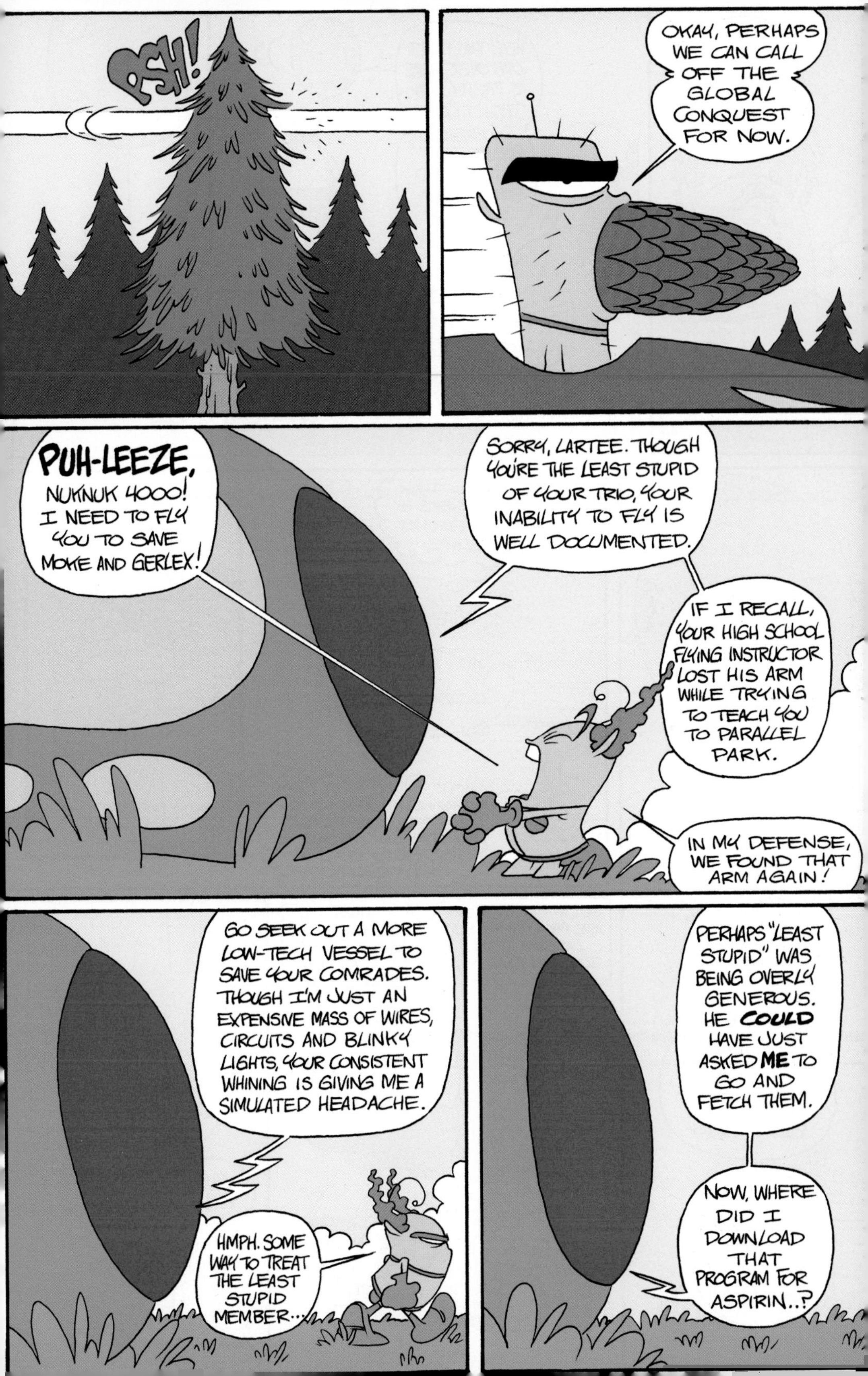
PSH!
OKAY, PERHAPS WE CAN CALL OFF THE GLOBAL CONQUEST FOR NOW.
PUH-LEEZE, NUKNUK 4000! I NEED TO FLY YOU TO SAVE MOKE AND GERLEX!
SORRY, LARTEE. THOUGH YOU'RE THE LEAST STUPID OF YOUR TRIO, YOUR INABILITY TO FLY IS WELL DOCUMENTED.
IF I RECALL, YOUR HIGH SCHOOL FLYING INSTRUCTOR LOST HIS ARM WHILE TRYING TO TEACH YOU TO PARALLEL PARK.
IN MY DEFENSE, WE FOUND THAT ARM AGAIN!
GO SEEK OUT A MORE LOW-TECH VESSEL TO SAVE YOUR COMRADES. THOUGH I'M JUST AN EXPENSIVE MASS OF WIRES, CIRCUITS AND BLINKY LIGHTS, YOUR CONSISTENT WHINING IS GIVING ME A SIMULATED HEADACHE.
HMPH. SOME WAY TO TREAT THE LEAST STUPID MEMBER...
PERHAPS "LEAST STUPID" WAS BEING OVERLY GENEROUS. HE COULD HAVE JUST ASKED ME TO GO AND FETCH THEM.
NOW, WHERE DID I DOWNLOAD THAT PROGRAM FOR ASPIRIN..?

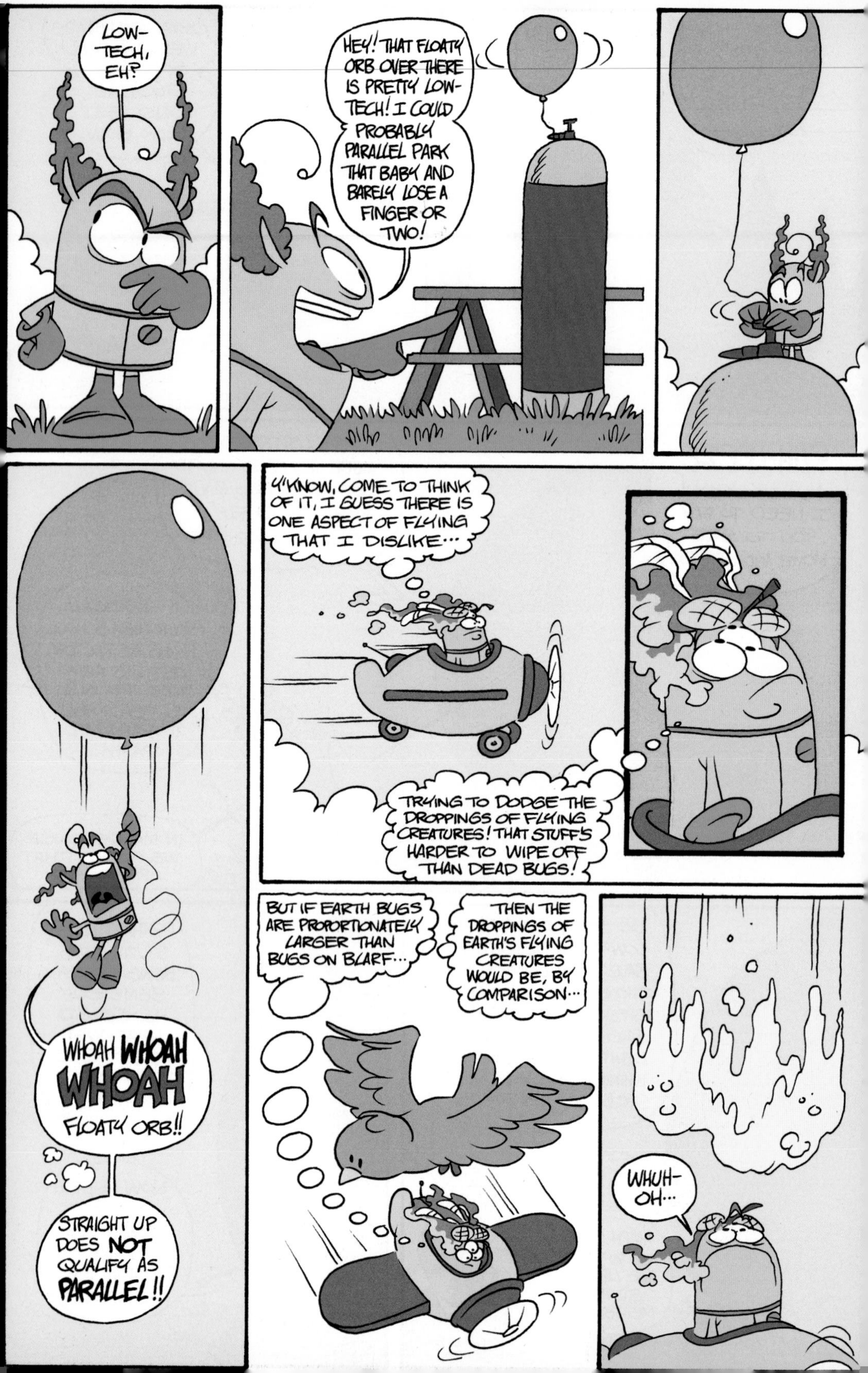

LOW-TECH, EH?
HEY! THAT FLOATY ORB OVER THERE IS PRETTY LOW-TECH! I COULD PROBABLY PARALLEL PARK THAT BABY AND BARELY LOSE A FINGER OR TWO!
WHOAH WHOAH WHOAH FLOATY ORB!!
STRAIGHT UP DOES NOT QUALIFY AS PARALLEL!!
Y'KNOW, COME TO THINK OF IT, I GUESS THERE IS ONE ASPECT OF FLYING THAT I DISLIKE...
TRYING TO DODGE THE DROPPINGS OF FLYING CREATURES! THAT STUFF'S HARDER TO WIPE OFF THAN DEAD BUGS!
BUT IF EARTH BUGS ARE PROPORTIONATELY LARGER THAN BUGS ON BLARF...
THEN THE DROPPINGS OF EARTH'S FLYING CREATURES WOULD BE, BY COMPARISON...
WHUH-OH...

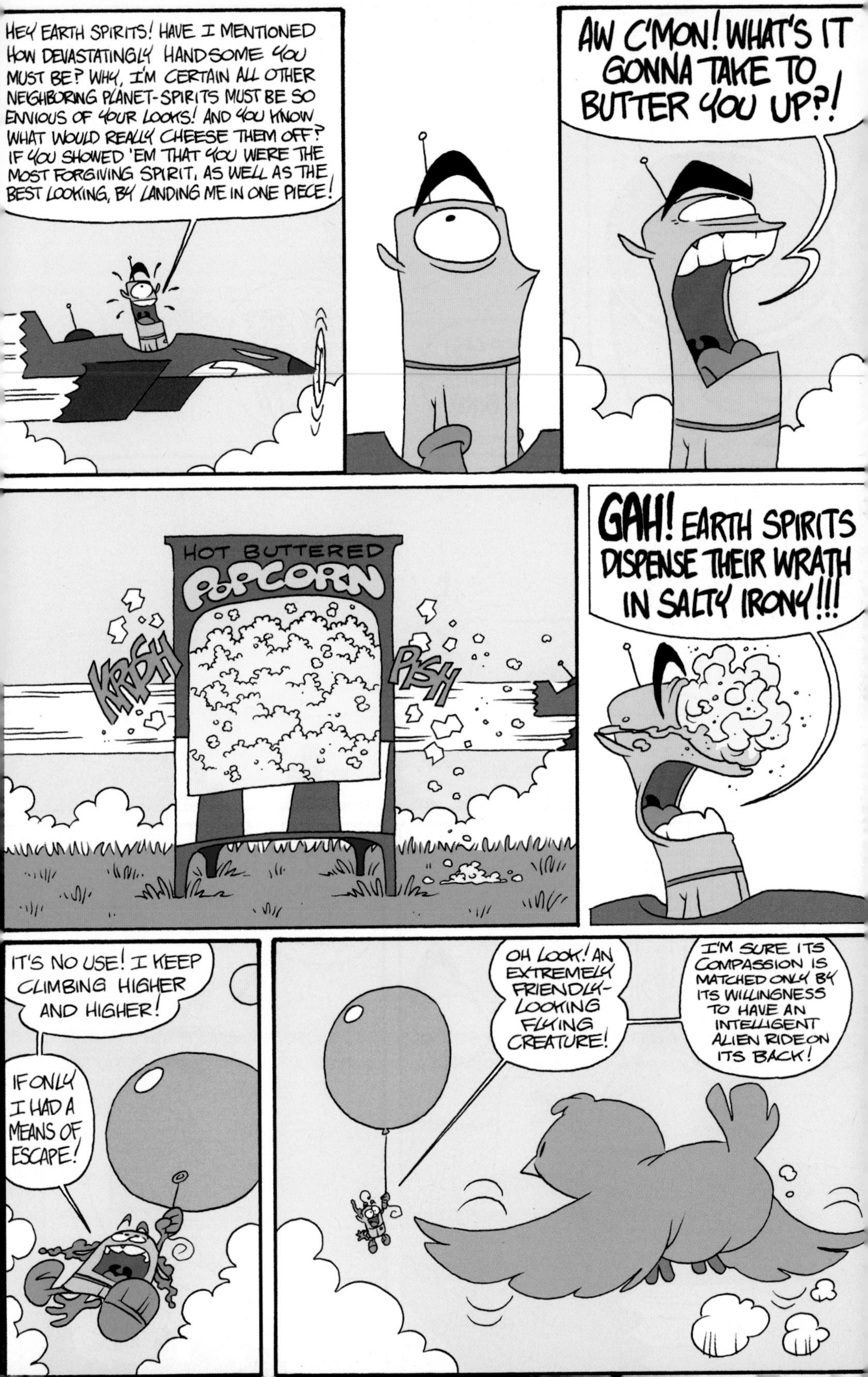
HEY EARTH SPIRITS! HAVE I MENTIONED HOW DEVASTATINGLY HANDSOME YOU MUST BE? WHY, I'M CERTAIN ALL OTHER NEIGHBORING PLANET-SPIRITS MUST BE SO ENVIOUS OF YOUR LOOKS! AND YOU KNOW WHAT WOULD REALLY CHEESE THEM OFF? IF YOU SHOWED 'EM THAT YOU WERE THE MOST FORGIVING SPIRIT, AS WELL AS THE BEST LOOKING, BY LANDING ME IN ONE PIECE!
AW C'MON! WHAT'S IT GONNA TAKE TO BUTTER YOU UP?!
HOT BUTTERED POPCORN
KRASH
PISH
GAH! EARTH SPIRITS DISPENSE THEIR WRATH IN SALTY IRONY!!!
IT'S NO USE! I KEEP CLIMBING HIGHER AND HIGHER!
IF ONLY I HAD A MEANS OF ESCAPE!
OH LOOK! AN EXTREMELY FRIENDLY-LOOKING FLYING CREATURE!
I'M SURE ITS COMPASSION IS MATCHED ONLY BY ITS WILLINGNESS TO HAVE AN INTELLIGENT ALIEN RIDE ON ITS BACK!

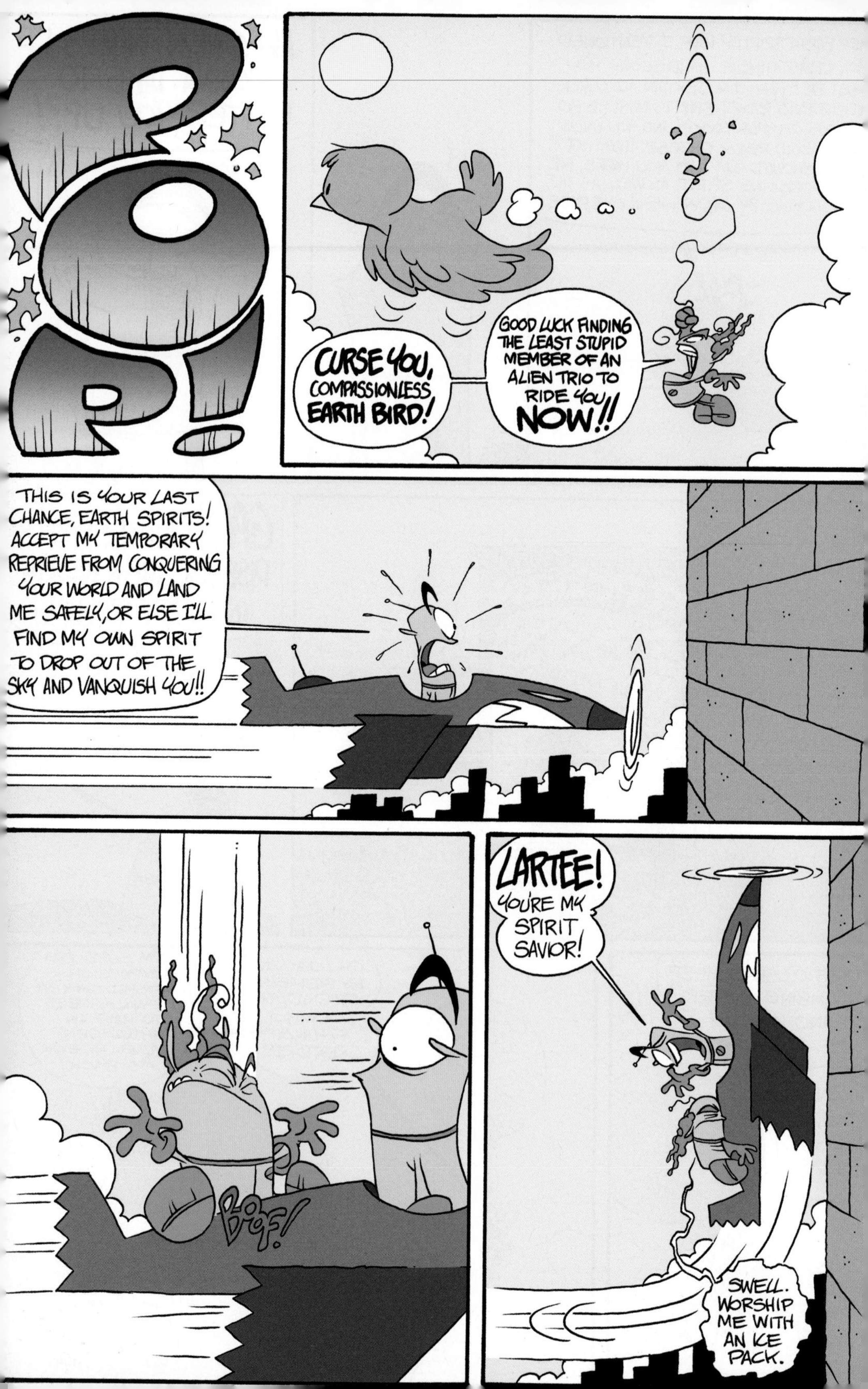
POP!
CURSE YOU, COMPASSIONLESS EARTH BIRD!
GOOD LUCK FINDING THE LEAST STUPID MEMBER OF AN ALIEN TRIO TO RIDE YOU NOW!!
THIS IS YOUR LAST CHANCE, EARTH SPIRITS! ACCEPT MY TEMPORARY REPRIEVE FROM CONQUERING YOUR WORLD AND LAND ME SAFELY, OR ELSE I'LL FIND MY OWN SPIRIT TO DROP OUT OF THE SKY AND VANQUISH YOU!!
BOOF!
LARTEE! YOU'RE MY SPIRIT SAVIOR!
SWELL. WORSHIP ME WITH AN ICE PACK.

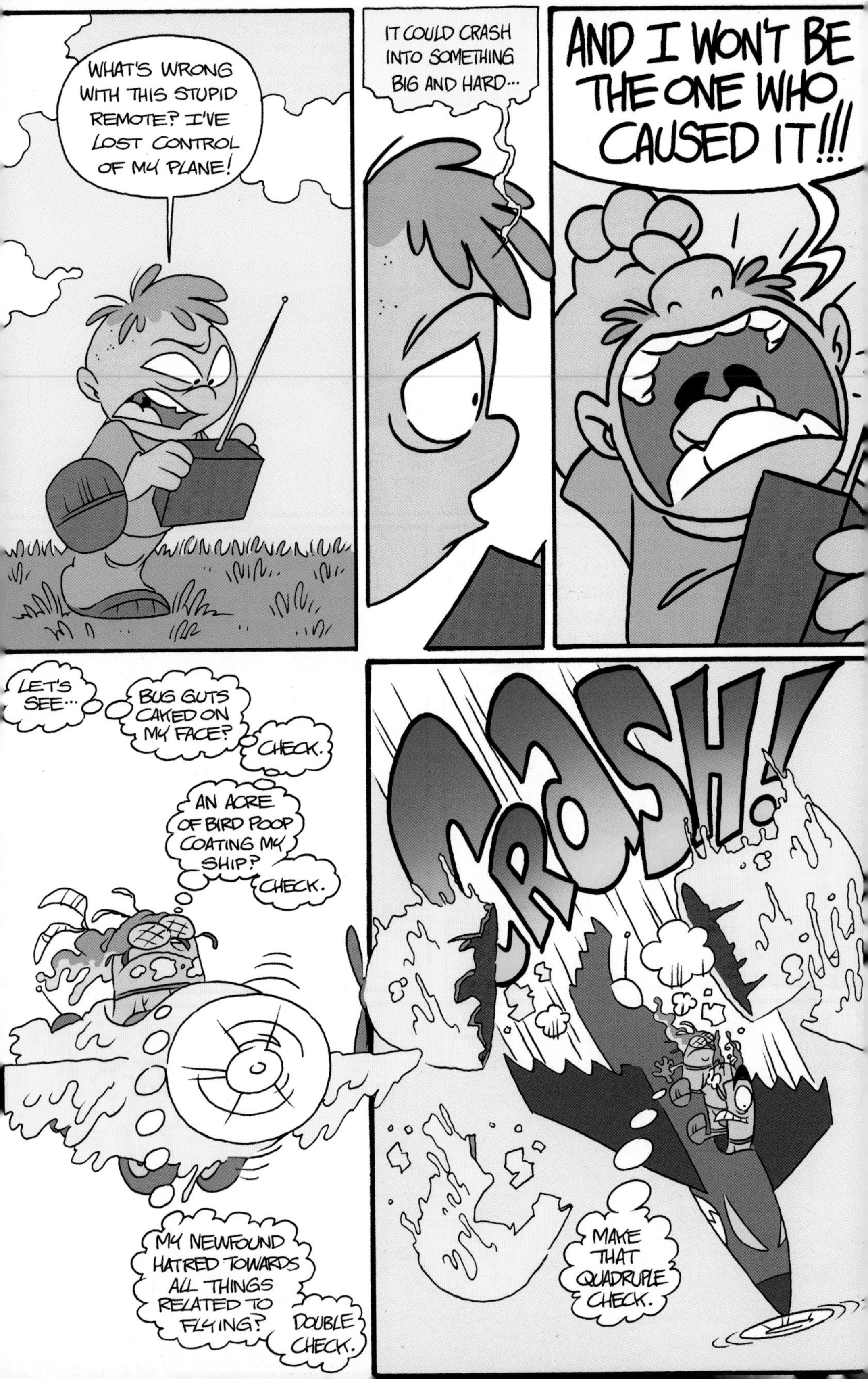
WHAT'S WRONG WITH THIS STUPID REMOTE? I'VE LOST CONTROL OF MY PLANE!
IT COULD CRASH INTO SOMETHING BIG AND HARD...
AND I WON'T BE THE ONE WHO CAUSED IT!!!
LET'S SEE...
BUG GUTS CAKED ON MY FACE?
CHECK.
AN ACRE OF BIRD POOP COATING MY SHIP?
CHECK.
MY NEWFOUND HATRED TOWARDS ALL THINGS RELATED TO FLYING?
DOUBLE CHECK.
CRASH!
MAKE THAT QUADRUPLE CHECK.

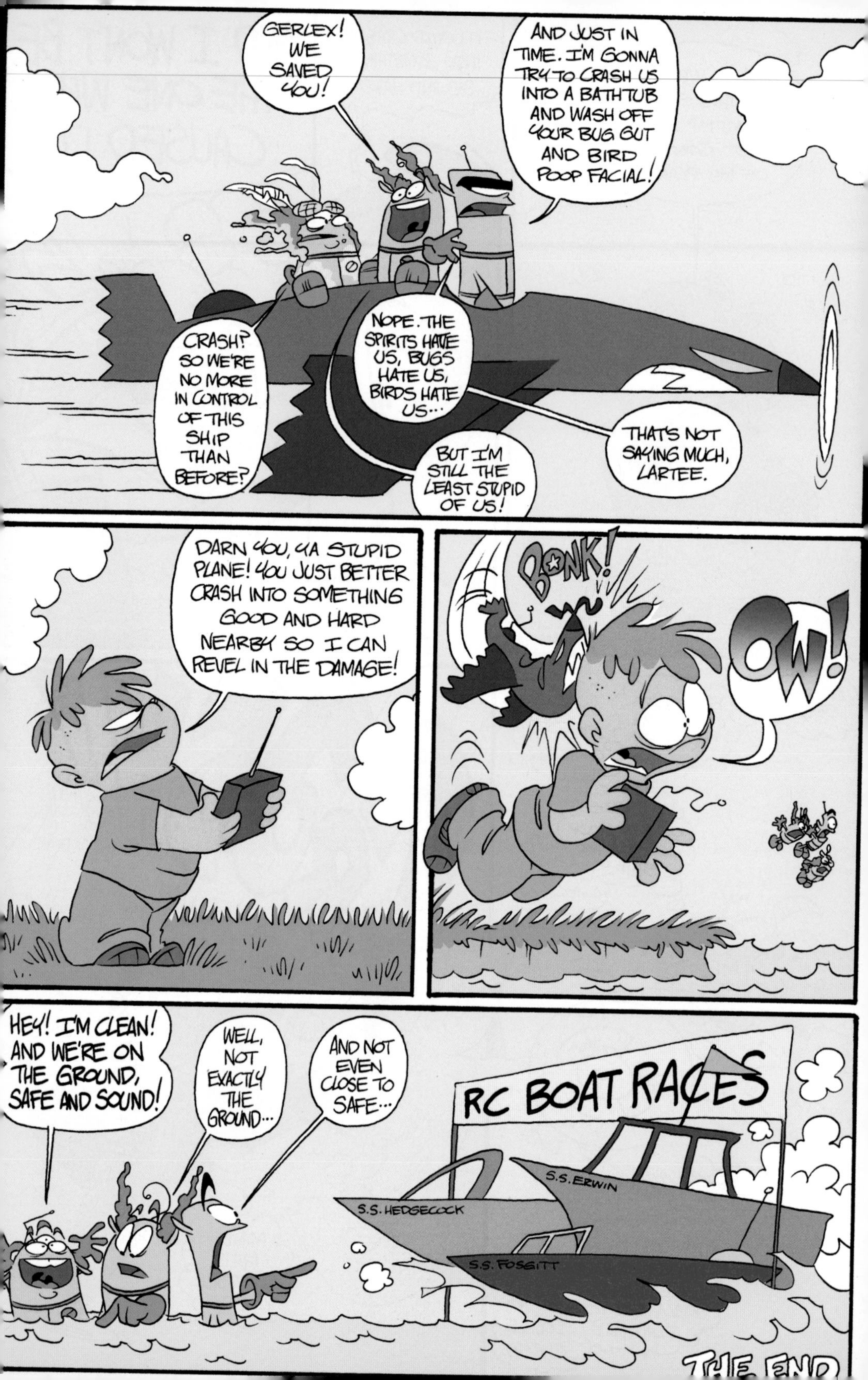
GERLEX! WE SAVED YOU!
AND JUST IN TIME. I'M GONNA TRY TO CRASH US INTO A BATHTUB AND WASH OFF YOUR BUG GUT AND BIRD POOP FACIAL!
CRASH? SO WE'RE NO MORE IN CONTROL OF THIS SHIP THAN BEFORE?
NOPE. THE SPIRITS HATE US, BUGS HATE US, BIRDS HATE US...
BUT I'M STILL THE LEAST STUPID OF US!
THAT'S NOT SAYING MUCH, LARTEE.
DARN YOU, YA STUPID PLANE! YOU JUST BETTER CRASH INTO SOMETHING GOOD AND HARD NEARBY SO I CAN REVEL IN THE DAMAGE!
BONK!
OW!
HEY! I'M CLEAN! AND WE'RE ON THE GROUND, SAFE AND SOUND!
WELL, NOT EXACTLY THE GROUND...
AND NOT EVEN CLOSE TO SAFE...
RC BOAT RACES
S.S. ERWIN
S.S. HEDGECOCK
S.S. FOSGITT
THE END

THE (NOT SO) SECRET ORIGIN OF...

Little GREEN Men

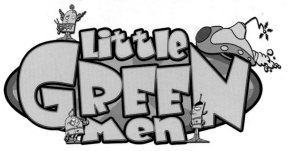

Brent called me up one day and said, “David, I have an idea.” I immediately got worried.

See, usually when Brent gets an idea it means that I am going to have to do a LOT of extra work. So, I did what any sane person should do and immediately began to throw my phone across the room. Brent must have sensed what I was up to, because as I began my wind up, I heard him shout two words that made me pause- “CANDY CORN!”

Candy corn? That sounds harmless enough. So, okay, I had to find out what he was on about. “I had a rough night last night.” Brent says, “Couldn’t sleep. So I stayed up watching a Three Stooges marathon.” Now, everyone knows that if you’re going to watch a Three Stooges marathon you MUST have a snack. Brent went on to tell me how the only snack he could find was some old candy corn from about three Halloweens back. Against his better judgement, he ate it... a lot of it. “So then,” Brent said, “I started thinking, what if the Three Stooges were only as tall as three candy corns stacked end to end?”

And thus began LITTLE GREEN MEN.

There was a lot more to it after that. And, of course, a lot more work for me.

But it was all worth it.

On the next page, you’ll see the very first LITTLE GREEN MEN story ever produced. It was written by Brent Erwin and drawn by the amazing Dave Perillo who also assisted us with the original designs of the characters. Shortly after this first story was done, Jay Fosgitt came on board and took the project, with Brent and I fussing over him like mother hens, to all new heights.

Hope you enjoy it as much as I know you’ve enjoyed the rest of the book!

We’ll see you again real soon but, until then, remember-
Big things come from the smallest of beginnings!

David Hedgecock
San Diego, CA

ape entertainment

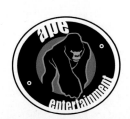

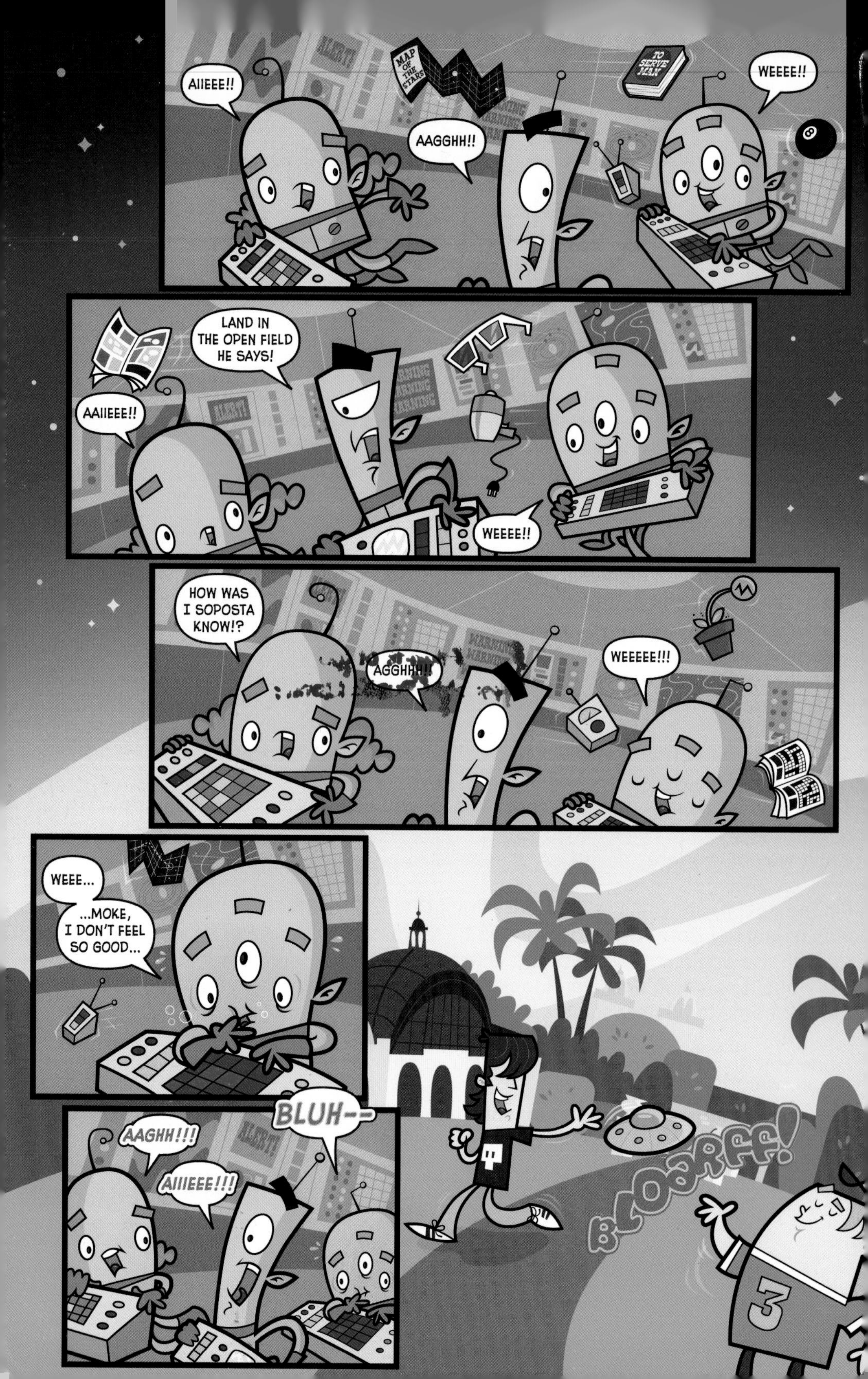

ALERT!
MAP OF THE STARS
TO SERVE MAN
AIIEEE!!
AAGGHH!!
WEEEE!!
LAND IN THE OPEN FIELD HE SAYS!
AAIIEEE!!
WEEEE!!
HOW WAS I SOPOSTA KNOW!?
AGGHHH!!
WEEEEE!!!
WEEE...
...MOKE, I DON'T FEEL SO GOOD...
BLUH--
AAGHH!!!
AIIIEEE!!!
BLOARFF!
3